CLASS ACTS
SIX PLAYS FOR CHILDREN

Tony Hamill, ed.

Playwrights Canada Press
Toronto

Class Acts - Six Plays for Children © 1992
Playwrights Canada Press 54 Wolseley St., 2nd fl.,
Toronto, Ontario CANADA M5T 1A5
Tel: (416) 703-0201 Fax: (416) 703-0059
e-mail: cdplays@interlog.com   http://www.puc.ca

The Secret Garden © 1991 Paul Ledoux
Mandy and The Magus © 1984 Brian Tremblay
Love and Work Enough © 1984 Peggy Sample & Collective
Beware the Quickly Who © 1973 Eric Nicol
The Copetown City Kite Crisis © 1973 Rex Deverell
My Best Friend is Twelve Feet High © 1972 Carol Bolt

Playwrights Canada Press operates with the generous assistance of The Canada Council for the Arts - Writing and Publishing Section and the Ontario Arts Council.

Front cover photo by Dick Luke.

Canadian Cataloguing in Publication Data
Main entry under title:
    Class acts: six plays for children
ISBN 0-88754-487-8
1. Children's plays, Canadian (English).* 2. Canadian drama - 20th century. I. Hamill, Tony - ed.

PS8307.C58 1992   jC812'.5408'09282   C92-095121-X
PR9196.7.C48C58 1992

First edition: September, 1992. Second printing: June 1997.
Printed and bound by Hignell Printing Ltd., Winnipeg, Manitoba, Canada.

Contents

The Secret Garden

by Frances Hodgson Burnett

Adapted for the stage by Paul Ledoux

Paul Ledoux was born in Halifax, Nova Scotia and educated at Dalhousie University, and the Nova Scotia College of Art and Design. His first play, *The Electrical Man,* won the 1975 Quebec Drama Festival Award. Since that time, 23 of his works have been produced across Canada, including *Honky Tonk Angels, The Children of the Night,* and two collaborations with David Young: *Love is Strange,* and the Dora Mavor Moore and Chalmers Award winning, *Fire.* He is past-chair of the Playwrights Union of Canada. In addition to his work for the stage, he has written extensively for radio and television.

The Secret Garden by Frances Hodgson Burnett was adapted for the stage by Paul Ledoux. The premiere production opened November 26, 1991 at Young People's Theatre, Toronto, with the following cast:

EILEEN	*Kalan Chung*
DICKON	*Tony Desmond*
BEN WEATHERSTAFF	*Denny Doherty*
MRS. MEDLOCK	*Kyra Harper*
MARTHA	*Lisa Hynes*
MR. CRAVEN/DR. CRAVEN	*Mervon Metha*
COLIN	*Greg Morris*
GERALDINE	*Martha Schabas*
MARY	*Sherry Smith*

Directed by Maja Ardal.
Set and Costume design by Shawn Kerwin.
Lighting design by Kevin Fraser.
Composer — Mario Marengo.
Movement Coach — Valerie Moore.
Stage Manager — Tony Ambrosi.
Assistant Director — Brenda Kamino.
Puppet Consultant — Robert More.

Music

A number of traditional folk songs are sung in the show. If needed, a tape of the songs is available from the playwright, through Playwrights Union of Canada. The soundtrack composed by Mario Marengo was also particularly successful in creating the great variety of moods called for in the script and the playwright heartily endorses it's use in future productions. Mr. Marengo may be contacted through the playwright.

Puppets

The robins, raven, squirrel, and fox who appear in *The Secret Garden* are puppets manipulated by the cast. The robin, a leading player is, a rod puppet manipulated by the children.

Act One, Scene One

A playroom at dusk. It's raining and a thunder storm is brewing. To one side a large doll house that looks like a manor sits near a gramophone. Two children dressed in outfits from the Twenties sit. EILEEN wears a sailor suit with a black arm band on her left arm and glumly looks at a costume. GERALDINE is already dressed up like a fairy from an old pantomime. EILEEN drops the costume by the doll house and sighs. GERALDINE cranks up the gramophone, puts on a record and hauls EILEEN to her feet, making her dance, but, after a moment, EILEEN pulls away and sits down by the doll house again. GERALDINE sits beside her and reaches into the doll house pulling out a cut-out doll of a little girl..

GERALDINE   Once there was a little girl called ...

EILEEN   Mary.

GERALDINE   She lived in...

EILEEN   India.

> GERALDINE *pulls out a soldier in a*
> *British Army officer's uniform and*
> *hands it to* EILEEN.

GERALDINE   Her father was a soldier.

EILEEN   She hardly ever saw her father because...He was
sick all the time.

> EILEEN *makes the father doll sway*
> *around like it's ill.* GERALDINE *pulls*
> *out another doll. This time it's a Lady*
> *in a ball gown.*

GERALDINE   But her mother...

EILEEN   She hardly ever saw her mother because her
mother cared only for...parties.

GERALDINE   She didn't love her?

EILEEN   She didn't care a bit.

GERALDINE   So Mary was raised by...

EILEEN   Servants.

> EILEEN *puts the mother down by the*
> *father.* GERALDINE *pulls out a doll of*
> *an Indian woman.*

GERALDINE   She had an Ayah who gave her everything she
wanted.

> EILEEN *takes the Ayah doll and puts in*
> *in front of the* MARY *doll.*

EILEEN   And kept her out of the way.

GERALDINE   By the time she was ten she was as selfish a
little pig as ever lived.

              EILEEN *laughs and makes noises like a*
              pig while animating the MARY doll.

GERALDINE   It's not funny. She didn't know how to do
anything for herself.

              EILEEN *hides the Ayah doll aside .*

EILEEN   One morning her Ayah didn't come to wake her.
No one came at all.

GERALDINE   Why not?

EILEEN   Mary didn't know, but she heard her mother
talking in the garden.

              EILEEN *plays with the Mother and*
              Father dolls, acting out the scene.
              GERALDINE *has the MARY doll 'spy'*
              on her parents.

EILEEN   (*as Father*) You should have gone to the summer
house two weeks ago!

(*as Mother*) I know. I only stayed to go to that
silly ball!

(*as Father*) What a fool you are.

(*as Mother*) Is it so very bad?

(*as Father*) Awfully. Hundreds have died in town
and now cholera has broken out among the
servants.

              EILEEN *begins a high pitched keening.*
              SOUND EFFECTS (SFX): Keening
              builds.

GERALDINE   What's that?

EILEEN   Someone has died.

(*as Mother*) Oh dear...I...I...

(*as Father*) Are you alright?

(*as Mother*) No, my head is sore and I'm thirsty all the time and...I'm afraid...

> *The Mother faints into the Father's arms.* GERALDINE *holds up the Mary doll. As* GERALDINE *speaks the actor playing* MARY *suddenly appears behind the dolls house, echoing her lines.*

BOTH   Where is my Ayah?

EILEEN   Her Ayah was dead.

> EILEEN *throws the* Ayah *back into the doll's house.* SXF: *The keening builds.*

BOTH   Mother!

EILEEN   Her Mother died too...

> EILEEN *throws the Mother doll back in the doll's house.*

MARY   I want my Ayah. Send her to me or I'll scream!

EILEEN   They all died.

> EILEEN *tosses The Father doll into the doll's house and goes for the* Mary *doll, but* GERALDINE *holds on to it.*

GERALDINE   Except for Mary.

> EILEEN *and* MARY *scream. Blackout.*

***

Act One, Scene Two

The corridor. Night. SFX: The sound of wind wuthering across the moor. SFX: A child's crying starts to bleed up in the mix. SFX: Thunder rattles the old house. Lightning flashes.

Lights fade up on a tableau. MRS. MEDLOCK, a housekeeper, is pointing to MARTHA, a maid. On the far side of the stage stands CRAVEN, an elegantly dressed Victorian with a hunched back. They all hold unlit candles. The children cross to them with lit candles, light the character's candles and thus bring them to life.

MEDLOCK and MARTHA scramble about trying to deal with some crisis. MARTHA exits and MEDLCOK crosses to CRAVEN.

CRAVEN   Death haunts this house. It wails like a great dark ghost outside my door. I cannot bear it!

The sound of a carriage pulling up. MEDLOCK crosses to him.

MEDLOCK   They've arrived.

CRAVEN	She must not hear it.
MEDLOCK	There's nothing I can do sir. If you'd go and ...
CRAVEN	No, I cannot bear to look into his eyes...his eyes...Oh, very well. Take her to her room and say nothing.

CRAVEN *starts to exit.*

MEDLOCK	Aren't you going to wait and meet her ?
CRAVEN	No. I am not to be disturbed .
MEDLOCK	But sir she'll expect to at least —
CRAVEN	I don't want to see her ! Do you understand me, madam!
MEDLOCK	Yes sir.

CRAVEN *exits.* MEDLOCK *opens the door.* BEN, *a big shaggy hulk of a man with his coat soaked with rain enters, carrying* MARY.

BEN	Shall I carry her up?
MEDLOCK	Yes, but softly. There is a disturbance in the house.

BEN *grunts sadly and shifts the weight of the burden in his arms. Suddenly...SFX: Thunder shakes the house.* MARY *begins to scream and flail about.*

MARY	No! No! I want my Ayah. My Ayah!

BEN *quickly stands her up. Coming out of her nightmare* MARY *looks around, confused. She is in mourning and dressed in black.*

MARY	Where am I?
MEDLOCK	Misselthwaite Manor.
MARY	My Uncle's estate?
MEDLOCK	Yes.
MARY	Are you my Aunt?
MEDLOCK	No, your Aunt is dead.
MARY	Dead?
MEDLOCK	Aye. My name is Mrs. Medlock and I am in the employ of your uncle.
MARY	(*disdainfully*) A servant.
MEDLOCK	(*disdainfully*) Yes.
MARY	(*looking around*) This is a queer place.
MEDLOCK	Aye, six hundred years old and near a hundred rooms in it. Most of them's shut up and locked, but there's a big park and gardens. (*waiting for a response*). Don't you care?
MARY	It doesn't matter whether I care nor not.
MEDLOCK	Right enough. It doesn't. Follow me.

MEDLOCK *holds a lamp high as she leads* MARY *down a long corridor dominated by huge spooky paintings.*

MARY	Are you taking me to my uncle?

MEDLOCK   No. Your uncle does not wish to trouble himself about you.

MARY   He will see me. He must.

MEDLOCK   He won't and you're not to go poking about the house looking for him either. He won't have it.

> *They approach a door hidden by a curtian SFX: Louder crying in the soundscape. MARY stops and listens.*

MARY   What is that sound?

MEDLOCK   The wind blowing across the moor.

MARY   The moor?

MEDLOCK   It's a desolate and dangerous place where nothing grows but heather and broom. The Manor sits on the moor and the wind howls like this all the time.

MARY   But there is something else besides the wind.

MEDLOCK   Don't be foolish.

MARY   It sounds like a child crying.

MEDLOCK   It is the wind!

MARY   No it isn't, it's ...

> *The curtain is snapped open. The dark figure of CRAVEN steps out from behind it. MARY screams. MEDLOCK's lamp is blown out.*
>
> *Blackout.*

***

Act One, Scene Three

MARY's *bedroom. Pale morning light streams into a gloomy room with a big table and a bed where* MARY *lies sleeping.* MARTHA, *a cheery young servant, enters the room pushing a tea trolly with a breakfast tray. She sings.*

MARTHA
She stuck a knife in the baby's head
A wella wella wallya
The more she stuck it the more it bled
Down by the river Solya.

Up and at it, girl. The sun's nearly shining.

MARY *sits up, rubs her eyes and looks around.*

MARY
Where am I?

MARTHA
In your room of course. Hope you're feeling better.

MARY
What do you mean by that?

MARTHA
Mrs. Medlock said you took fright last night and fainted dead away in the corridor.

MARY
I wasn't frightened. I was exhausted...from my trip.

MARTHA	Have it your way, Miss.
MARY	Who are you?
MARTHA	I'm Martha.
MARY	Are you my servant?
MARTHA	Your servant! No, Mrs. Medlock said I was to carry up your breakfast, tea, and dinner but a big girl like you don't need that much waiting on.
MARY	You will find that I shall need a great deal of waiting on. You may dress me.

MARTHA stares in amazement.

MARTHA	Can you not dress yourself?
MARY	I've never tried.
MARTHA	(*laughing*) You'll turn out a fair fool being tended to as if you was an untrained puppy!
MARY	Fetch me my dress — you — you insolent daughter of a pig!

MARTHA looks offended.

MARTHA	I won't. It will do you good to wait on yourself for a change. Mistress - Mary - Quite - Contrary.
MARY	What did you call me?
MARTHA	(*singing*) "Mistress Mary, quite contrary How does your garden grow."

MARY growls at her.

MARY	Fetch my dress or I will slap you very hard indeed.

MARTHA   Keep it up and I'll be the one doing the
                slapping — on your bottom.

                        MARY *throws herself face downward on
                        the bed and bursts into passionate
                        sobbing. Concerned,* MARTHA *bends
                        over* MARY.

MARTHA   Eh! You mustn't cry like that!

                        MARY *screams even louder.* MARTHA
                        pales.

MARTHA   Alright. Alright. I didn't know you'd be so vexed.
                I'll help with your clothes.

                        MAR *stops crying in a split second and
                        stands up, waiting to be dressed.*
                        MARTHA *fetches a new white outfit
                        from a chair.*

MARY   Those are not mine. Mine are black.

MARTHA   Your uncle says a little girl dressed in black
                running about the place would be too depressing
                to bear.

MARY   My uncle is a very strange man.

MARTHA   He's got a crooked back. They say it set him
                wrong, though he treats us well enough.

                        MARY *looks the white dress over with
                        cool approval.*

MARTHA   It's a pretty dress isn't it?

MARY   I had things that were much prettier in India. Put
                it on me.

MARTHA *tries to dress* MARY *who stands still and waits as if she has no hands or feet of her own. As* MARTHA *fumbles about,* MARY *fidgets.*

MARTHA   Hold still now.

MARY *crosses to the window and looks out.*

MARY   Is that the moor?

MARTHA   Aye.

MARY   I hate it.

MARTHA   That's because you're not used to it.

MARY   You don't like it do you?

MARTHA   Aye. I wouldn't live away from the moor for anything. It's fair lovely in spring when the heather's bloomin'. It smells of honey and the sky's so high and the bees and skylarks are humming and singing...

MARTHA *has her dressed by now.* MARY *walks back to the bed, sits on it and holds out a foot.*

MARY   Shoes.

MARTHA   Why don't you put on your own shoes?

MARY   My Ayah always did it.

MARTHA   Now what an inconvenience that must have been for you.

MARY   I don't know what you mean.

MARTHA   There must have been times when your Ayah
                wasn't there and you wanted to put on your shoes
                and go about wasn't there?

MARY   I won't talk about my Ayah. You must never ask
                about her ! Do you hear me?

MARTHA   My Lord, ya haven't been here a day and you're
                already talking like a Craven, born and bred. Slip
                your foot in.

                        MARY *slips into her shoes.*

MARY   (*a snotty lady*) You managed quite well once you
                decided to try, didn't you Martha?

MARTHA   I've been dressing little brothers and sisters for
                years. Come and have your breakfast.

MARY   I don't want any.

MARTHA   You don't want your porridge!

MARY   No.

MARTHA   You doesn't know how good it is with a bit of
                treacle.

MARY   I don't want it.

MARTHA   Eh! I can't abide to see good victuals go to waste.

MARY   What difference does it make?

MARTHA   It makes a difference to my brothers and sisters.
                There's twelve of 'em and they've scarce had their
                stomachs full in their lives.

MARY   Well you can put it in a box and send it to them
                by post for all I care. I don't know what it is to
                be hungry.

MARTHA   (*indignant*) Well, it would do you good to try it.
                I can see that plain enough.

MARY	"Man does not live by bread alone".
MARTHA	Oh do eat something or we'll both be cranky all day long.

> MARY *drinks some tea and eats a little toast.*

MARTHA	That's good, and when you're done we'll wrap you up warm and you can run out and play in the gardens.
MARY	I don't want to go out.
MARTHA	If you doesn't go out, you'll have to stay in and what has you got to do?
MARY	You will fetch me my toys.
MARTHA	Mrs. Medlock does not approve of such amusements.
MARY	That's ridiculous!
MARTHA	Aye, but there you have it.
MARY	Oh, very well then, come along. We will play in the garden. (*pointing*) Hat. Coat.
MARTHA	Sorry, but I've got too much work to do to go playing about with you.
MARY	My servants always played with me in India.
MARTHA	You'll have to learn to play alone like other children does when they haven't got sisters or brothers or servants.
MARY	One cannot play by oneself.
MARTHA	Our Dickon goes off on the moor by himself and plays for hours.
MARY	Who is Dickon?

MARTHA	He's my brother and the whole wide world is his friend. Foxes and squirrels and birds come and eats right out of his hand.
MARY	(*fascinated*) Wild things eat from his hand?
MARTHA	Aye.
MARY	Are there animals in the garden ?
MARTHA	Oh, I reckon you might see a bird or two if you keep your eyes open.
MARY	Then I shall explore the gardens.
MARTHA	Aye, explore to your heart's content. It's none of my business.
MARY	I suppose the crying I heard in the hall last night is none of your business either.
MARTHA	I've got nothing to say about no crying.
MARY	I heard it quite clearly. Who was it?
MARTHA	It's a long day and a busy day I've got ahead of me Miss. Excuse me.

> MARTHA *exits. Frustrated,* MARY
> *struggles to pull on her own coat and*
> *manages it with some difficulty.*

MARY	This is the queerest house in the world and I suppose the garden is every bit as strange.

***

Act One, Scene Four

*The kitchen garden. Day. A bare, vine-
covered wall. The children run on.
GERALDINE is playing with a stick
puppet of a robin. The bird flits about.
EILEEN tries to whistle like a robin.
She's useless. GERALDINE laughs and
flies the robin away. It sits on the wall
looking down at EILEEN. She tries the
call again and fails.*

EILEEN   I want the bird to sing.

GERALDINE   Then whistle.

EILEEN   I can't.

GERALDINE   Well I know somebody who can — just like a
bird.

EILEEN   Who?

GERALDINE   Dickon.

*The sound of a penny whistle playing
the song of the robin is heard. The
shadow of* DICKON *playing the pipe
appears. The robin soars into the sky
and flys around. .*MARY *enters, drawn
by the sound of the robin. The children
hide. The bird sits on top of the wall. It
sings.*

MARY   Hello.

The bird sings a reply.

MARY   My name is Mary. What's yours?

The bird whistles and flies off.

MARY   Wait! Don't go! (*sighing*) Oh alright, go! I don't
care. People never like me and I never like
people. Why should it be any different with
you ? (*kicking at the ground, dejected*). It's just
that I'm so lonely. (*to herself*) You silly little
fool. He's just a stupid bird and he's gone behind
that wall.

MARY *goes to the wall and looks for a
gate. No luck. From beyond she hears
the mocking call of the robin. She tries
to climb the ivy and doesn't notice* BEN
enter.

BEN   Get down from there!

MARY *is startled, loses her grip and
falls to the ground.*

BEN   What do you think you're doing?

MARY   Exploring.

BEN   Snoopin' about is more like it.

MARY	Where is the gate into the garden on the other side of this wall?
BEN	What makes you think there's a garden there?
MARY	Because a bird flew over there and disappeared.
BEN	A bird you say?
MARY	A bird with a red breast. He sang.

> *BEN's surly old weather-beaten face changes. A slow smile spreads over it.*

| BEN | Oh, he sang did he? Like this was it? |

> *BEN begins a low soft whistle. MARY looks at him as if he's acting just a bit insane.*

| MARY | Yes... |
| BEN | The cheeky little beggar — I've not seen him before today. |

> *The robin appears again on the wall.*

| BEN | Ah, and where have you been these last five months? To Africa and back I suppose. |

> *The bird whistles a reply.*

| MARY | What kind of bird is he? |

> *BEN ignores her, whistling to the bird.*

| MARY | What kind of bird is he! |
| BEN | (*irritated*) He's a robin redbreast. |

> *The bird calls again.*

BEN	(*to robin*) Ya knows I'm talkin' about you don't you?
	The bird trills again.
MARY	He couldn't.
BEN	(*irritated*) Of course he does. (*to robin*) Always comin' to see what I'm plantin' ain't ya? Like you was the head gardener.
	BEN *whistles. The robin replies.*
MARY	(*in a whisper*) Will he always come when you call him?
BEN	Most times. See — he gets lonely.
	MARY *moves a step nearer to the robin and looks at him very hard.*
MARY	I'm lonely too.
BEN	Aye. I'm not surprised — losin' your ma and pa...
MARY	(*snapping*) You are not to mention my mother and father. No one is.
BEN	(*sour*) No wonder you're lonely. With that sour look upon your face, you'll be lonely a good long time too.
MARY	(*insulted*) What is your name?
BEN	Ben Weatherstaff. And there's no need to screw up your face so.
MARY	Why shouldn't I? I have no friends at all. Not even a robin.
BEN	Why, should ya? You act like a sharp old woman.

MARY	I am not an old woman!

> *The robin whistles, gives a little shake of his wings then flies over the wall.*

MARY	There, look what you've done. He has flown back into the garden behind the wall.
BEN	That's not my doin' and you know it.
MARY	Well I want to go in there and see him. Where is the door?
BEN	There is no door as anyone can find, and none as it's anyone's business to look for.
MARY	(*standing right up to him*) A door just doesn't disappear.
BEN	You stay away from that wall, girl, or I'll be tellin' your uncle and he won't like it.

> *BEN storms off. MARY stands there looking frustrated and then the robin appears on the wall, singing again. She looks at him with longing.*

MARY	Hello again. Would you be my friend too?

> *The robin trills happily.*

MARY	Yes, that's right you can be my friend instead of that mean old man's and you can tell me all about the garden. (*to* BEN, *offstage*) Just because he won't!

> *The robin sings and the song becomes spooky. Lights shift. MARY is transfixed. SFX: Sound of a woman and man laughing.*

LILLIAS	(*voice over*)) Where you tend a rose my love A thistle cannot grow.

MARY	Something awful happened there, didn't it ?
MARTHA	(*worried*) Now how in the world would you come to think something like that?
MARY	I was in the kitchen garden and I heard something — a woman's voice and laughter and then the sound of something breaking and a man cried out in terrible pain. The garden's haunted, isn't it Martha?
MARTHA	(*blanching*) It's not to be talked about. Mrs. Medlock's orders.
MARY	Tell me or I shall tell her all I have deduced and blame it on you!
MARTHA	You wouldn't.
MARY	Oh yes I would, you know I would. I will tell and you will be discharged!
MARTHA	You're a demon you are.

MARY *grins nastily.*

MARY	Mr. Craven locked it up because someone died there — didn't he? (*as* MARTHA *hesitates*) Tell me.
MARTHA	It was before my time! All I know is that something happened and he locked the door to that garden and buried the key and forbade anyone to ever mention it again.
MARY	It was my Aunt. It must have been.

Pause. The sound of the wind comes up a bit, and with it the crying.

MARY	Listen.

MARTHA	(*nervous*) The wind's wutherin' louder than ever now.
MARY	Not that.
MARTHA	What?
MARY	The crying.
MARTHA	It's just the wind, child. Sometimes it sounds like some poor soul wailing out on the moor .
MARY	No. The sound is in the house.
	MARY *crosses and opens the door to her room. The sound is louder.*
MARY	There. Someone is crying and it isn't a grown-up. What is it Martha? Is it a ghost?
MARTHA	You know about the garden. That's enough!
	MARTHA *exits.*
MARY	Martha! You come back here!

***

Act One, Scene Six

In the corridor. Night. Lights shift to the children at the doll's house. They are holding candles. SFX: The wind still wuthers and we hear the crying.

EILEEN   The clock struck twelve. The wind wuthered and howled around the house. And the crying wouldn't go away.

GERALDINE   What did Mary do?

EILEEN   What would you have done?

GERALDINE   Put my head under the covers and not come out 'till morning.

EILEEN   Well Mary was a much braver little girl than you. She got up and took a candle and...

MARY enters. EILEEN lights MARY's candle and pushes her into the next scene. MARY walks down the empty corridor, scared. As she approaches the curtained door she turns to look back down the corridor and as she does, a figure steps out of the shadows and grabs MARY who screams and struggles until MEDLOCK lets her go.

MEDLOCK   What are you doing girl!

MARY	I heard crying.
MEDLOCK	You heard nothing of the sort! Do you understand! You heard nothing!

The crying continues.

MEDLOCK	Back to your room before I box your ears.
MARY	There is crying.

> MEDLOCK *grabs her arm and gives it a*
> *yank.* MARY *fights her.*

MEDLOCK	Hush. You will learn to stay where you are told or you will find yourself locked up.
MARY	Yes, that's right. Lock me up like the little child who's sobbing. Anyone with ears could hear!
MEDLOCK	Oh ! I told Mr. Craven not to let you come here. He didn't want you, you can be sure of that, but he said, "It is my duty". As if he's ever done his duty!
MARY	Let go of me!
MEDLOCK	The master had better get you into a boarding school and soon. I've too much to do taking care of this house and him and...

> MARY *bites her hand and breaks free.*

MEDLOCK	Go to your room! Go!

> MARY *runs off.*

***

Act One , Scene Seven

In the kitchen garden. Daytime. BEN and MARTHA enter and freeze. The children cross to them and give BEN a carpet bag and MARTHA a shawl .

MARTHA You've got to tell me Ben. I heard stories, but I was nothing but a child when it happened. You was here. Tell me.

BEN There's little to tell.

MARY appears, snooping, as usual.

MARTHA Ben, I got to know. I'll go crazy if I don't. Tell me about Mrs. Craven and the garden.

BEN She loved it, that's all. And her and the master used to go in and shut the door and stay there hours and hours, talkin' and tendin' her roses.

MARTHA But what happened to her?

BEN There was an old tree with a branch bent down like a seat and she used to love sittin' there. Then one day...

MARTHA The branch broke ! Oh Lord. The garden's haunted Ben. (*as BEN grunts*). It is. She heard it!

MARY That's right. And now I know what happened too.

MARTHA	Oh Lord!
BEN	Why I could...ya sneakin', slippin', slidin', little spy!
MARY	I don't like you Weatherstaff.
BEN	How does you like yourself!

> MARY *is brought up short by this question. Pause. There's the sound of a horse cart offstage.*

BEN	Butcher's cart's leavin'.

> BEN *gives* MARTHA *her bag and she starts to go.*

MARY	Where are you going?
MARTHA	To see my family — if it's any of your business. It's my day off.

> MARTHA *exits.* BEN *grunts and starts digging with a small trowel near the base of the wall. An uncomfortable pause.* MARY *plots her next move.*

MARY	The moor has changed.
BEN	Aye. It does that this time of the year.
MARY	Everything smells so fresh and damp.
BEN	It's spring. Things are stirring around in the dark waiting for the sun to wake them.
MARY	What are you doing?
BEN	Digging.
MARY	(*pointing*) What's that?

BEN	A trowel.
MARY	(*pausing*) Are things stirring in the other garden?
BEN	What other garden?
MARY	(*frustrated*) The secret garden ! Are the roses dead, or do some of them still come in the summer?

> *The robin appears, singing.* BEN *points at him.*

BEN	(*sour*) Ask him why don't ya, 'cause I don't know.
MARY	You call me sour, well I think you are the sourest man in the whole world.
BEN	Aye, we are cut from the same cloth ain't we!

> BEN *exits.* MARY *looks up at the robin perched on the wall.*

MARY	Did you hear what Ben said Mr. Redbreast ? He asked me how I liked myself. (*hesitating a moment and thinking it over*).
MARY	I never thought of that before. (*pausing*). Not much really.

> *The bird sings again.*

MARY	I like you better.

> *The bird sings again .*

MARY	And I believe I would like your garden too — if I could just see it.

> *The robin flies down to the ground and lands in the dirt near where* BEN *was digging.* MARY *watches and sees something glint.*

MARY   What? What is it?

> MARY *picks up an old key that looks as if it has been buried a long time.*

MARY   Is this the key to the garden? It must be!

> MARY *is interrupted by the arrival of* MEDLOCK.

MEDLOCK   Girl.

> *The robin flies over and "buzzes"* MEDLOCK *who shoos it away.* MARY *quickly hides the key.*

MADLOCK   Get out...Shoo! Shoo! (*to* MARY) What are you doing there?

MARY   Nothing. Digging!

MEDLOCK   Getting filthy. Come here!

MARY   What is it?

MEDLOCK   Mr. Craven wants to see you.

MARY   Why?

MEDLOCK   You're snooping about has something to do with it I should expect.

MARY   But that was nothing I was...sleepwalking!

MEDLOCK   It's the boarding school for you now and lying won't help a bit.

MARY	Oh no, dear, sweet, kind Mrs. Medlock, boarding school would be terrible. I promise I won't snoop anymore and...
MEDLOCK	Hush. Mr. Craven is waiting for you. Come along. Lord you look a sight. Fix your hair.
	MEDLOCK *leads her off. The children appear.*
GERALDINE	Why did she have to show up now? Mary found the key and the robin was going to show her the garden too.
EILEEN	That's what grown-ups do isn't it ? They get in your way or ignore you — like her Uncle has...
GERALDINE	Well, he wants to see her now.
EILEEN	That's right and he's a hunchback. He must be planning something horrible.
GERALDINE	Why?
	CRAVEN*enters. The scene shifts. A chair is brought on .*
EILEEN	Because hunchbacks are always horrible.
GERALDINE	That's just not true.
	EILEEN *hauls a book of poetry out of the doll's house, crosses and hands it to him . He sits and begins to read.*
EILEEN	It is.
GERALDINE	You are a stupid, ignorant, little pig.
	GERALDINE *stomps back to the doll house.* EILEEN *chases after her.*

***

Act One, Scene Eight

MARY's room. Daytime. CRAVEN sits in his chair brooding over his book of poetry. He reads from Keat's "The Eve of St. Agnus".

CRAVEN

"They glide like phantoms, into the wide hall;
Like phantoms, to the iron porch, they glide;
By one, and one, the bolts full easy slide;
The chains lie silent on the foot worn stones;
The key turns,
and the door upon its hinges groans."

"And they are all gone aye, ages long ago
These lovers fled away into the storm.
That night the Baron dreamt of many a woe,
And all his warrior-guests, with shade and form
Of witch, and demon, and large coffin-worm
Were ..."

*MEDLOCK leads MARY in.
CRAVEN closes the book.*

MEDLOCK

Here she is sir.

*MEDLOCK hovers by the door .
MARY stands nervously waiting to see what he's got to say.*

CRAVEN

Come here girl.

MARY	I'm sorry about last night sir...I...

CRAVEN *gestures for her to be silent.*

CRAVEN	I cannot give you time or attention. I am too ill, and wretched and distracted...(*looking at her for the first time he is alarmed by how she looks*) You are very thin.
MARY	I am getting fatter.
CRAVEN	Mrs. Medlock says you should be in school. I have been meaning to ...
MARY	(*frightened*) Oh no sir. Please not yet. I must get stronger first and...I don't mean to do any harm.
CRAVEN	(*irritated*) Don't look so frightened. It depresses me.
MARY	(*tremulously*) I'm sorry. I can't help it.
CRAVEN	I am going away to the continent and I can't say for how long. Is there anything you need or want? Toys? Dolls?
MARY	That would be lovely sir but...what I really want...Might I...Might I...have a bit of earth?
CRAVEN	(*looking quite startled*). Earth! What do you mean?
MARY	I want to plant seeds and make things grow .
CRAVEN	(*passing his hand quickly over his eyes*). Do you care about gardens so much?
MARY	I'm starting to.
CRAVEN	You remind me of someone else who loved the earth and the way things grow.

> CRAVEN *lets his memories fill him for a moment and his mood shifts. He smiles.*

CRAVEN Yes ! When you see a bit of earth you want take it, child, and make it come alive!

MARY May I take it from anywhere if it's not wanted?

CRAVEN Anywhere. Anywhere at all!

MEDLOCK Sir? If she's to go away to school...

CRAVEN You heard her Medlock. She must be stronger before she begins lessons.

MARY Yes. I need liberty and fresh air and romping about.

MEDLOCK Sir, the girl is driving us all mad. She'll be snooping and prowling and...

MARY I will not! I will play in the garden and that is all!

MEDLOCK The garden. Aye — you know where that will lead, don't you sir?

MARY What do you mean by that! If...

> *The cloud descends.* CRAVEN *suddenly becomes angry.*

CRAVEN I'll hear no more about it! (*in a torrent of emotion*) Don't you understand ? She's suffered. She's suffered and if she can find some relief in this futile, rotten...If she can find the peace that eludes me...then...then...

> *Realizing he's on the verge of raving,* CRAVEN *reins himself in. The life goes out of him.*

CRAVEN   Oh, what does any of this matter? I am tired and
                begin my travels this afternoon. Do as I've said
                Mrs. Medlock.

MEDLOCK   (*coldly*) Yes sir.

CRAVEN   (*afterthought*) And give her some money.

MARY   Money sir?

CRAVEN   A shilling a week.

MEDLOCK   Sir there is nothing to spend it on and...

CRAVEN   Give her money. I can give her nothing else.

                As CRAVEN *exits, the children slip in.*
                MEDLOCK *glares at* MARY *who
                sticks out her tongue and runs out. The
                children look at each other and laugh
                with delight, their own little squabbles
                forgotten.* MEDLOCK *sighs and exits.
                The children start to sing.*

                            ***

Act One, Scene Nine

The kitchen garden. Day. The children run singing into the garden.

CHILDREN
Mistress Mary quite contrary
How does your garden grow ?
With silver bells and cockle shells
And pretty maids all in a row!

MARY enters looking glum and starts to look for the door.

GERALDINE   Now she's going to find the garden.

EILEEN   She can't find it yet.

GERALDINE   Why not?

EILEEN   Because she hasn't earned it.

GERALDINE   What nonsense.

EILEEN   In all the old fairy stories you have to do something good before you get what you want.

GERALDINE   Like kiss a frog?

EILEEN   She has to do something good.

> *Frustrated in her search,* MARY *sighs
> and sits down.* MARTHA *enters
> carrying her bag and sneaks up on
> * MARY. *She taps her on the shoulder.*

MARTHA   Boo!

> MARY *gives a little involuntary scream
> and glares at* MARTHA *who smiles in
> return.*

MARTHA   Beautiful morning isn't it Mary? The moor has
turned such a heavenly colour! I think
springtime's coming at last!

MARY   I thought perhaps it always rained or looked dark
in England.

MARTHA   Yorkshire's the sunniest place on earth when it's
sunny at all. Just wait until you see the heather
flowerin'. (*getting no response*) Well...My visit
was such fun. I made doughcakes with a bit of
brown sugar in it and me and Mother had 'em
pipin' hot when the children came in. And they
just shouted for joy. (*still no response*) And in
the evening we all sat round the fire, and I told
them about the little girl who didn't know how
to put on her own clothes at all.

MARY   You told them about me?

MARTHA   Couldn't tell 'em enough. Dickon 'specially.
When I told him you was from India his eyes
nearly started right out of his head,

MARY   Dickon wanted to hear about me?

MARTHA   Aye and Mother, well, she was put out about
your bein' all by yourself.

MARTHA (*as her mother*) "Now, Martha you just think how you'd feel in a big place like that, with no family at all to love you.", she says, "You do your best to cheer her up," and I said I would. And she sent you a present.

MARY A present!

MARTHA Aye, it cost us tuppence, but Mother said it's worth it.

> MARTHA *gives* MARY *the package.*
> MARY *opens it and looks at the rope with a mystified expression.*

MARY Thank you. It's lovely. What's it for?

MARTHA For! Skippin', that's what for.

> MARTHA *tucks up her skirts, then takes the rope.*

MARTHA Mother says skippin'll stretch your legs and arms and give you some strength in 'em. And that you'll be needin' it too round these parts. Now, watch me. (*beginning to skip*).

> Cinderella dressed in yella
> Went upstairs to kiss a fella
> By mistake she kissed a big snake
> How many doctors does it take ?

(*triple time*) One, two, three, four, five, six, seven, eight, nine...etc...

> MARTHA *finally flubs it, laughs and hands the rope to* MARY.

MARTHA I skipped five hundred when I was twelve, but I wasn't as fat then as I am now.

MARY Do you think I could ever skip like that?

MARTHA	Of course. You just try it. (*handing her the rope*)
MARY	It was your twopence bought the rope, wasn't it Martha? It was your wages.
MARTHA	Aye, it was.
MARY	Thank you.

> MARY *holds out her hand because she doesn't know what else to do.* MARTHA *gives her hand a clumsy little shake, as she's not accustomed to this sort of thing either. Then she laughs.*

MARTHA	Eh! You are a queer, old-womanish thing. If you'd been our 'Lizabeth Ellen you'd have given me a kiss.
MARY	Do you want me to kiss you?
MARTHA	(*laughing again*) If you was different, you'd want to do it yourself.
MARY	Oh Martha...So many things have happened since you left...and I had no one to tell and it's made me feel so...Oh, I don't know...
MARTHA	Well, I'm back and you can tell me anything you want.
MARY	I have met my Uncle and he said I won't be sent away to school.
MARTHA	Eh. That was nice of him wasn't it?
MARY	(*solemnly*) Martha, he is so sad he doesn't know what to do about anything at all. I feel sorry for him. And her.
MARTHA	Her?

MARY	My Aunt who died.

                    Pause.

MARTHA	You know, something good has happened to you since you come here.
MARY	What?
MARTHA	Guess.
MARY	I met the robin and I think he understood me when I talked to him.
MARTHA	That's good, but that's not it.
MARY	I ran in the wind until I was out of breath and I could feel the blood rushing through me and it gave me an appetite for the first time in my life.
MARTHA	That's good, but that's not it.
MARY	I got dressed all by myself for the first time in my life! See.

                    Her jacket is buttoned up all wrong.
                    MARTHA *laughs.*

MARTHA	That's good...
TOGETHER	...but that's not it.
MARY	(*thinking of the key*) I'm...I'm not sure what it is then.
MARTHA	You felt sorry for him and her.
MARY	(*thinking about it*) You're right. I don't think I ever felt sorry for anybody before.
MARTHA	Aye, except perhaps for yourself.

MARY	I'm not going to ever feel sorry for myself again. I promise. Any time I start to feel sorry for myself I'll...I'll skip!

> *MARY begins to skip. She's awful. She sort of walks over the rope when she isn't tangled up in it, but she is determined. MARTHA smiles and exits.*

CHILDREN	One, two buckle my shoe Three, four open the door Five, six pick up sticks Seven, eight open the gate. Open the gate, open the gate!

> *The children laugh and run off. MARY keeps skipping.*

MARY	...nine, ten, eleven twelve, thirteen, fourteen, fifteen...(*not seeing* BEN *entering and watching her*)...seventeen, eighteen, twenty!
BEN	Well. You've got more than sour buttermilk in your veins after all.
MARY	Why do you say that?
BEN	Because you're skippin' red into your cheeks, ya young plucked crow.
MARY	I never skipped before. I'm just beginning but I can go up to twenty already.

> BEN *whistles for the robin.*

MARY	(*pausing*) Ben, I'm sorry I spied on you. I promise not to do it anymore.

> BEN *grunts, unsure how to respond and whistles again. The robin appears.*

MARY	There's the robin!

BEN   Aye, there you are!

MARY   He's friends with me now!

BEN   Aye. There's nothin' he wouldn't do for the sake
of showin' off his tail-feathers.

> *The robin sings.*

BEN   Ah, don't you come cozening up to me now. I
can see you've been reddening' up your waistcoat
and polishin' your feathers and I know what
you're up to. You're courtin' out on the moor.
Soon you'll be payin me no mind at all.

> *In a bold mood, the robin flies right
> over to BEN and lands on his head.*

MARY   Oh!

> *BEN shushes MARY and stands
> without stirring, listening to his song
> until the robin gives another flick to his
> wings and flies back up on the wall.*

BEN   Now ain't that something to melt your heart.

> *BEN begins to dig, breaking into a slow
> grin. He sings "The Little Streams of
> Dounna" as he works.*

BEN   Oh it's over the world I've wandered
It's over the world I've roamed
And oh with ships and sailor man
I made the sea my home
But I'm weary of the Trade Winds
And I'm weary all the day

And the little streams of Dounna
They run clean
The little streams of Dounna
They run clean

MARY	Have you a garden of your own Ben?
BEN	No. I'm bachelor and lodge with Martin at the gate.
MARY	If you had one, what would you plant?
BEN	Bulbs and sweet-smellin' roses.
MARY	You like roses?
BEN	I was learned it by a young lady I was gardener to. She had a lot in a place she was fond of and she loved 'em like they was children. Used to bend over and kiss 'em.
MARY	Where is she now?
BEN	According to what the parson says, heaven.
MARY	Did the roses in her garden die too Ben?
BEN	You know nothing about keepin' secrets, do ya?
MARY	Well, if you know about something it isn't a secret is it ?
BEN	You should learn to let things come out natural like, instead of always pushing at them.
MARY	What do you mean?
BEN	I mean you are the worst girl for askin' questions I ever come across.
MARY	If one doesn't ask questions then how can one learn ?
BEN	Ya already know all you need to know about that place. Oh....Skip. It's better for ya.

BEN *starts to walk off.*

MARY	(*calling after him*) I like you Ben Weatherstaff!

> BEN *stops, looks back at her, grunts and starts to exit.*

BEN   (*under his breath, exiting*) Snoop herself to death that one will. Snoop, snoop, snoop.

MARY   Or at least I would if you weren't such an old bear!

> *Suddenly the robin bursts into song and flies in a great circle around the wall. He hovers in one spot and calls to MARY. She goes to him.*

MARY   What? What is it?

> *A gust of wind swings aside some loose ivy trails. MARY jumps towards it and catches it in her hand. She parts the ivy to reveal a round knob which had been covered by the leaves hanging over it.*

MARY   The door!

> *MARY pushes the ivy aside. She pulls the key out of her pocket, puts it in the lock, turns it with both hands and opens the door into the secret garden. MARY stands looking inside.*
> *SFX: a rush of sound - birds and squirrels and the hint of laughter. Then everything stops.*

MARY   (*whispering*) How still it is! How still!

> *MARY enters the garden. The children come out singing the round "White Coral Bells" and moving us into the next scene.*

CHILDREN   White coral bells upon a slender stalk
Lilies of the valley line my garden walk
Oh don't you wish that you could hear them
ring
That can only happen when the fairies sing.

***

Act One, Scene Ten

The kitchen garden. Day. The round continues as MARTHA *bounces on with* MARY *who is practicing her skipping. She's getting better, but has a way to go yet.* MARTHA *joins in the singing.* MARY *skips around the garden.*

CHILDREN & MARTHA   White coral bells upon a slender stalk
Lilies of the valley line my garden walk
Oh don't you wish that you could hear them ring
That can only happen when the fairies sing.

MARY   Martha, what are those white roots that look like onions?

MARTHA   They're bulbs. In spring flowers grow from 'em. Dickon's got a whole lot of 'em planted in our bit of garden.

MARY   Does Dickon know all about flowers too?

MARTHA   (*laughing*) 'Course. Why our Dickon can whisper things right out of the ground. Why? You goin' to take to diggin'?

MARY   Yes. My uncle said I could have a bit of earth and I plan to take him up on his offer. How much would a ...'trowel' cost — just a little one?

MARTHA	Well at Thwaite village I saw little garden sets with a trowel and a rake and a fork all tied together for a shilling.
MARY	I've got more than that in my purse.
MARTHA	My word. That kind of riches can buy anything in the world. (*thinking for a moment*). You know we could write Dickon a letter and ask him to go and buy them garden tools for you.
MARY	But....But, what would I say?
MARTHA	Say;
	"My dear Dickon; This comes hoping to find you well as it leaves me at present. Will you go to Thwaite and buy me some seeds and a set of tools to make a flower bed? "
MARY	"And pick the pretty ones that are easy to grow as I've never done it before".
MARTHA	Good, and then tell him that Martha sends love to mother and...tell him all about India — the elephants and camels and gentlemen going hunting lions and tigers.
MARY	There's no lions in India.
MARTHA	Write that too! We're ignorant when it comes to the place, you know, and it'll be good to learn something new.
MARY	Martha will Dickon bring my tools himself?'
MARTHA	Aye. He'll bring 'em — soon as it's time for plantin'.
MARY	Then I shall see him! I shall like that.
MARTHA	Well I dare say he'd like to see you too.

MARY *stops skipping.*

MARY   (*amazed*) No one ever wanted to see me ever in
my whole life!

> *"White Coral Bells" underscores the
> bridge into the next scene as* MARY *and*
> MARTHA *exit.*

***

Act One, Scene Eleven

The kitchen garden. Day

GERALDINE   Mary visited the garden whenever she could and watched and waited for Dickon.

> EILEEN *brings* DICKON *on, then* MARY *re-enters. Time is passing . She begins to skip and by now she skips quite well.*

EILEEN   And the sun shone and the rain came down.

> EILEEN *goes to the doll house and pulls out a toy squirrel. She makes it race up* DICKON's *leg and perch on his shoulder.*

DICKON   And the squirrels as was sleeping snug in their nests came out to see what was about to eat. And a little fella called Nut went looking for his friend Dickon.

> MARY *stops and looks around, then begins to skip again.The pace and skill of* MARY's *skipping goes up a knotch.*

GERALDINE   And Mary watched and waited.

EILEEN   And the sun shone and the rain came down.

> EILEEN *leads* DICKON *back to the*
> *doll's house and pulls out a puppet fox.*

DICKON   And out on the moors the two of 'em found a
little baby fox as was ailin' and all alone. And
quick as that Dickon picked him up and gave him
a hug. And he called him Captain and put him in
his sack and took him home to make him well.

> DICKON *slips the fox into the bottom*
> *of his sack.* MARY *stops and looks*
> *around again.*

GERALDINE   And still Mary watched and waited.

> MARY *starts to skip again and is*
> *skipping up a storm.*

EILEEN   And the sun shone and the rain came down.

> EILEEN *rushes to the doll's house and*
> *hauls out a toy raven which she flies*
> *over and sits beside* DICKON.

DICKON   Then one day the old black raven what sat in the
eaves of the manor all winter, grumpy and rude
as a bird can be, came down and sat in the
kitchen garden as if he was waiting for an old
friend to visit.

> MARY *stops again and looks around,*
> *then starts to skip once more.*

GERALDINE   And still Mary watched and waited for Dickon.

> EILEEN *sets the raven to cawing and*
> *fluttering.* GERALDINE *rushes over to*
> DICKON, *pulls a penny whistle out of*
> *her pocket and gives it to him.*

EILEEN   But the raven knew...

GERALDINE	She didn't have to wait no more.

>DICKON *begins to play.* MARY *stops*
>*skipping, sees him and rushes over.*

MARY	Dickon?
DICKON	(*smiling at her*) Yes I'm Dickon and these are my friends Nut (*the squirrel*) and Soot (*the raven*).
MARY	Hello. Hello. Hello. Martha said you'd come if I wrote, but it was weeks and weeks ago and I thought you'd never come, not really.
DICKON	Well, here I am Mary.

>*An awkward pause.*

MARY	I'm sorry about the lions.
DICKON	It's true then is it? There's no lions in India.
MARY	No, but there are tigers and they are twice as fierce!

>MARY *beams at* DICKON *who shifts*
>*about shyly.*

DICKON	Ah, well, that's good. I guess. (*showing her a little bundle of tools*). I've got the tools and the woman in the shop threw in a packet of white poppies when I bought the other seeds.

>*The children take Nut and Soot and sit*
>*them on the wall as* DICKON *gets*
>*down to business.*

DICKON	So...Where's your garden? I'll help you plant 'em.

>MARY *doesn't know what to say. She*
>*looks away.*

DICKON	What's the matter?
MARY	I don't know anything about boys.
DICKON	Aye? Well I don't know much about girls neither — 'cept for my sisters and that don't count.
MARY	Could you keep a secret, if I told you one?
DICKON	'Course I could.
MARY	It's a great secret and if any one found it out I believe I should die!
DICKON	Mary if I couldn't keep secrets about the wild things as is my friends, there'd be nothing safe on the moor.
MARY	I want to tell you but...but I'm afraid.
DICKON	Well I promise...You are as safe as a thrush in it's nest upon the moor.
MARY	I've stolen a garden. Nobody wants it. They're letting it die ! And...and nobody has any right to take it from me when I care about it and they don't.

> MARY *throws herself down with her back to* DICKON *and bursts out crying.* DICKON *is taken aback.* DICKON *thinks for a minute, then hauls Captain, the fox out of his bag and takes him to show* MARY.

DICKON	Here Mary. Look. This here is Captain. He's a little fox I found left alone out on the moor. An orphan he was and half-starved...so I had to take care of him.

> MARY *can't resist the little fox. She*
> *holds her hand out nervously to pet it.*
> *The fox looks at her curiously and*
> MARY *pulls it back, but then he*
> *snuggles up for a pat.*

MARY   He's strong now.

> DICKON *gives the fox to* MARY *who*
> *takes him gingerly.*

DICKON   That's right he is. See I thinks when something
like a fox...or a garden as has been left by itself
starts to get tended to again...why it's bound to
grow and get better.

MARY   Do you think my garden can still grow?

DICKON   Well now, that's hard to say 'till I see it.

MARY   (*giggling*) Well...It's right over here...

> *The robin trills away excitedly.* MARY
> *parts the ivy, opens the door and leads*
> *him inside.* MARY *leads* DICKON
> *through the garden door.*

***

Act One, Scene Twelve

In the secret garden. Continued from preceeding scene. DICKON and MARY look around in wonder. The garden is a spooky place. It's grey and everything looks dead, except for a few sprouts poking up here and there. In one corner there is a big tree with a broken limb hanging down on the ground.

DICKON   (*whispering*) I never thought I'd see this place.

MARY   (*loudly*) You knew about it!

DICKON   (*shushing her*) Aye, Martha told us about the garden . She said no one was allowed inside on account of the great sadness that happened.

MARY   Yes. It was tragic. (*pointing*) That's the tree where Mrs. Craven fell. It must be. It's sad in here, isn't it Dickon?

DICKON   Aye, it's a gloomy enough place now, but come summer — the nests as'll be here!

MARY   Nests!

DICKON   Aye. It'd be the safest nestin' place in England. No one never comin' near and tangles of roses to build in.

MARY   I thought the roses were all dead.

DICKON   Not all of 'em! Look.

> DICKON *steps over to the nearest rose
> vine. It's old with gray lichen all over
> its bark, but with a curtain of tangled
> sprays and branches.*

DICKON   This here's as wick as you or me.

MARY   It's alive?

DICKON   There'll be a fountain of roses here this summer.

MARY   I'm glad! I want them all to be "wick". (*pausing*)
                  Do any of the flowers look like bells?

DICKON   Lilies does. Why?

MARY   I just remembered a silly rhyme...

DICKON   Mistress Mary, quite contrary,
                  How does your garden grow?
                  With silver bells and cockle shells,
                  And pretty maids all in a row.

MARY   That's what Martha called me when I first came
                  here. Mistress Mary - Quite - Contrary.

DICKON   I know, we all laughed so hard when she told us.

MARY   It's not funny.

DICKON   Of course it is. How could anybody be contrary
                  in a place where flowers bloom and robins are
                  buildin' nests and singin' and whistlin'?

> MARY *rushes towards him, excitedly.*

MARY   I like you! I do. I never thought I would ever like
                  so many people.

DICKON	You like lots of people now do ya?
MARY	Three and a half!
DICKON	Three and a half?
MARY	(*checking them off on her fingers*) You and Martha and the robin. That's three, and Ben Weatherstaff...but he's only nice to me half the time. DICKON *laughs.*
MARY	You're laughing. Don't you like me?
DICKON	I like you wonderful.

> MARY *beams up at him.* DICKON *reacts shyly.*

DICKON	Well, there's a lot of work to do here!
MARY	Will you help me?
DICKON	Sure. It'll be fun — wakenin' up a garden!
DICKON	You don't want to make it look all clipped and spic and span, do you?
MARY	Oh no. It wouldn't seem like a secret garden if it was tidy. (*melodramatic*) Just think, this door was locked and the key buried ten years ago.
DICKON	But...this here bush has been pruned not more than two year ago!
DICKON	(*looking up*) Storm comin'...

> SFX: *The wind slowly builds to a howl..* MARY *and* DICKON *sneak out, nod goodbye, and run off in opposite directions.*

***

Act One, Scene Thirteen

MARY's *room. Daytime.* MARY
*enters, out of breath. The wind is
building.* MARTHA *is waiting, looking
nervous. Off to one side stand*
MEDLOCK *and* DR. CRAVEN, *a
serious-looking, bearded gentleman who
looks a lot like his cousin.*

MARY   Martha! Martha! I've seen Dickon I've seen
            Dickon! Oh Martha!, I just love him! Oh!

            MARY *gasps, for the first time
            noticing* MEDLOCK *and* DR.
            CRAVEN *standing in her room.*

MEDLOCK   Mistress Mary This is Doctor Craven, your
            guardian's cousin.

DR. CRAVEN Hello Mary.

MARY   Good day sir.

DR. CRAVEN My cousin asked me to look in on you. He said
            you were very thin.

MARY   I am getting fatter. Look — there are no wrinkles
            in my stockings anymore.

            MARY *shows him. He smiles thinly.*

MEDLOCK   Martha, have you been shrinking Mistress
              Mary's hose?

MARTHA   No m'am I...

MARY   They are not shrinking. I am growing in girth.

DR. CRAVEN   (*producing a tonge depressor*) Well let's take a
              look at you then. Stick out your tongue.

              MARY *sticks out her tongue.*

MEDLOCK   She's excellent at that Doctor.

DR. CRAVEN   (*checking her tongue*) Mrs. Medlock I believe
              you have formed a dislike for the child.

              DR. CRAVEN *pulls out a stethoscope.*

MEDLOCK   She's a holy terror sir.

DR. CRAVEN   Breathe in.

              MARY *inhales and holds it.* DR.
              CRAVEN *listens, but keeps on talking.*

DR. CRAVEN   (*to* MEDLOCK) That's to be expected Mrs.
              Medlock. After what she's been through it would
              be strange if she wasn't a borderline hysteric.

              MARY *exhales.*

MARY   I'm not hysteric.

DR. CRAVEN   Inhale girl. Inhale.

              MARY *inhales.*

MEDLOCK   She plain bad, Doctor. It's simple as that.

DR. CRAVEN   Well she's healthy enough.

> DR. CRAVEN *packs up.* MARY
> *stubbornly refuses to exhale until told*
> *to do so, but makes enough noise to*
> *insure the doctor notices.*

DR. CRAVEN   Exhale.

MARY   I'm not hysteric!

DR. CRAVEN   Little girl, you have absolutely no idea what an hysteric is.

MARY   It's somebody who's sick. Isn't it ?

DR. CRAVEN   In a manner of speaking but...

MARY   Well I'm not sick, you just said so.

DR. CRAVEN   I said you were healthy enough but ...

MARY   If there's somebody sick in this house it isn't me.

DR. CRAVEN   What are you talking about?

MARY   There is a child here who cries almost every night.

> DR. CRAVEN *looks at* MEDLOCK
> *accusingly.*

MEDLOCK   Mary...

MARY   She's heard it, everybody has, but they won't admit it. You're a doctor — it is your duty to do something.

DR. CARVEN   (*hauling a bottle and spoon out of his bag*) You know what an hysteric is Mary ? It's someone who hears voices that do not exist. (*to* MEDLOCK) A tablespoon daily, Mrs. Medlock. That should help. Open up girl.

MARY   What is it?

DR. CRAVEN   Cod liver oil.

> MARY *tries to dodge, but* MEDLOCK
> *gets her.*

DR. CRAVEN   (*to* MEDLOCK) Good for both her colour and
her nerves.

> DR. CRAVEN *pours the spoonful of*
> *medicine into* MARY *who makes a*
> *horrible face.*

MARY   You know about him too. Don't you!

> DR. CRAVEN *looks guilty and makes*
> *a fast exit followed by* MEDLOCK.
> MARY's *right on their tail.*

MARY   Answer me. Answer!

MARTHA   Mary.

MARY   You do. You do know. Answer!

MARTHA   MARY!

> MARY *glares at* MARTHA, *then*
> *rushes out.*
> SFX: *The wind howls louder. The*
> *howling of a child gets very loud.*

***

Act One, Scene Fourteen.

The corridor. Night. The children are gathered around a candle at the doll house.

GERALDINE Who do you think is crying ?

EILEEN It's a ghost.

GERALDINE But Mary said it was a child!

EILEEN It's the ghost of a child that the hunchback killed.

GERALDINE It isn't!

EILEEN It's not fair is it ? All the grown-ups know what's going on and we don't .

GERALDINE Mary doesn't know eiither.

EILEEN Well she better find out soon or I'm not going to play anymore.

GERALDINE Fine then.

> MARY *appears.* GERALDINE *lights
> her candle and* MARY *heads down the
> corridor.*
> *SFX: The crying is heard even louder,
> along with the wind.*
> MARY *gets all the way to the curtain
> without being caught and is just about
> to open it when* DR. CRAVEN *and*
> MEDLOCK *step out !* MARY *hides.*

MEDLOCK   Is there nothing else you can do?

DR. CRAVEN   I've done everything that is medically possible.

MEDLOCK   But he is getting worse.

DR. CRAVEN   Well what do you expect? It would be a blessing
if the poor little chap were just to die and get it
over with.

MEDLOCK   Aye. (*interested in the idea*) Then you'd inherit
the manor.

DR. CRAVEN   Mrs. Medlock! The boy's not an orphan! My
cousin is alive after all.

MEDLOCK   Aye, but he'll be dead before his time with all his
gloomy carryin' on.

DR. CRAVEN   (*pleased, but trying not to show it*) For God's
sake Mrs. Medlock.

MEDLOCK   I'm sorry sir, but I can't help but thinking we'd
all be a sight better off with you in charge of
Misslethwaite.

DR. CRAVEN   Perhaps, but this is hardly a conversation one has
right outside the sick room. Come along.

MEDLOCK *and* DR. CRAVEN *exit
into the darkness. MARY steps out of
the shadows and pulls back the curtain.
A glimmer of eerie light pours out.
Summoning all her strength, she steps
into the room beyond. A scream tears
the night. MARY throws herself back
against the door frame in horror.*

Blackout.

End of Act One.

***

Act Two, Scene One

COLIN*'s room. A curtained painting
hangs over a fireplace mantle.* COLIN, *a
ghostly pale boy of* MARY's *age, lies
in bed, propped up by lioows.*MARY
stands looking at him.

EILEEN   (*whispering*) Are you a ghost?

COLIN *and* MARY *come to life.*

COLIN   Are you a ghost?

GERALDINE   No, who are you ?

MARY   No. Who are you?

COLIN   I am Colin. Who are you?

MARY   I am Mary Lennox. Mr. Craven is my uncle.

COLIN   He is my father.

MARY   Your father! No one ever told me he had a boy!

COLIN   Of course not.

MARY   But why wouldn't they?

COLIN   Come here.

> MARY *crosses to the bed and he puts out his hand and touches her.*

COLIN   You are real, aren't you? I have such real dreams. You might be one of them.

MARY   Why were you crying?

COLIN   Because I can't go to sleep when the wind wuthers so. It's lonely and cold and my head aches.

MARY   I imagined that you were crying because you were locked up.

COLIN   Locked up! I will have you know that I stay in this room because I am ill. (*almost proud of it*). I have to lie down all the time. Tell me your name again.

MARY   Mary Lennox. Did no one ever tell you I had come to live here?

COLIN   No, they wouldn't dare.

MARY   Why?

COLIN   Because I would have been angry. You might have seen me and said something. I won't have it when people talk me over.

MARY   Oh, what a queer house this is!

> SFX: *The howling of the wind goes up a notch. COLIN shivers.*

COLIN   Do you hate the moor? I hate the moor.

MARY   I hate it on nights like tonight. It's enough to make one miss India.

COLIN   India? You have come from India?

MARY	Yes, and I could do whatever I wanted there.
COLIN	(*bragging*) Well I can do whatever I want here, but I don't bother because I hate everything.
MARY	How do you like yourself?
COLIN	What ?
MARY	You can't like anything else unless you like yourself — just a little bit.
COLIN	Why should I like myself ? I am going to die.
MARY	Why do you think that?
COLIN	I have heard people say I will die ever since I can remember.
MARY	Dr. Craven?
COLIN	For one.
MARY	I would not believe a word he says. When you're gone he will inherit Misselthwaite so he wants you to die.
COLIN	Well I don't want to die. When I lie here and think about it I cry and cry.
MARY	That's what you were crying about tonight wasn't it?
COLIN	Oh I dare say...Let's talk of something else. Do you see that rose colored silk curtain hanging on the wall over the mantelpiece?
MARY	Yes.
COLIN	There is a cord hanging from it. Go and pull it.

> MARY *gets up, much mystified, and*
> *finds the cord. She pulls it and the silk*
> *curtain runs back on rings and uncovers*
> *a picture of a girl with a laughing*
> *face, hair tied up with a blue ribbon.*
> *She is standing in a garden festooned*
> *with roses.*

MARY   She's beautiful.

COLIN   She is my mother.

MARY   I'm sorry she died.

COLIN   I hate her for it. If she had lived my father would not hate looking at me and I would have a strong back and might have lived too.

MARY   She is much prettier than you but her eyes are just like yours.

COLIN   I am not like her. Draw the curtain.

MARY   But it's a pretty painting. She's in the garden isn't she?

COLIN   Yes she's in a garden, what of it? Draw the curtain.

MARY   Why?

COLIN   She smiles too much and I am ill and miserable.

MARY   But the picture should cheer you up.

COLIN   Draw the curtain. She is mine, and I don't let just anyone see her.

MARY   But...

COLIN   Draw it or I shall become scream!

> MARY *draws the curtain.*

MARY	You are a very strange little fellow
COLIN	(*frowning*) I am strange?
MARY	Always having your own way makes anybody strange.
COLIN	I like having my own way very much so you needn't say any more on the subject.
MARY	(*miffed*) Very well.
COLIN	And why are you so interested in my painting anyway?
MARY	Because I believe it was painted in the secret garden.

            COLIN *half sits up, turning toward her,*
            and leaning on his elbows.

COLIN	The secret garden?
MARY	It was your mother's favourite place but years ago your father locked it up and buried the key. It's a terrible mystery.
COLIN	Oh that garden. My mother had an accident in there and I was born and she died because of it. Everyone knows that. So the garden isn't a secret at all.
MARY	It is! It's locked and no one will talk about it!
COLIN	Oh don't get angry. If you want to see it I will make them let you in.
MARY	(*frightened*) No, you couldn't!
COLIN	I could too. I am going to make them find the door and break it down.
MARY	No, you can't!

COLIN	Why not?
MARY	(*almost sobbing*) If you make them open the door like that it will never be a secret again.
COLIN	I don't understand you at all.
MARY	Don't you see ? If I can find the door on my own I can get inside and no one will know. Then it really would be a secret...and...and it could be our secret and we could play there every day and dig and help the flowers grow and make it come alive. Oh, don't you see how much nicer it is if it's a secret?
COLIN	I never had a secret before, except for knowing I'm going to die. They all think I can't hear when they talk about it.
MARY	Then they are all horrid, stupid beasts.
COLIN	(*laughing*) Yes, they are. I want you to come to see me every day. And we shall keep the garden secret. And you shall be a secret, too.
MARY	But what will Mrs. Medlock do if she catches us ?
COLIN	She will do as I tell her. (*yawning*) Oh, I wish I could go to sleep.
MARY	In India my Ayah used to sing to me when I couldn't sleep.
COLIN	(*drowsily*) I should like that.
MARY	Well then...Shut your eyes

> MARY *sits beside* COLIN, *strokes his hair and sings an Indian lullaby. Slowly he drifts off to sleep.*

***

Act Two, Scene Two

*The secret garden. It's a beautiful day—
things are turning green and buds are
beginning to pop open on the vine.
DICKON is inside, pruning the roses.
Captain is curled up sleeping in the sun
near the wall. Soot and Nut are perched
nearby. MARY rushes in.*

MARY   Dickon! Dickon! There's a boy living in the
house and his name is Colin and he's Mr.
Craven's son and he lives in a big room in the
east wing and

DICKON   Never comes out at all.

MARY   You know about him?

DICKON   Aye.

MARY   Why didn't you tell me!

DICKON   I told you I was good at keepin' secrets.

MARY   Dickon they're trying to kill him!

DICKON   Kill him? Who?

MARY	Everybody! Except for me.. and Martha and you of course...and Ben...and...Oh, it's Doctor Craven and Mrs. Medlock. They talk over him and say he's going to die and he believes it. And his father does nothing. He just runs away to Italy!
DICKON	Do you think Mr. Craven wants him to die too?
MARY	No, but I think he wishes he'd never been born.
DICKON	That's the worst thing on earth for a child.
MARY	Why do you say that?
DICKON	Them as is not wanted scarce ever thrives - like flowers left untended in a garden.
MARY	Well I'm not going to let them kill him. We have to do something.
DICKON	Aye, but what?
MARY	I...I...I don't know, but Dickon you can help. I know you can. Why, you're always finding sick things out on the moor and helping them get better. Like you did with Captain.
	Captain hears his name and looks at them.
DICKON	But Mary you got to know something about a creature 'fore you can help it much. Ya got to know what it likes to eat and where it likes to sleep and all of that.
MARY	Well I know all about Colin.
DICKON	Aye? What does he like?
MARY	Nothing. He hates everything.
DICKON	Ah, now that's what he might say, but I don't believe it for a minute. He likes you doesn't he?

MARY   (*surprised*) You know I think he does. He said I must come and visit every day...and I sang to him and he must have liked that because he fell asleep...

DICKON   Aye and what else?

MARY   Secrets. He likes secrets. When I told him about the garden...

DICKON   You told him about the garden?

MARY   Well no, not exactly. I didn't tell him I'd found the way in, just that it was a secret and I said it could be our secret together. He liked that very much.

DICKON   Well that's the answer isn't it? If Colin came out here it'd be right good for him. The whole world's workin' and hummin' and scratchin' and pipin' and nest-buildin' and breathin' out scents. Why he wouldn't be thinkin' about being sick out here. Not with us.

MARY   Oh, I don't know Dickon. Could he keep the secret? If he tells I'd lose the garden for myself.

DICKON   Nobody ever did no good thinking only of themselves Mary.

MARY   (*thinking on it*) You're right. We'll bring Colin into the garden.

> *The robin flies into the garden with something hanging from its beak.*

MARY   It's the robin!

DICKON   He's building his nest.

> MARY *starts towards him, but* DICKON *stands quite still and puts his hand on* MARY's *shoulder.*

DICKON	We mustn't seem as if we was watchin' him too close or he'll be out with us for good.
MARY	Don't be silly. He's my friend!
DICKON	Aye, but he's building a nest. He'll have nothing to do with us 'till he's done.
MARY	Don't be silly Dickon, we're nest building too!

> *The robin takes off and soars above them singing. Bridge music swells as they begin to play with Soot and Captain.*

***

Act Two, Scene Three

> COLIN's *room. Day into night.* COLIN
> *lies in his bed with* MARTHA *hovering*
> *over him nervously.*

COLIN   Where is she?

MARTHA   I don't know sir. I've looked all over the grounds. Oh me. Oh my. Oh me...

COLIN   Stop fretting!

MARTHA   That's fine for you to say Master Colin but when Mrs. Medlock finds out Mary's been coming here she'll think I told and then I will be sent away.

COLIN   I'll send Medlock away if she dares to say a word about it. Now go and find my cousin!

> MARTHA *bows and begins to exit.*
> MARY *enters.*

MARTHA   Eh! Miss Mary! You shouldn't have done it! When Mrs. Medlock finds out...

COLIN   Shut up about Medlock and get out!

> MARTHA *scurries out.*

MARY   Colin ! You shouldn't treat Martha like that.

COLIN   (*sulky*) Why didn't you come?

MARY	I was in the gardens with Dickon, he's Martha's brother and...
COLIN	I know all about Dickon! Martha's forever prattling on about him — out on the moors talking to the beasts like a madman.
MARY	Colin!
COLIN	I won't let that boy come here if you go out with him instead of coming to see me.
MARY	It's a beautiful day and Dickon...
COLIN	Shut up about Dickon! He's a selfish boy. Keeping you playing in the dirt when he knows I am all by myself.

MARY's eyes flash fire.

MARY	He's nicer than any other boy that ever lived! He's — he's like an angel!
COLIN	(*scornful laugh*) He's a common cottage boy off the moor!
MARY	He's a thousand times better than you — you selfish little brat.
COLIN	How dare you call me selfish!
MARY	It's true. You're the most selfish boy in the world.
COLIN	I'm not as selfish as you. There is a lump coming on my back. I am going to die and you abandoned me.
MARY	I didn't and you're not going to die! You just say that to make people feel sorry for you.
COLIN	I do not, you horrible little lying orphan ! I am going to have Dickon sent away for ever!

MARY	If you send Dickon away, I'll never come into this room again!
COLIN	I'll make them drag you in.
MARY	If you do I'll sit and clench my teeth and...I won't talk. I won't even look at you!

> COLIN *sits up in bed in quite a healthy rage.*

COLIN	Get out of my room!

> COLIN *grabs a pillow and throws it at her.*

MARY	I'm going and I won't come back!
COLIN	Good !

> MARY *stomps out and* COLIN *throws himself back on his pillows . Registering what he's just done* COLIN *begins to sob softly to himself.*

COLIN	I'm going to die.

> COLIN *closes his eyes and buries his head in the pillows. Lights shift. As* COLIN *tosses and turns the lights begin to fade.* EILEEN *and* GERALDINE *appear on either side of the bed with candles. They whisper.*

EILEEN	He's going to die.
GERALDINE	That's what all the grown-ups say.
COLIN	No. I don't want to die.
EILEEN	He's going to die.

GERALDINE   That's what all the grown-ups say.

COLIN   My father hates me. I have her eyes.

EILEEN   His back. His eyes.
It's better if he dies.

COLIN   My back!

> COLIN *moans in fear and screams. As the scene continues,* MEDLOCK *rushes on with a candle. She looks down at* COLIN *then rushes off.* MARTHA *enters, also holding a candle. She frets over* COLIN, *doesn't know what to do and rushes off to find* MARY.

EILEEN   His back. His eyes.
It's better if he dies.

COLIN   I can't bear it!

EILEEN   His back. His eyes.
It's better if he dies.

GERALDINE   Stop it!

> Spotlight on COLIN *who sits up in bed and lets out a hideous shriek.*

COLIN   I'm dying!

***

Act Two, Scene Four

The corridor. Night. MARTHA *drags* MARY *by the arm.*

MARTHA You've got to.

MARY I won't do it.

MARTHA He keeps screaming,"I can't bear it".

MARY If you don't like it make him to stop.

MARTHA He's worked himself into hysterics. He'll do himself harm.

MARY Then somebody ought to beat him!

MARTHA Mary, he's screaming like the world's comin' to an end!

MARY Good. I hate him.

MARTHA Girl this is not funny! You don't understand how sick he is.

MARY So you think he will die too.

MARTHA He gets no fresh air and lies in bed all day. What's gonna make him live?

MARY begins to soften

MARTHA   Do it Mary, for me, who sent you out of doors
to play.

MARY   Oh, very well.

> MARY *screws up her face in*
> *determination, takes* MARTHA's *candle*
> *and enters* COLIN's *room, followed by*
> MARTHA.

***

Act Two, Scene Five

COLIN's *room. Night.* COLIN *is having a major panic attack.* MARY *crosses to the bed.*

MARY   You stop!

COLIN   I'm dying.

MARY   Stop it! I hate you!

COLIN   (*screaming*) I'm dying!

MARY   Everybody hates you! They all want to run out of the house and let you scream yourself to death!

COLIN   (*screaming*) I'm dying!

MARY   If you don't stop I'll scream — and I can scream louder than you ever heard. I'll frighten you!

COLIN *takes a big breath as if he's going to scream.* MARY *screams first and* COLIN *stops, startled by both* MARY's *volume and tone. The tears are streaming down his face and he shakes all over.*

COLIN   I felt a lump on my back. I felt it. I'm going to die.

MARY You're not. It's just hysterics — hysterics! Oh...Let me see.

> MARY *climbs on the bed with him.* DR. CRAVEN *and* MEDLOCK *burst into the room.*

DR. CRAVEN Good Lord!

MEDLOCK Martha!

MARTHA He was in a fearful state and I thought Mary...

MEDLOCK You told her about Colin!

MARY I found him myself so you leave her alone!

COLIN My back! My back!

MARY There's nothing the matter with your horrid back!

DR. CRAVEN Get away from him!

MARY I won't!

MEDLOCK Leave him alone!

COLIN No!

> COLIN *yells with such force that they pull back.*

COLIN Look. Look. You'll see!

> COLIN *holds himself in while* MARY *looks at his back.*

MARY There's not a lump as big as a pin! If you ever say there is again I shall laugh!

> DR. CRAVEN *picks* MARY *up off the bed and sets her aside so he can examine* COLIN.

MARY	Put me down. Put me down!
COLIN	(*to* DR. CRAVEN) You said...I was a hunchback.
DR.CRAVEN	I told you your back was weak because you wouldn't try to sit up.
MARY	You're lying. You said he was going to die, I heard you.
COLIN	You told Medlock I would get a hump ! I heard you too!
DR. CRAVEN	(*to* COLIN) I was speculating.
MARTHA	Oh Lord, you said that with him lying right there before ya?
DR CRAVEN	I didn't think he could hear me.
MARTHA	Did you think he had no ears!
MEDLOCK	Martha!
MARTHA	Children is humans the same as you or me. They got ears. They understand. Ah, all of ya have been trying to kill the poor boy for years.
MEDLOCK	Martha, you are discharged!
COLIN	Leave her alone! It's true! Everything she says is true.
MARY	Tell them Colin. You tell them!
MEDLOCK	Mary — go to your room — immediately!
COLIN	No!
DR.CRAVEN	Master Colin don't forget that you are very ill.
COLIN	I want to forget it. She makes me forget it.

DR. CRAVEN	You need rest — sleep.
COLIN	I can't sleep. You know I can't!
MARY	Hush now Colin. If you're quiet I'll sing you to sleep again.
COLIN	Would you?
MARY	Of course.
COLIN	You can all go.
DR. CRAVEN	But Colin...
COLIN	Go!

> COLIN *glares at* MEDLOCK *who turns and points at* MARTHA.

MEDLOCK	Go!

> MARTHA, *still in a rage, in turn yells at* DR. CRAVEN.

MARTHA	Go!

> DR. CRAVEN, MEDLOCK, *and* MARTHA *exit.*

COLIN	Oh Mary, I'm sorry.
MARY	Hush.

> MARY *starts to sing her Indian lullaby to him and he settles down a bit.*

COLIN	I get so frightened Mary. I don't want to die. I'd do anything to get well. Anything.

> MARY *stops singing.*

MARY	Can I trust you? Can I trust you for sure?

COLIN   I promise.

MARY   I found the way into the garden.

COLIN   Tell me what it's like. Please tell me.

                   MARY *begins to speak.* COLIN *closes
                   his eyes and begins to drift off. Lights
                   shift and become dreamlike. Music
                   underscores the monologue.*

MARY   Well...It has been left alone so long that it has
                   grown all into a lovely tangle. The roses have
                   climbed and climbed until they hang from the
                   branches and walls and creep over the ground.
                   Some have died but many are alive and when the
                   summer comes there will be curtains and
                   fountains of roses.

                   And the ground ...well it's full of daffodils and
                   snowdrops and lilies working their way out of
                   the dark. They are coming up in clusters of
                   purple and gold and leaves are beginning to
                   uncurl. And everything smells of sunshine and
                   honey and butterflies.

                   COLIN *is nearly asleep.* MARY *speaks
                   more softly.*

MARY   It is safe and still and the robin has found a mate
                   and is building a nest.

                   COLIN *is asleep. The lights fade to
                   black then shift to next scene.*

                   ***

Act Two, Scene Six

> COLIN's *room. Morning.* DICKON *sits on the wide side of* COLIN's *bed with Captain in his hands.* MARY, *on the other side, shakes him awake.*

MARY Colin. Wake up. Dickon is here.

> COLIN *sits up startled. He looks around unsure what in the world is going on.*

DICKON Good day Master Colin.

> COLIN *suddenly sees Captain and gives a little scream.*

COLIN A fox!

DICKON That's right. He wanted to meet you special.

> DICKON *hands him Captain who nuzzles his arm.* COLIN *squirms, rather frightened.*

COLIN What does it want?

DICKON He's hungry.

COLIN Take him. Take him Mary.

DICKON It's alright...he's friendly.

MARY	He won't hurt you Colin.
DICKON	Here I brought a bottle so you can feed him.

> DICKON *gives him a baby bottle and the little fox snaps at the nipple.*

COLIN	Oh no, he's...oooo!
MARY	Colin will you...
DICKON	It's O.K., he won't hurt you.

> COLIN *screams a little excited scream and pulls the bottle away, the little fox is too fast for him. He snaps a couple of times then gets the nipple and with a contented growl settles down to drink.*

COLIN	He' likes it.
DICKON	He'll be fine there now Colin.
COLIN	Look Mary. I'm feeding a fox.
MARY	Yes. Fun isn't it? Now, let's get down to business. Dickon is going to help us get you into the garden.
COLIN	How?
DICKON	I could push you in your chair, but what with you never going out, every grown up on the property is going be peeking round corners to see you.
MARY	We'd get caught for sure.
COLIN	Nonsense. I know how to handle the people who work around here and I shall fix it so they don't know a thing.
DICKON	But how?

COLIN	I shall have Mrs. Medlock order everyone to stay away from the gardens whenever you take me out in my chair and I shall warn her that if I so much as see one person I shall become very, very cross and so ill that my father will have to be called back from the continent. He hates that worse than anything.

> MARY *and* DICKON *laugh.* COLIN *looks at them curiously, not quite getting the joke.*

COLIN	What's so funny?
MARY	You are.
DICKON	You talk like you was king of the world.
COLIN	I feel like the king of the world.

> COLIN *smiles. Captain, finishing his bottle nuzzles up to his face.*

COLIN	He smells like flowers and — and cool and warm and sweet all at the same time.
DICKON	It comes of the springtime smelling so grand.
COLIN	I can't help thinking — about what it will look like.
MARY	The garden?
COLIN	No. The springtime.

***

Act Two, Scene Seven

>*The secret garden. Daytime. Music swells as the two robins fly about finishing their nest on the wall. They lay their eggs and the season progresses. COLIN is wheeled on in a chair by DICKON and given a tour of the garden by MARY.*
>
>*The "mother" sits on the nest, then she flies away and out pop five little birds - hatched in the nest. COLIN points at them and laughs in delight .*
>
>*MARY kneels down and begins kissing flowers.*

MARY   Daffodils and snowdrops and lilies. I'm kissing flowers ! You can never kiss people like that.

DICKON   Aw now, I kiss me ma like that most every day.

MARY   You do?

>*COLIN looks at the broken tree. MARY catches his glance and looks at DICKON.*

COLIN   That old tree over is quite dead, isn't it Dickon?

DICKON	Aye.
MARY	(*quickly*) But roses have climbed all over it and will hide every bit of the dead wood when they're full of leaves and flowers.
COLIN	See how the big branch has broken off...

> *The awkward moment is broken by the robin's song as it flutters up to the nest with a worm in it's beak. The little ones cry for food.*

MARY	Oh ! Look at the robin! He's been foraging for his little ones.

> *MARY wheels COLIN towards the robin and leaves him there.*

COLIN	Mary!

> *MARY takes DICKON aside. They whisper.*

DICKON	Mary, what are you doing?
MARY	We must not talk about the tree.
DICKON	Why not?
MARY	Because this place isn't about death any more. It's about life. He can't start thinking about his mother's death, not in here or he will never get well.
DICKON	But Mary you can't just pretend things didn't happen either.
COLIN	Mary!

> *Ignored, COLIN wheels himself back to a place where he can look at the tree.*

MARY	If he says anything about it we must try to look cheerful.
DICKON	But things live and things die, that's just the way of it.
MARY	(*fiercely*) Don't say that.
COLIN	There is no need for all this whispering! That broken tree is where my mother fell and I know it.
MARY	Colin!
COLIN	It's the truth. It's a haunted tree. Isn't it Dickon?
DICKON	Aw...well now, maybe it is.
MARY	Dickon!

> GERALDINE *scowls at* EILEEN *who beams at her.* GERALDINE *then flies her robin off to sit on the far wall. As the scene progresses her robin whistles up a cheery storm.*

DICKON	Why shouldn't Mrs. Craven come back to this garden to look after Colin.
MARY	Yes, why not?
DICKON	I think mothers always come back to look after their young ones when they're took out of the world too soon.
MARY	That's not true. Some mothers never care. They never care at all.

> MARY *wheels* COLIN *away from the tree.*

DICKON	But you heard Colin's Mam yourself, Martha said so.

> *Shocked by* DICKON's *statement*
> MARY *spins to address him, letting*
> COLIN *roll on. He stops himself before*
> *he hits the garden wall and comes back.*

MARY   I didn't. I was...hysterical.

COLIN   You heard her. What did she say ?

MARY   Nothing.

COLIN   My mother is here Mary. I'm sure of it. What did she say?

MARY   She said; "Where you tend a rose my love
A thistle cannot grow."

> *They look around at the flowers*
> *growing where they've been tended.*

DICKON   And just look at her roses now.

COLIN   This place is full of magic.

DICKON   That's the word for it.

COLIN   There is magic here Mary, and you know it. When I look up through the trees at the sky, I feel something pushing and drawing in my chest and making me breathe fast and feel...happy.

DICKON   That's magic sure enough. It's always pushing and drawing and making things grow.

COLIN   I'm growing too!

DICKON   Aye. We'll have you walking round here 'fore you know it, won't we Mary?

MARY   Of course we shall.

COLIN   But my legs are so thin and weak that I'm afraid to try to stand on them.

DICKON	When you stops bein' afraid you'll stand on 'em.
COLIN	Will I?
MARY	Of course you will.
	BEN, *drawn by the robin's persistent whistle suddenly appears on the far side of the wall. He's on a ladder.*
BEN	What in blazes!
MARY	Ben!
BEN	(*shaking his fist at* MARY) If you was a girl of mine I'd give you a hidin'!
MARY	You don't understand.
BEN	I understand me own eyes, don't I? I should have expected such treachery...
MARY	Ben listen...
BEN	I will not listen! Ya scrawny, buttermilk-faced busy body . Always pokin' your nose where it wasn't wanted. You'd have never got around me if it hadn't been for the robin — drat him.
MARY	But it was the robin who showed me the way in!
BEN	(*outraged*) Layin' your badness on a robin! You scamp!
MARY	He did. Oh, I can't explain with you up there shaking your fist at me.
BEN	It's the scruff of your neck I'll be shaking if I come down there.
COLIN	Gardener! Do you know who I am? Answer!
BEN	(*in a shaky voice*) Aye, that I do.

COLIN	Then what are you doing poking about ? I gave orders that no one is to come to the gardens when I am outside.
BEN	You wasn't out here and I figured...
DICKON	You're the one who did the prunin'!
BEN	Aye.
MARY	But no one could get in. The door was locked.
BEN	I'm no one and I come over the wall. (*to* COLIN) Your ma, she told me: "Ben Weatherstaff, if ever I'm ill or if I go away you must take care of my roses."
COLIN	But my father ordered everyone to keep away.
BEN	She'd gave her order first! (*overcome with emotion*). Oh God look at you. Your mother's eyes starin' at me out of your face — you poor little cripple.

COLIN's *face flushes and he sits up.*

COLIN	I'm not a cripple!

COLIN *tears the blanket off his legs and tries to stand.*

BEN	Steady there boy.

BEN *climbs down the ladder in a flash.*

MARY	You can do it! You can do it! You can!

COLIN *stands just as* BEN *bursts through the door.*

BEN	Oh my Lord...

COLIN   Look at me! Am I a cripple?

BEN   (*overwhelmed*) Nothing like it sir...Oh...Why
            have you been hidin' away from folk, lettin' 'em
            think you was on death's door?

COLIN   Well...well because...everyone said I was going to
            die.

BEN   Never! You've got too much pluck in you for that.

                        BEN *chokes and tears run down his*
                        weather-wrinkled cheeks.

COLIN   There is magic in this garden Weatherstaff. It
            made me stand up. Do you believe?

BEN   You're the proof sir.

COLIN   I'm going to walk to that broken tree. Watch me.

                        COLIN *tries to walk but stumbles and*
                        falls to the ground. They rush to him,
                        put him in his chair and wheel him off .

GERALDINE   Why did he fall ?

EILEEN   He's been lying in his bed for years and he's too
            weak to walk.

GERALDINE   No, the magic cured him.

EILEEN   It's not that kind of magic.

GERALDINE   It is. It's magic like in the earth.

EILEEN   Things don't grow out of the earth over night.

GERALDINE   Never-the-less they grow.

                        ***

Act Two, Scene Eight

COLIN's *room. Daytime.* MARY *and*
COLIN *are lying on the bed, apparently*
asleep. The curtain is drawn back on the
painting of COLIN's *mother.*
MARTHA *enters with a tray of*
muffins.

MARTHA   Wake up now. I got hot muffins. Cook made 'em
special.

They don't move. MARTHA *bends over*
them to see what's the matter. They
scream and tickle her. COLIN *grabs a*
muffin and gobbles it down.

MARTHA   Ah, it's good to see you eating like that Master
Colin.

COLIN   I must eat to build up my strength.

MARTHA   I just wish you'd let me tell Mrs. Medlock.

COLIN   You mustn't. This is the biggest secret of all
time and if you weren't Dickon's sister we
wouldn't have told you.

MARTHA   I wish you hadn't sir. When we're caught...

COLIN   We won't be caught. No one is going to know anything about it until I have grown so strong that I can walk and run like any other boy.

                    MARTHA *looks at* MARY *nervously.*

MARTHA   Aw now sir, don't you think your father would be pleased to know you're gettin' better?

COLIN   No. He wouldn't believe it Martha. He's too...sad. And if he sees me, and doesn't believe, it will kill the magic. I know it will. So until I can walk into his study and say; "Here I am — just like any other boy", nobody will say a word to my father.

MARTHA   Yes sir, but if you write to him...

COLIN   Not yet Martha. (*to* MARY) Pass the muffins.

MARY   There's only three left.

COLIN   I know. That's two for me and one for you.

MARY   Three for me. None for you.

COLIN   No, none for you!

                    COLIN *makes a grab for the muffins.* MARTHA *snatches the tray away from* MARY.

MARTHA   Lord, wastin' food! It vexes me!

                    MEDLOCK *and* DR. CRAVEN *enter catching* MARY *and* COLIN *laughing and screaming.*

MEDLOCK   Colin!

                    COLIN *freezes.*

MEDLOCK	I don't know what's got into the boy. All he does these days is eat and laugh.

> COLIN *groans and lays back in the bed.* MARY *tries not to giggle.*

DR. CRAVEN	Come, let me look at you Colin.

> DR. CRAVEN *crosses to* COLIN *who does his best to look wan.*

DR. CRAVEN	And how are we feeling?
COLIN	Terrible. I always feel terrible when you arrive.

> MARY *almost giggles.* MEDLOCK *glares at her. The doctor makes a quick examination of* COLIN.

DR. CRAVEN	You're gaining weight and there's color in your cheeks.
MEDLOCK	No wonder, the way he's been eating.
COLIN	It's an unnatural appetite.

> MARY *gags with suppressed laughter.*

DR. CRAVEN	What is the matter?
MARY	(*severe in her manner*) It was something between a sneeze and a cough and it got into my throat.
DR. CRAVEN	Has she been taking her cod liver oil Martha?
MARTHA	Well sir...
MARY	Twice a day. It tastes so good!

> COLIN *laughs. The doctor goes back to examining him.*

DR. CRAVEN   Yes...well if this rapid recovery keeps up I shall
              have to send for Mr. Craven.

                        COLIN *looks at* MARY *in a bit of a
                        panic.*

COLIN   But I'm not recovering! I'm not recovering at all!

                        DR. CRAVEN *doesn't seem to hear
                        him at all. He and* MEDLOCK *exit.
                        Lights shift to the children.*

GERALDINE   He can't write yet. Colin's not ready.

EILEEN   He doesn't care. Grown-ups never do.

GERALDINE   All you ever do is make trouble! If Mr. Craven
              comes back too soon everything will be ruined.

EILEEN   Well then, Colin had better keep him from
              writing somehow.

GERALDINE   He will!

                        ***

Act Two, Scene Nine

	In the secret garden. Daytime. COLIN, MARY, *and* DICKON *being lead through exercises by* BEN. *The robins sing happily in their nest.*
BEN	Alright now. Tall as a house. Small as a mouse. Tall as a house. Small as a house. Tall as a...
	BEN's *back gives out and he stops, out of breath.*
MARY, COLIN & DICKON	House!
BEN	Enough, enough. Master Colin needs to catch his breath.
COLIN	Fiddlesticks.
MARY	Did you really learn those exercises in the navy Ben?
BEN	Of course. Why the Admiral himself did "Tall as a house, small as a mouse".
	The three laugh and BEN *smiles at them.* COLIN *sits down in his chair, looking quite tired.*

COLIN	I am famished.
MARY	So am I.
COLIN	It's terrible Ben. We're hungry all the time, but we can't let anybody catch us eating.
BEN	That makes no sense. You'll not get strong that way..
COLIN	But we have to pretend we've no appetite or Dr. Craven is going to send for father and I'm not ready.
DICKON	You know I've been givin' this problem some thought. And so I talked to my mother.
MARY	What did she say we should do?
DICKON	Eat. She says: "You can trifle with your breakfast and disdain your dinner if you are full to the brim with frothy new milk and buns and heather honey."
	DICKON *hauls two tin pails — one full of rich new milk and the other with cottage-made currant buns out of his bag. They all dive in. As they eat COLIN gets ever so thoughtful.*
COLIN	What day of the month is it Mary?
MARY	The first of May.
COLIN	Good. We must all remember this day because I am going to tell you all something very important. (*assuming a military air*) Are you with me Midshipman Weatherstaff?
BEN	Aye, aye sir!
COLIN	Excellent. I am going to give you a lecture.

BEN	(*nervously*) A lecture?
COLIN	Don't worry Midshipman Weatherstaff. It will be a short lecture because I am very young, and I don't want to put you to sleep.
BEN	Ah Master, I only fall asleep in church.
	COLIN *laughs and* BEN *joins in.*
COLIN	I am growing strong Ben. I can feel it in my bones and I know why. Magic. I can prove it too.
MARY	How?
COLIN	You know how you learn things by saying them over and over until they stay in your mind forever ?
MARY	Yes I suppose I do.
COLIN	Well I suspect it is the same with magic. I think that if you keep calling it, it will come. So as often as I can remember I am going to say, "Magic is in me!" And that will make me strong. Do you think it will work Dickon?
DICKON	Aye. It'll work for sure.
COLIN	Then let us begin. We must sway backward and forward...
BEN	I can't do no swayin' back and forward. I've got the rheumatics.
COLIN	(*in a High Priest tone*) The magic will take them away. (*regular voice*) But we won't sway until it has done it. We will only chant.
BEN	(*testily*) I can't do no chantin'. They turned me out of church choir only time I ever tried.
COLIN	Then I will chant for you.

          COLIN *chants.*

COLIN

The sun is shining.
The sun is shining.
The magic is alive.

          COLIN *falters, but the robin pipes in.*

DICKON

Look. The robin has come to help us.

          COLIN *smiles.*

COLIN

The robins are singing
The roots are stirring.
The flowers are growing.
Magic is alive.

I'll grow tall as a tree
There's magic in me.
Tall as a tree.
There's magic in me.

ALL

Tall as a tree
There's magic in me.
Tall as a tree.
There's magic in me.

          As they chant COLIN *stands.*

COLIN

It's in Ben Weatherstaff's back too. (*waving his hand at* BEN) You will get better.

          BEN *stands and does a comic dance step.*

COLIN

The magic is in us Ben! The magic is making us strong! I shall live for ever and ever and ever! I shall find out about people and creatures and everything that grows and I shall never stop making magic.

***

Act Two, Scene Ten

In the kitchen garden. MEDLOCK *and*
DR. CRAVEN *enter.*

MEDLOCK They are eating next to nothing and yet they look so healthy.

DR. CRAVEN They'll die of starvation if they can't be persuaded to take some nourishment.

MEDLOCK They're a pair of young Satans that's what they are. Bursting their jackets while they're turning up their noses at the best meals Cook can tempt them with. Why the poor woman fair invented a pudding for them yesterday and back it's sent. She almost cried .

DR CRAVEN Cried?

MEDLOCK She's terrified she'll be blamed when they starve themselves into their graves.

DR. CRAVEN Is there any way in which those children can get food secretly?

MEDLOCK Not unless they dig it out of the earth.

The sound of laughing off. DR.
CRAVEN *and* MEDLOCK *hide beside
the wall.* MARY *pushes* COLIN *on.
He's got his blanket over his head and is
pretending to be a
ghost - having a grand old time. They
laugh furiously until* MEDLOCK *and*
DR. CRAVEN *step out of hiding.*

DR CRAVEN   Master Colin.

Seeing the doctor COLIN *assumes a
languid pose.*

COLIN   Oh, hello Uncle.

DR. CRAVEN   I am sorry to hear that you do not eat anything.

COLIN   I can't.

DR. CRAVEN   That won't do. You will lose all you have gained.

COLIN   Yes, I suppose I shall waste away.

MEDLOCK   You ate so well a short time ago.

COLIN   I told you it was an unnatural appetite.

MARY *bursts out laughing.*

MEDLOCK   Listen to her. The glummest, ill-natured little thing she used to be, and now her and Master Colin laugh like a pair of crazy people all day long!

COLIN   Perhaps we're growing fat on laughing.

DR. CRAVEN   Perhaps you are. (*to* MEDLOCK) But I doubt it.

COLIN *hoots and laughs as* MARY
pushes him off.

DR. CRAVEN   I'm writing my cousin tonight.

                 They exit. EILEEN *rushes forward,*
                 angry at GERALDINE.

EILEEN   No, no, no. He wouldn't write to Mr. Craven not
                 now!

GERALDINE   Why not?

EILEEN   Because he thinks Colin is getting sick again.
                 That would make him happy.

GERALDINE   But Colin is well now. It's time for his father to
                 come home.

EILEEN   There is no magic in a letter from an evil doctor
                 and it will take magic to make Mr. Craven love
                 his son.

                 They think.

GERALDINE   Then we will have to send the robin.

EILEEN   No, the ghost.

GERALDINE   It was late summer and Mr. Craven was in...

EILEEN   ...Italy.

                 GERALDINE *hauls a blue scarf out of*
                 the doll house and gives it to EILEEN.

GERALDINE   At Lake Como.

                 GERALDINE *rushes off and* EILEEN
                 lays the cloth out on the ground. It
                 becomes a stream.

EILEEN And as he walked in the hills he heard a robin singing.

> *SFX: The song of a robin.*
> GERALDINE *enters with the robin.*
> CRAVEN *comes on following the bird as* EILEEN *sprinkles flower petals around.*

***

Act Two, Scene Eleven

At Lake Como and in the kitchen garden at night. CRAVEN *sits among the flowers watching the robin. He re-reads the letter he holds in his hands and noticing the flowers begins to drift.*

CRAVEN Forget-me-nots.

CRAVEN *laughs wearily and lays back.*

CRAVEN How differently I looked at flowers years ago when I felt as if I was alive.

CRAVEN *falls asleep to the song of the robin. The lights shift. Something magical is happening as* CRAVEN *dreams. Special on* COLIN *off to one side.*

CHILDREN (*singing*) White coral bells upon a slender stalk

COLIN (*whispering*) Father. Come home. I miss you.

CHILDREN Lilies of the valley line my garden walk

COLIN Father! I love you.

CHILDREN Oh don't you wish that you could hear them ring?

COLIN   I love you, like my mother did.

CHILDREN   That can only happen when the fairies
            sing.

            SFX: a new voice is heard joining the
            children, who gradually fade out in the
            mix.

COLIN   I have her eyes.

            COLIN, *The Children and a woman's*
            voice on tape are all heard
            simultaneously. This round builds, then
            fades as CRAVEN *wakes.*

LILLIAS   When you tend a rose my love
            A thistle cannot grow.

CHILDREN   When you tend a rose my love
            A thistle cannot grow.

COLIN   Come home...to the garden.

            CRAVEN *sits up and looks around,*
            confused.

CRAVEN   Lillias? Lillias, where are you?

ALL   (*whispering*) In the garden.

            The robin sounds like a golden flute.

ALL   (*whispering*) In the garden.

CRAVEN   In the garden!

            CRAVEN *stands and follows the robin*
            off.

       ***

Act Two, Scene Twelve

> *In the secret garden. Daytime.* BEN,
> DICKON, MARY *and* COLIN *are in
> the garden. The whole family of robins
> are singing. Rose bushes have exploded
> around the broken tree but above the
> bushes the tree barren. After a moment*
> COLIN *stands.*

COLIN   Do you remember that first morning you brought me in here Dickon?

DICKON   Aye, that I do.

COLIN   Just this minute, all at once I remembered you wheeling me in and I looked at my hand digging with the trowel and I had to stand up on my feet to see if it was real. And it is real!

> EILEEN *appears on the wall adding a
> beautiful single budding flower to the
> top of the dead tree.*

DICKON   Aye, the magic worked!

COLIN   I wish...I wish my father was here. I wish he could see me. The waiting is terrible now.

MARY   I remember in India how I used to wish my mother would come and see me, but she never came.

DICKON	Ah, now Mary.
MARY	It's true. She never spoke to me and never wanted to ever see me and when everybody got sick with the cholera and were dying, even then she didn't come for me. She just went off and died on her own and left me alone.
COLIN	Well you're not alone anymore, are you Mary?
MARY	No.
DICKON	Now you have friends.
BEN	And the garden.
MARY	It's strange you know. Before I couldn't even think about her. It was like the tree. Remember I thought if we talked about it Colin would be afraid and get sick again, but you talked about it Dickon and then it wasn't so awful any more.
CHILDREN	Colin, look up!
COLIN	(*looking at the top of the tree*) The tree. Look! Something is blossoming. There on the highest branches!
BEN	(*squinting up*) Ah, it couldn't boy, the tree's long dead.
DICKON	I don't know Ben. Look...
COLIN	I'm going up there.
BEN	She's too brittle Colin.
COLIN	Believe Ben. Watch.
	COLIN *runs over to the tree and begins to climb.*
MARY	Colin!

BEN	It won't hold boy!
COLIN	It will Ben. I am going to climb all the way to heaven!

> COLIN *climbs to the top and looks at the flowers.*

COLIN	Look at it Mary. It is alive! Everything is alive and oh the view of the garden from up here...and the moor I can see across the moor for hundreds and hundreds of miles!
CRAVEN	(*off*) Colin? Colin!

> COLIN *looks across the kitchen garden and sees his father. He explodes with joy.*

COLIN	Father ! Father !

> CRAVEN *runs in and beams up at* COLIN.

COLIN	I wished for you ! I wished and now you're here! Come! Come in and see the garden!
CRAVEN	Oh my boy. My boy, look at you!
COLIN	Yes father. Here I am. Just like any other boy.
CRAVEN	You are well! You are!
COLIN	Yes. (*a shy pause*). Look at Mother's tree father. It's alive.

> COLIN *beams at his father.* CRAVEN *moves towards him.*

CRAVEN	Your mother...She came to me in a dream and...and she said she was in the garden.
COLIN	She is here father. She is...with us.

CRAVEN   Oh Colin, when she died I missed her so I let my soul fill up with blackness and I...I was afraid if I let you into my heart I would lose you too and I couldn't bear it...

I abandoned you. That was wrong, so very wrong. Can you ever forgive me ?

COLIN   Of course I forgive you, father. It doesn't matter now. You're home. (*looking around the garden*)

> COLIN *looks around the garden and "sees"* EILEEN *and* GERALDINE. *He smiles at them and they smile back.*

COLIN   We all are.

CRAVEN   I love you Colin.

COLIN   And I LOVE YOU !

> COLIN *swings down off the wall lands at his father's feet and hugs him.*

COLIN   I have so much to tell you ...about Mary and Dickon and Ben and the robin and the secret garden...

> MARTHA *appears climbing over the wall.*

MARTHA   Oh Lord, Master Colin where are you ? Your father's back and Mrs. Medlock is looking all over for you. He'll have me hide he will if he finds out...

> MARTHA *gets a look inside the garden and gapes at the scene below.*

MARTHA   Oh me, oh my, oh me, oh my....

MEDLOCK   (*off*) Martha get down from there!

> MARTHA *falls off the wall and*
> *disappears for a moment as* MEDLOCK
> *bursts into the garden.*

MEDLOCK   Oh my Lord, Master Colin Have you gone mad boy! Your father has come and...

MEDLOCK   (*as she sees them all*) Mr. Craven...Colin... Ben...I...I...

BEN   Aye look at him darlin'. The Master of Misselthwaite, eyes full of laughter and as strong and steady as any boy in Yorkshire!

> BEN *crosses to* MEDLOCK, *picks her*
> *up, spins her around and kisses her as*
> DICKON *and* MARY *close the garden*
> *wall.* DICKON *smiles, takes* MARY's
> *hand and squeezes it tight.*

DICKON   Would you fancy a walk on the moors, Mistress Mary?

MARY   Aye Dickon. I would that.

DICKON   Then I will take you home for tea and you can tell my Ma this story and she'll be cryin' and laughin' before we're done!

> *Impetuously* MARY *kisses* DICKON
> *who blushes and smiles, then takes her*
> *hand. They run off.*

> *The End.*

Mandy and the Magus

A play for children in one act

by Brian Tremblay

Music by Leslie Arden

Brian Tremblay completed a three-year theatre studies program at Camosun College in Victoria, British Columbia, and then went on to a career as an actor at many of Canada's regional theatres. His first play, *Two for the Show*, debuted at the Kawartha Summer Theatre in 1982, and his first play for children, *Fezwick*, premiered in Toronto and toured the Western provinces the next year. Later works include *The Shadow Walkers, Caught in the Act, The Promise* and *R.I.P Mr. G.I.C.* In 1985, he started directing for stage in Canada and the U.S. He is currently the Artistic Director of the Kawartha Summer Theatre, in Lindsay, Ontario, and is also writing for television.

The Characters

ACTOR ONE   Mother, The Magus

ACTOR TWO   Mandy

ACTOR THREE   Mr. Davenport, Max/Father

ACTOR FOUR   Michael, Captain Tanglewood

Production Notes

At one point in the play, Mandy's bed is tipped on its side to become a
wall. If this bed is made for your production it would be nice to have it
constructed with supports. If a regular bed is to be used, that will also
work well providing the mattress and springs are secured to the frame.
For convenience you may wish to consider underdressing MOTHER
when she plays the MAGUS, and MICHAEL when he plays CAPTAIN
TANGLEWOOD. If the bedspread on Mandy's bed could be doublesided
it would also help. One side for MANDY, the other as a cover or
dressing for the Magus' throne with, perhaps, an emblem on it. The
character of MUGWORT is designed to be a hand puppet and easily
carried by the MAGUS or CAPTAIN TANGLEWOOD.

Mandy and the Magus premiered at The Kawartha Summer Theatre, Lindsay, Ontario, 1988, with the following cast:

MOTHER/MAGUS	*Jody Howz*
MANDY	*Debra Drakeford*
MAX/FATHER	*Darren Hill*
MICHAEL/CAPT. TANGLEWOOD	*Kevin Ryder*

Directed by Janet Feindel.
Stage manager — Chris Chenier.
Set design by Jane Wild.

Scene One

The bedroom of MANDY *on a rainy day. The only essential furnishings are her bed and one chair which will double as the* MAGUS' *throne. There are a few toys scattered about on the floor. On the bed is a distinctive looking doll Mr. Davenport. He is dressed in a red suit with a matching cape and small pillbox hat. There is thunder in the distance.*

At rise, MANDY *is laying on her bed talking to the doll, Mr. Davenport.*

MANDY   I don't know Mr. Davenport. I don't think it's ever going to stop raining. What a crummy day to have a birthday.

MOTHER *enters.*

MOTHER   I'm sorry Mandy, but it's raining so hard I don't think we can go to the zoo today.

MANDY   It's the only thing I wanted to do on my birthday.

MOTHER   (*sympathetically*) I know dear, but there's nothing we can do about it.

MANDY   It's just not fair. I waited a whole year for this day and now its ruined.

MOTHER	We'll do something else Mandy. When your father comes home how about we all go to a movie?
MANDY	No. There's nothing on I want to see.
MOTHER	I'll tell you what. The very next sunny day we will go to the zoo. We'll pretend *that* day is your birthday.
MANDY	It's no use pretending because it won't be my birthday. This is my birthday.
MOTHER	Pretending can be fun Mandy.
MANDY	Pretending is for little kids.
MOTHER	I don't think so. I'm your mother and I still pretend.
MANDY	If I pretend the rain will stop, will it stop?
MOTHER	I can't change the weather Mandy.
MANDY	Then why should I pretend? What's the use?
MOTHER	Well then, we'll just have to settle with what we have. (*moving to the door*) I want you to look after your brother Michael while I go to the store.
MANDY	Oh Mom. Do I have to baby-sit on my birthday?
MOTHER	It will only be for a few minutes while I get some cake and ice-cream. Won't that be nice? (*calling*) Michael!
MICHAEL	(*off*) Yea!
MOTHER	(*calling*) Come up to your sister's room!
MICHAEL	(*off*) Do I have to? *Killer Robots* is on!
MOTHER	(*calling*) Do as I say young man!

MANDY   Be as fast as you can. I hate looking after him.

MOTHER   Why?

MANDY   He never listens to what I say. If I could pretend,
               I'd pretend he lived in another country.

MOTHER   He's your brother Mandy.

MANDY   That's not *my* fault.

MOTHER   Honestly! I don't know what's gotten into you
               Amanda.

                         MICHAEL *enters.*

MOTHER   I ask you to do the smallest things around this
               house and you'd think I had asked you to fly to
               the moon!

MANDY   I wish I could.

MICHAEL   I wish you could too.

MANDY   (*starting for* MICHAEL) You Little Wart!

MICHAEL   (*avoiding her*) Bird Brain!

MOTHER   (*stopping the confrontation*) Now look you two,
               just calm down! Michael, you listen to your
               sister while I'm out.

                         MANDY *sticks her tongue out at*
                         MICHAEL *without* MOTHER *seeing.*

MOTHER   And Mandy, don't provoke your brother into any
               fights.

                         MICHAEL *sticks his tongue out at*
                         MANDY *without* MOTHER *seeing.*

MOTHER   Now, I'll be back in a few minutes. Try not to
                wreck the house while I'm gone. Mandy, why
                don't you read your brother a story. Something
                nice and quiet.

                        MOTHER *exits. A moment passes as
                        the two glare at each other.*

MICHAEL   Well, "Gorp Head", what do you want to do?

MANDY   Nothing with you, "Nerd Face"! What a crummy
                birthday.

MICHAEL   Mom said you had to read me a story.

MANDY   She did not.

MICHAEL   Did.

MANDY   Did not.

MICHAEL   Did.

MANDY   She said, "Why don't I?" Remember, I'm the one
                who's in charge.

MICHAEL   Well then what do you want to do? (*picking up
                Mr. Davenport*) Sit around and talk to a dumb
                doll. (*shaking the doll*)

MANDY   (*taking the doll from* MICHAEL) You leave this
                alone and mind your own business. I wish it
                wasn't raining. I'd shove you outside.

MICHAEL   I know what we can do. Let's play, "War In
                Space"!

MANDY   I don't want to play, "War In Space".

MICHAEL   Then how about, "Battle Of The Dead Planets"!

MANDY   No.

MICHAEL   How about throwing flys into a spider's web?

MANDY	You're disgusting.
MICHAEL	I am not. You're disgusting.
MANDY	You don't even know what it means.
MICHAEL	I do too!
MANDY	What then?
MICHAEL	It means...(*stuck*) It means...Well, what ever are, that's what it means.
MANDY	See. I told you. You don't have any idea what it means.
MICHAEL	Why don't you tell me then?
MANDY	It means...(*not exactly sure*) It means ....something that's not very nice.
MICHAEL	(*not letting go*) Like what?
MANDY	Like anything. Like school on a Monday and needles from the doctor and little brothers.
MICHAEL	I saw a dead rat yesterday.
MANDY	Oh! That's gross!
MICHAEL	Do you have to be such a "Grump" all the time?
MANDY	You would be too if you had to look after a little brother who always played with ickey dead things. Why don't you do something else?
MICHAEL	I do. Sometimes I go on great adventures.
MANDY	Oh ya? Like where?

SONG: "I CAN'T SIT STILL".

By the end of the song, MICHAEL has messed up the bed, upset the chair and broken one of MANDY's toys which was on the floor. The damage is not done maliciously, but just seems to happen as MICHAEL gets carried away with himself.

MICHAEL
I'm a hero near a Death Star,
That is hurtling through space.
My assignment is to save us,
From an ugly Alien race.
My space ship's going warp speed plus,
Oh gee, it's so much fun.
The Aliens can't go quite as fast,
They crash into the sun.

MICHAEL
Bam!

I can't sit still. I can't be quiet.
I thought I could once, so I tried it.
I had to squirm, I had to prance.
It's like I got ants in my pants.

I'm a knight in shining armour,
With a splendid flashing sword.
My duty is to save you ,
From a drooling nasty Lord.
I scale the mighty castle wall,
And fight a hundred men.
I find the maid and, coming out,
I fight them all again.

Bash!

I can't sit still. I can't be quiet.
I thought I could once, so I tried it.
I had to squirm, I had to prance.
It's like I got ants in my pants.

MANDY

I don't want to be the oldest.
It's no fun to baby-sit.
I always have to be in charge.
Well I'm just sick of it.

MICHAEL

I'm Captain of a pirate ship.
I look for Spanish gold.
My pirate friends don't question me.
They all do what they're told.
I sail far to the east and west.
It doesn't bother me.
No other ship can catch my craft.
I'm master of the sea.

Bang!

I can't sit still. I can't be quiet.
I thought I could once, so I tried it.
I had to squirm, I had to prance.
It's like I got ants in my pants.

Bam! Bash! Bang!

End of SONG. MICHAEL looks down
and realizes he has broken one of
MANDY's *toys.*

MICHAEL

Oh no!

MANDY

Look what you've done! I've had that since I was
six.

MICHAEL

It was an accident.

MOTHER *enters carrying a bag of*
groceries.

MOTHER

What's all the noise? (*slowly taking in the scene*
of devastation) What has been going on here?

MANDY *and* MICHAEL *try to answer*
at the same time. The following lines
all overlap each other.

MANDY	Michael broke my toy.
MICHAEL	It was an accident!
MANDY	You know? The one..
MICHAEL	I was just showing...
MANDY	...had since I was six
MICHAEL	...Mandy some pretend...
MANDY	...years old. He never cares...
MICHAEL	...games and somehow this...
MANDY	...about my things. He just...
MICAHEL	...silly toy got under my...
MANDY	...does what he likes.
MICHAEL	...feet. I don't know how...
MOTHER	Enough! Mandy, I left you in charge. What happened?
MANDY	Michael just started jumping around and, before I knew it, he wrecked my room and broke my toy.
MOTHER	Just look at this mess.
MANDY	But Mom...
MOTHER	Just a moment "Young Lady". I ask you to do one small thing for me while I'm out and look what you let happen. Amanda, I'm very disappointed in you. (*looking at* MICHAEL *and pointing toward the door*) Go to your room Michael and stay there.

MICHAEL *exits.*

MOTHER	You will clean up this mess Mandy. And you will stay in this room until I tell you to come out.
MANDY	But it's my birthday.
MOTHER	Birthday or no birthday, you will stay in this room until you clean up this mess.

> MOTHER *exits.* MANDY *reluctantly begins to tidy her room, straightening her bed, and righting the chair*

MANDY   (*to herself*) It's not fair. Why do I get blamed for everything that happens around this house. I hate living here. I hate this room and I hate my brother. If it wasn't for him none of this would have happened. This is the worst birthday of my life. The very worst. It's pouring rain outside, Michael breaks one of my oldest toys and I can't leave my room.

> MANDY *has now finished her cleaning. She smooths the covers of her bed, picks up her doll, Mr. Davenport, and settles herself at the top of the bed.*

MANDY   (*to the doll*) You don't know how lucky you are Mr. Davenport. No mother to yell at you. No little brother to drive you crazy. It must be great to be a toy. Always ready to play. I think you have a great life Mr. Davenport. I wish there was one thing in my life I didn't hate. Oh what's the point in talking to this stupid doll!

> MANDY *violently throws the doll off, picks up one of her pillows, covers her head on the bed,a nd begins to cry. A moment later Mr. Davenport enters full-size from the direction* MANDY *threw the doll. He is rubbing his head and his behind from the rough landing he had as a doll.*

> *He is a little wobbly as he makes his way toward the bed. MANDY does not see his approach. He must not be frightening, but rather timid and jovial.*

MANDY What am I going to do? What ever am I going to do?

> *Mr. Davenport (MAX) sits on the bed and tries to comfort MANDY by patting her on the shoulder.*

MAX There, there.

MANDY I have no friends...

MAX I know, I know.

MANDY I have to stay in my room on my birthday...

MAX (*continuing to pat*) It will all be better, you'll see.

MANDY It's pouring rain outside...

MAX It will stop soon.

> *MANDY suddenly realizes that someone has been answering her complaints. Without looking, MANDY reaches behind and finds Mr. Davenports's hand on her shoulder. She spins around to see him sitting there smiling at her. She screams. Mr. Davenport, frightened by the scream, screams back thinking there is something behind him. In terror he crams himself under the bed. Pause as they consider their positions.*
>
> *After a moment, MANDY looks under the bed and sees him, but does not scream. She remains wary of MAX who forces a smile and waves at her.*

MAX	Hello.
MANDY	Who are you?
MAX	Who do I look like?
MANDY	I'm not sure. What are you doing here?
MAX	I live here.
MANDY	Oh no you don't.
MAX	Oh yes I do.
MANDY	I would remember someone as big as you if you lived here.
MAX	I have lived in this house longer than you. I used to belong to your mother when she was a little girl and your grandmother when she was a little girl too.
MANDY	(*recognizing him*) Mr. Davenport?
MAX	That's me. Maxwell Davenport. But you can call me Max.
MANDY	But you're a doll.
MAX	Thank you. I think you are kind of sweet too.
MANDY	No. I mean you are not real.
MAX	(*hurt*) Well that's a heck of a thing to say to somebody. I have feelings too you know. I've been with you since you were born. Helped you through the measles, the chickenpox, the mumps, two bouts of the flu, and ten colds and you can sit there and tell me I'm not real. (*pouting*) I'm hurt.

MANDY	I'm sorry.
MAX	Well you should be. After all I've been through with you. I've been thrown up on and wet on but I'm still here. How many other friends do you have who would put up with that?
MANDY	Not many I guess.
MAX	Not many is right. You can bet your icebox on that.
MANDY	My what?
MAX	Your icebox. You know, where you keep all your cold food.
MANDY	Oh, you mean the fridge.
MAX	Is that what they call it now. (*to himself*) What a funny name.
MANDY	Why did you call it an "icebox"?
MAX	Well, that's what they called it the last time I was here. You see Mandy, I get to come to life once for every little girl that owns me.
MANDY	You do?
MAX	Yes. Before they stop believing such a thing is possible.
MANDY	But this is impossible.
MAX	(*worried*) Please don't tell me I'm too late?
MANDY	Well...
MAX	You see, there is so little magic left in the world just knowing when to come to life is a real problem for me. It's so easy to overshoot it.
MANDY	I don't believe in magic.

MAX   Oh you don't? Then why were you talking to me just before you threw me rather harshly over there?

MANDY   I don't know.

MAX   You were wishing that you were a doll. Well take it from me, that's not such a great wish. You have to play whether you feel like it or not. I have no control over my life and I have already pointed out the other moist disadvantages of the job. In spite of what you say, I still think there is some magic left in your life.

MANDY   What does wishing have to do with magic?

MAX   When you wish you use your imagination. And imagination and magic are two peas in a pod. (*stopping*) Do you know what peas are?

MANDY   Of course.

MAX   Thank heavens. At least that hasn't changed. You see Mandy, imagination lets you pretend and the magic lets you believe.

MANDY   I don't understand?

MAX   (*thinking*) Have you ever been afraid of something under your bed?

MANDY   Sometimes.

MAX   Did you ever find anything?

MANDY   Well, no.

MAX   That's because nothing lives there. The next time you think there is something hiding under your bed, use the magic of your imagination to turn it into a big white rabbit or a golden pony. Whatever you want it to be. After all, you are the boss of your own imagination.

MANDY	I've never thought of it that way. I think you are very smart for a doll.
MAX	I'm not as smart as you think.
MANDY	Why?
MAX	I wasn't always a doll. A long, long time ago when there was still lots of magic in the world I was a person just like you. I didn't like my life very much so I made a deal with...(*whispering*) the Magus.
MANDY	What's a Magus
MAX	It's a rare and powerful creature that creates magic. I went to the Magus and asked it if it would turn me into a doll. I thought it would be wonderful to be a doll. Everybody always wanting to play with me....I wish now that I'd never made that deal because sometimes I don't feel like playing. But I don't have a say in that anymore.
MANDY	Why don't you ask the Magus to turn you back?
MAX	It's not that simple. To get a wish from the Magus you have to buy it and I have nothing left to sell to the Magus. So I guess I'll have to be a doll for ever.
MANDY	What kind of things does the Magus buy?
MAX	Thoughts. The Magus collects thoughts. And in return for a thought or two, it will grant you a wish.
MANDY	How do you give the Magus a thought?
MAX	Some thoughts can be caught inside words. For example, why do you say, "please" and "thank you"?
MANDY	Mostly because I'm told to.

MAX   So when you say, "thank you" to your aunt who gives you a pair of slippers for a gift when you really wanted a toy, you don't mean it?

MANDY   I guess not.

MAX   That's the kind of thing you sell to the Magus. If you don't really mean your "thank yous" why not sell them for a wish. That sort of thing.

MANDY   I think if I could have any wish, I'd like to have a perfect brother and be free from all the trouble he causes in this house. Would the Magus do that for me?

MAX   I don't think it's such a good idea to get mixed up with the Magus. Look what happened to me.

MANDY   Please Max. This is my birthday and it's been just about the worst day of my life. Please? Just one little wish.

MAX   I don't know.

MANDY   Pleeeeeease?

MAX   Well, it is your birthday. I guess one little wish wouldn't hurt.

MANDY   Oh thank you Max! Thank you! How do we start?

MAX   (*taking out a small book*) Let me see. It says here that you have to give up three things to get your first wish. How about giving away your "thank yous" if you don't mean them?

MANDY   Alright. What else?

MAX   How about the phrase, "I'm sorry"? When you say those words how often do you really mean them?

MANDY   To be honest, not too often. I say it mostly so I won't get in to more trouble.

MAX	Good. You won't miss that, so you can give that up as well. Now let me see (*looking at the book*) That's all your "thank yous" and all your "I'm sorrys". You need one more thing.
MANDY	How about "happy" or "sad"?
MAX	I don't think so. According to this book it has to be someone's smile.
MANDY	Mom hardly ever smiles at me. Can I give her smile away?
MAX	You can, but are you sure you want to?
MANDY	I'm sure. You know what I think? I think she won't miss smiling one bit.
MAX	Well then, if you are sure, all that's left is to say these few words and the deal is done. But remember once a deal with the Magus is done sometimes it's very hard to get it undone. Are you ready?
MANDY	I sure am. I'll never get blamed for anything my brother does again.

MAX reads as it gets dark.

MAX	Oh Magus of the long ago. Oh Magus of today. I call to beg a wish from you. And for it we will pay. We give you all the "thank yous" That were lightly sent. We give you all the "I'm sorrys" That were never meant. And last of all we give you The smile from her mother. If you will free Amamda from The troubles of her brother.

There is a great flash of lightning and a crash of thunder. The lights restore.

MAX	There, I think that did it.
MANDY	I don't feel any different.
MAX	Why don't we try it out.
MANDY	How?
MAX	Well, try to say, "thank you".
MANDY	All right. Here goes. (*taking a deep breath and trying with all her might but the words "thank you" will not come out*) Thhhhaaakkk...Thhkkk. (*delighted*) Max! I can't say it!
MAX	Try to say, "I'm sorry".
MANDY	(*trying to say it, but with the same difficulty*) I'mmmmmSeerrr...I'mmmmmSeeeerrr...It worked! The Magus has taken my...my...
MAX	"Thank yous"?
MANDY	Yes. And my...my...
MAX	"I'm sorrys"?
MANDY	Yes! That must mean that my wish has come true! (*delighted*) Oh Max, this is wonderful! I wonder what it will be like living with a brother that never gets into trouble. I'm free. I'll never be blamed for anything again.
MOTHER	(*off*) Mandy! Mandy, are you up there?
MANDY	That's mother. Quick, you had better hide.
MAX	There's no need. Your mother will only see me as a doll like all other adults do. She can't see me the way you can.
MANDY	This has turned into the best birthday I have ever had.

MAX *sits on the chair motionless.*
MOTHER *enters. For the rest of this*
scene MOTHER *will look very sad and*
down in the mouth in spite of what she
may say.

MOTHER	Mandy, I've got some good news for you. The rain has stopped. We can go to the zoo after all. Isn't that wonderful?
MANDY	Is something wrong Mother?
MOTHER	Why no Mandy. Why do you ask?
MANDY	You look so sad.
MOTHER	Do I? I don't feel sad. I don't feel anything at all.
MANDY	Aren't you happy it's my birthday?
MOTHER	Why yes Mandy. I'm very happy. And your father and I love you very much.
MANDY	But you don't look happy.
MOTHER	I can't help how I look Mandy. Now, come down stairs and put your coat on. You and I are going to have a wonderful time at the zoo.
MANDY	Isn't Michael coming with us?
MOTHER	Who?
MANDY	Michael, my brother.
MOTHER	What are you talking about Mandy. You don't have a brother.
MANDY	What!?
MOTHER	You never have had a brother by the name of Michael or any other name.

MANDY   Yes I have. He's nine years old and always in trouble.

MOTHER   What has put such a thought into your head?

MANDY   Don't you remember him?

MOTHER   No. I should think if I had another child I would remember. Who told you you had a brother?

MANDY   No one. I remember him.

MOTHER   It is just your imagination Mandy. Don't be silly.

MANDY   I'm not being silly mother. Can't you remember?

MOTHER   No I can't and neither can you. You are just making all this up.

MANDY   (*turning to* MAX) Max, help me.

MOTHER   Why are you calling your doll Max?

MANDY   Because that's his real name.

MOTHER   You are not making any sense at all Mandy. You must have had a dream. Honestly, if you had a brother to look after perhaps you wouldn't be making up such wild stories.

MANDY   It's not a "wild story" mother. Honest.

MOTHER   Well, it is your birthday I suppose. So if you want to imagine you have a brother I guess there's no harm done.

MANDY   But he is real!

MOTHER   (*patronizingly*) If you say so Mandy. (*reaching into her pocket and handing* MANDY *money*) Now here is some money for you to spend at the zoo on whatever you like.

MANDY	(*taking the money*) Is this all for me?
MOTHER	It's a birthday treat for my Mandy. What do you say?
MANDY	(*trying to say "thank you"*) Oh thhhh...I mean thhhh...
MOTHER	Can't you even say a simple "thank you"?
MANDY	Let me try again. (*trying with all her might*) Thhhh... Thhhhhhkkkkk...It's no use.
MOTHER	You would think I had asked you for the earth. Really Mandy. I think you are a very spoiled child not to be able to give your mother a little "thank you". Now let's get started before it gets too late.
MANDY	But I can't go until I find out what happened to Michael.
MOTHER	You would rather stay in this room than go to the zoo?
MANDY	I have to. Don't you see? I'm the one that made him go away. It's all my fault. Everything is my fault. I'm so sooorrrr...I'm sorrrr.
MOTHER	What are you trying to say Mandy?
MANDY	I said I'm srroooo...I can't say it.
MOTHER	Oh! I've had enough of this nonsense. Stay in your room if that's what you want. But when your father gets home we are all going to sit down and have a long talk.

> MOTHER *moves to leave, then turns back to* MANDY.

MOTHER	I hope you are not coming down with something.

MOTHER *moves to leave again.*

MANDY   Mother?

MOTHER   (*stopping*) Yes?

MANDY   Would you give me a smile?

MOTHER   Why?

MANDY   Just to let me know everything is alright.

MOTHER *tries to make a smile but it is hopeless.*

MOTHER   I'm sorry Mandy. I just don't feel like it. I don't think I can.

MANDY   Why?

MOTHER   I don't know. Maybe if you could say "thank you" once in a while, I could find my smile.

MOTHER *exits.*

SONG: "I'M NOT FEELING VERY GOOD".

MANDY   I'm not feeling very good just now.
I think I've made a big mistake somehow.
I don't know what to do or say.
I have taken her smile away.

MAX   A smile can be warm or funny.
A smile can be full of love.
A smile can say, "How are you?"
A smile can part the clouds above.

MANDY   I didn't think it would be all that bad,
To take away the smile I never had.
But now I see it's more than that.
It has made my whole world so flat.

MAX	A smile can say, "I'm sorry." A smile can say, "I care." A smile can say, "I miss you." A smile can fill the air.
MANDY	I have learned a lesson very clear. And for a price that's cost me dear. A smile's not just to show your teeth. It shows how you feel underneath.
MAX	A smile can say, "I'm happy." A smile can say, "I'm shy." A smile can say, "Hello there." A smile can light the sky.
MANDY & MAX	We're not feeling very good just now. I think we've made a big mistake somehow. We don't know what to do or say. We have taken her smile away.

SONG ends.

MANDY	Oh boy! What have I done?
MAX	This is not working out at all well is it?
MANDY	I didn't mean for Michael to disappear.
MAX	I guess that's the only way you can make a nine-year-old boy perfect.
MANDY	What am I going to do?
MAX	I don't know.
MANDY	Did you see the way my mother looked at me? It was like I was a stranger to her.
MAX	I guess that's how people look without smiles.
MANDY	Max. I've made a big mistake. I have got to get things back to the way they were.

MAX   I don't know how.

MANDY   There must be a way.

MAX   If there was, I would have stopped being a doll
                    years ago.

MANDY   Is it really that bad?

MAX   It was alright for the first thirty years, but now
                    it's kind of boring. Nothing ever changes.
                    Believe you me, if I could stop being a doll and
                    be a person again, I'd be the first one in line.

MANDY   Max, I have got to see the Magus.

MAX   Nobody has ever seen the Magus and come back
                    to tell about it.

MANDY   Where does it live?

MAX   In The Valley Of Dark Things.

MANDY   How do we get there?

MAX   What do you mean we!? I'm not going. It's a
                    damp, dark and dangerous place.

MANDY   Please!? You are the only one who knows
                    anything about the Magus. I would be lost
                    without you.

MAX   (*softening*) Well

MANDY   If you come with me I'll do all I can to help you.

MAX   Oh you can't do anything for me. I traded
                    everything I had to become a doll. Now I have to
                    live with it.

MANDY   (*sadly*) Oh.

MAX   On the other hand, what have I got to lose?

MANDY	Then you will come with me?
MAX	I do feel kind of responsible for you.
MANDY	Oh thakkkkk...I mean thakkkkk.
MAX	You mean "thank you"?
MANDY	Yes.
MAX	Don't mention it.
MANDY	How do we get there?
MAX	(*looking at the book*) Well now, let me see. It says here that the only way is to make a wish and pretend.
MANDY	Alright. I wish —
MAX	Just a moment. You have to buy the wish with a word.
MANDY	Which word do I have to sell?
MAX	Please.
MANDY	Alright, which word do I have to sell, "please?"
MAX	No you don't understand. "Please" is the word you have to sell.
MANDY	And that will get us to the Magus?
MAX	It will get us to The Valley Of Dark Things.
MANDY	I'll do it.
MAX	Then, here goes. (*reciting the incantation*)

Oh Magus of the long ago.
Oh Magus of today.
I call to ask a wish of you.
And for it, we will pay.

The lights fade to a lower level.

MAX	To your valley we must go.
We have the special keys.
And we offer them to you.
These magic words called "please"!

>*There is a flash of lightning and a crash of thunder. MANDY and MAX transform the bedroom to The Valley of Dark Things by quickly dismantling or tipping the bed to form a wall.*

>*CAPTAIN TANGLEWOOD enters with a sack with a string tied around the top, a stool, and a halberd—an axe and spear together on a long pole. He is dressed in costume elements of a pirate, a knight and a space traveller. At the top of this scene he is hooded to mask his face. CAPTAIN TANGLEWOOD helps with the change from the bedroom to The Valley Of Dark Things. He places MANDY's chair centre left and puts the stool beside it. MANDY's bedspread is thrown over the chair to become the MAGUS' throne. With the aide of a lighting change we are now in the Valley Of Dark Things. On one side of the wall crouch MAX, who holds a coil of rope, and MANDY. On the other side of the wall is the throne room where CAPTAIN TANGLEWOOD walks guard duty.*

***

Scene Two

MAX	This is it Mandy, The Valley Of Dark Things. On the other side of this wall lives the Magus.
MANDY	Let's climb over and get in.
	MANDY and MAX look over the wall and see CAPTAIN TANGLEWOOD who does not see them. They quickly pop down.
MANDY	There is a guard over there. What are we going to do?
MAX	I don't know.
	The MAGUS enters the throne room. She is darkly dressed in rich looking clothes. Her hair is covered with a veil and she wears a small coronet. In her arms she carries her pet, MUGWORT, a mean, nasty, ferret-like creature. CAPTAIN TANGLEWOOD falls to one knee in homage. MANDY and MAX clearly hear what is to follow.
CAPTAIN	Good morning your Magusty.
MAGUS	Good morning Captain Tanglewood. What a lovely morning.
CAPTAIN	Yes, your Awfulness.

MANDY	It's the Magus!
MAX	Shhhhhhhh!
MAGUS	(*not hearing*) Do you like the colour I chose for the sky this morning?
CAPTAIN	(*rising*) Very much your Magusty.
MAGUS	Mugwort likes it too, don't you Mugwort? (*the creature nods*) Was it a quiet night Captain?
CAPTAIN	Yes, your Magusty. (*pulling back his hood*)
MAGUS	Did anything come in?
CAPTAIN	Yes your Awfulness. I caught a fresh "please" which came in last night. I think it's from that same little girl.
MAGUS	My, what a good customer. Where did you put it?
CAPTAIN	It's in the sack with all the other words.
MAGUS	(*moving to the sack*) Let me see.

> CAPTAIN TANGLEWOOD *opens the sack for the* MAGUS *to look in.*

MAGUS	(*looking in the sack*) Very good Captain Tanglewood. A fresh "please". We don't see many of them anymore. What do we have left in there?
CAPTAIN	(*looking into the sack*) We have three "thank yous", seven "I'm sorrys", four "I'll never do that agains" and at the very bottom one "mother's smile".

> MUGWORT *becomes excited at hearing there is a mother's smile in the sack.*

MAGUS	There, there my little treasure. Are you hungry?

MUGWORT *nods.*

MAGUS   Would you like to eat that nice delicious "mother's smile" for dinner?

MUGWORT *nods enthusiastically.*

MAGUS   Then you shall have it today.

MANDY   Oh no! So that's what she does with them.

MAX   Shhhhhh!

MAGUS   I'm so glad you came to stay with me Captain. Do you like it here?

CAPTAIN   Yes, your Magusty.

MANDY   I know that voice. It's Michael!

MAX   Be quiet or the Magus will hear.

MAGUS   Keep up the good work and soon you will be my general.

MANDY   She has taken Michael and turned him into one of her guards.

MAGUS   *(freezing)* I have a feeling there is danger near.

MAX   Oh no! Now you've done it!

MAGUS   I had better take a walk around the palace. Come Mugwort, let's put you back into your box until it's time to eat.

> *The* MAGUS *exits.* CAPTAIN TANGLEWOOD *crosses to the throne and sits. Unseen by* MANDY *and* MAX, CAPTAIN TANGLEWOOD *has slipped a noose of string around his wrist. The other end of the string is attached to the sack. He settles down for a nap.*

MANDY	What are we going to do?
MAX	We have got to get that sack. Your mother's smile is in there.
MANDY	Do you think we can talk Michael into giving it to us?
MAX	I don't think so. He is under some kind of spell.
MANDY	Then we will just have to be very careful. Are you ready?
MAX	I guguguess.
MANDY	Then let's go.

> MANDY *takes the rope and throws it over the wall.* Carefully MANDY *and* MAX *climb over the wall into the throne room unseen by* CAPTAIN TANGLEWOOD *who has fallen asleep on the throne.* MANDY *and* MAX *quietly sneak up to the sleeping* TANGLEWOOD *and take the sack from beside the throne.* MANDY *and* MAX *start to move back to the wall. As* MANDY *and* MAX *rush to leave, they inadvertently yank* TANGLEWOOD *from the throne by pulling on the string attached to his wrist. He lands on the floor with a thud.* TANGLEWOOD *wakes up quickly, retrieves the sack, and takes* MANDY *and* MAX *prisoner with his halberd.*

CAPTAIN	Well, well, well. What have we here?
MANDY	Michael. Don't you recognize me?
CAPTAIN	Never seen you before in my life.

MAX   (*nervously*) My, my. You sure look like
                 Michael. (*to* MANDY) Doesn't he look like
                 Michael? I sure thought you were Michael. Why
                 I could have

CAPTAIN   Quiet! My name is Tanglewood. Captain
                 Tanglewood. Loyal bodyguard to the most high
                 and exalted Magus in TheValley Of Dark Things.
                 What are you doing here?

MAX   Actually, we just dropped in to see if we could
                 borrow a cup of sugar. (*laughing nervously*)

CAPTAIN   Silence! I don't think so. I think you came here
                 to steal this sack of words from the Magus.
                 (*pointing the halberd at* MANDY) What do you
                 say?

MANDY   I...I...I...

MAX   (*thinking quickly*) Oh look! One of your "thank
                 yous"is getting away.

CAPTAIN   (*looking around*) Where?

                         MAX *and* MANDY *take this
                         opportunity to grab the rope and quickly
                         tie the distracted* TANGLEWOOD. *They
                         sit him on the throne.*

CAPTAIN   What do you think you're doing!? Let me go!
                 You're going to be in a lot of trouble. Let me
                 go!

MAX   (*taunting* TANGLEWOOD *with the halberd*)
                 You're not so brave now are you? Not without
                 this oversized toothpick. I knew I had you all
                 along.

                         TANGLEWOOD *growls at* MAX *and
                         he jumps back in fright.*

MANDY   Quick. Let's get out of here.

> MANDY *picks up the sack which is no longer attached to* TANGLEWOOD, *and heads for the wall.*

MAX　　What's the rush. I think I've got everything under control here. (*sweeping the halberd at* TANGLEWOOD) Yessiree. That was a pretty smooth move even if I do say so myself.

> *Unseen by* MAX *the* MAGUS *has entered behind him.* MANDY, *seeing the* MAGUS *is frozen with fear.*

MAX　　Old Maxwell has not lost his touch. (*seeing* MANDY'*s frozen look*) What's wrong with you? You'd think you had seen a ghost.

> *Smiling,* MAX *turns around to come face to face with the* MAGUS. *He screams and drops the halberd.*
>
> MAX *and* MANDY *scramble for the wall and the* MAGUS *raises her hand.*

MAGUS　　Tumblewell!

> *At this command* MANDY *and* MAX *are frozen in their tracks like statues. The* MAGUS *points her finger at* TANGLEWOOD.

MAGUS　　Tumblewell!

> *The rope falls like magic from* TANGLEWOOD.

MAGUS　　Quickly. We must tie them up!

> *The* MAGUS *and* TANGLEWOOD *quickly move to* MAX *and* MANDY. *They position them back to back. If their arms are raised in flight the* MAGUS *and* TANGLEWOOD *will be able to bring them down to their sides.*

> *Quickly they are tied securely. Once they are firmly bound the* MAGUS *points her finger at them.*

MAGUS   Tumblewell!

> MAX *and* MANDY *become animated once again. They struggle but are firmly bound.*

MANDY   (*together*) Let me go!

MAX!   Please! We didn't mean...

MANDY   You can't do this to...

MAX   ...any harm. Let us go!

MANDY   ...me. You have no right!

MAX   We'll leave right away.

MAGUS   Silence!

> MANDY *and* MAX *sink to the floor.*

MAGUS   Good work Captain. It looks as though we have captured a couple of thieves. And you know what we do with thieves.

MANDY   I'm not a thief! You are the one who took my brother. That was never part of the deal.

CAPTAIN   She thinks I'm her brother your Magusty. Isn't that a laugh?

MAGUS   Very funny indeed. Captain, why don't you go and get my little pet Mugwort. I think we'll give him his dinner right now.

CAPTAIN   Yes, your Magusty.

> TANGLEWOOD *exits.*

MAGUS	I think it will be fun to feed your mother's smile to Mugwort in front of you.
MANDY	No!
MAX	Please your Awfulness, don't do it.
MAGUS	(*mimicking* MAX) "Please your Awfulness, don't do it." Let's hear a "please" from her and I might consider it.
MANDY	(*struggling to say the word*) Your Magusty pppllleeee...pppllleeee...It's no use. I can't say it.
MAGUS	Of course you can't. That's because you gave it to me didn't you. And it's here in this sack. Well, I'll feed that to Mugwort as well.
MANDY	I never would have given them to you if I had known you were going to take my brother.
MAGUS	I gave you what you wanted, a perfect brother that never bothers you.
MANDY	But you took him away. You tricked me.
MAGUS	He is happy enough here.
MANDY	But he doesn't know who he is.
MAGUS	That's why he's happy.
MAX	So the guard *is* Michael.
MAGUS	Quiet! Or I'll use you as a pin cushion! Hummm, that's not such a bad idea.
MANDY	Please your Terribleness, won't you let us go? We don't belong here and neither does Michael.
MAGUS	He is my slave and I'm going to keep him just as he is.

MAX You mean you are never going to let him grow
up?

MAGUS He will stay as my slave the same way you are
going to stay a doll, 'Button Head'! (*to* MANDY)
Tell you what, my little 'Dumpling', I'll make
you a deal. To show you that I'm not such a bad
person I'll give you three wishes if you can say
"please" or "thank you" just once.

MANDY You know I can't. You have them all in that
sack.

MAGUS (*feigning surprise*) Well, so I have. Isn't that too
bad.

> The MAGUS *laughs.* TANGLEWOOD
> *enters with* MUGWORT's *box.*

CAPTAIN Your Magusty, Mugwort's box is empty!

MAGUS He can't be far. You search the tower I'll look in
the dungeon. He's probably playing down there
again.

> TANGLEWOOD *exits.*

MAGUS And you two can sit here for a minute and
imagine how nice it will be to spend forever with
me.

> The MAGUS *exits.*

MANDY What a rude person. She called you a "Button
Head."

MAX Well I am. I never wanted to grow up so now
I've got to stay a doll forever. Sometimes getting
exactly what you want is not a good thing.

MANDY I think you are right. Look at the mess I've
caused.

MAX	I don't know what we're going to do now. Things look terrible.
MANDY	(*remembering*) Yes Max, things *look* terrible. But they only seem terrible because that's how we feel.
MAX	I don't understand.
MANDY	The Magus has given us the key to get out of here.
MAX	She has?
MANDY	What did she say just before she left?
MAX	Let me think. She said "Sit here and imagine how nice it will be spending forever with her."
MANDY	Max that's it! Don't you remember? You are the one that told me.
MAX	Told you what?
MANDY	Remember when I said that I was afraid of things under my bed?
MAX.	Yes.
MANDY	You said there was nothing to fear because it was only my imagination. I can turn bad thoughts to good because I am the boss of my own imagination!
MAX	You mean the Magus is only powerful because we imagine she is?
MANDY	That's exactly what I mean. A bully always seems stronger if you are afraid of him.
MAX	What shall we do?
MANDY	Stop being afraid of her. That's her only power over us. Quick, let's get out of these ropes.

> *They free themselves.*

MAGUS (*off*) I'm glad you found him.

MAX It's them! What are we going to do?

CAPTAIN (*off*) He was in the tower.

MANDY We are going to have fun with our imagination.

> *The MAGUS and TANGLEWOOD enter. The MAGUS carries MUGWORT.*

MAGUS Well, I see you got free of the rope. What's the matter too afraid to run? Tanglewood check the sack.

> *TANGLEWOOD does so.*

CAPTAIN Everything is still there your Magusty.

MAGUS Hummm, you got free and had a chance to get away with the sack and yet you stayed. Are you that afraid of me?

MANDY Not any more.

MAGUS We'll see if feeding your mother's smile to Mugwort won't take that smirk off your face. Here Captain, you hold Mugwort.

> *The MAGUS reaches deep in the sack and fumbles at the bottom for something. All of a sudden, the MAGUS gives a loud scream and pulls her hand out shaking it violently.*

MAGUS It bit me! Your mother's smile bit me! I have never been bitten by a smile before. What's going on here?

MANDY It worked! Just like I imagined. Now, let me imagine you making a silly sound.

MAGUS	Me make a silly sound? Ha! Don't be foolish. I would never make a silly sound. (*making an involuntary raspberry sound*) Oh! my goodness was that me? (*doing it again*) Stop this! Stop this at once! (*doing it again*) What are you doing to me!?
MANDY	I am imagining just how much fun it will be here.
MAGUS	I want you to stop using your imagination right now, do you here!
MANDY	But I've just started.

> TANGLEWOOD *puts* MUGWORT *in his box.*

MAGUS	Oh no! (*making the raspberry sound again*)
MANDY	Now, let me imagine you hopping on one foot while going around in circles.

> *The* MAGUS *does so.*

MAX	That's very good.
MAGUS	Double drat! She has figured out the secret of my power.
MANDY	Yes I have. Fear is the secret of your power and I'm not afraid of you any more. Now sit!

> *The* MAGUS *crashes to the floor.*
> MANDY *looks at* TANGLEWOOD.

MANDY	Michael, do you recognize me?
CAPTAIN	(*not really sure*) I don't think so.
MAGUS	(*to* TANGLEWOOD) You have never seen her before have you.
CAPTAIN	I'm not sure now. She does look a little familiar.

MAX	It's working! He's starting to remember. Imagine harder!
MANDY	Michael, please remember me!
MAGUS	You can't say "please". You gave them all to me!
MANDY	Michael, I'm sorry I got mad at you.
MAGUS	You can't say, "I'm sorry". I have them all.
MANDY	You had all the ones I never meant. I couldn't say them again until I started meaning them. Well now I do.
CAPTAIN	Mandy, is that you?
MANDY	Oh yes, Michael, yes!
	MANDY *and* MICHAEL *rush to embrace each other.*
MANDY	I'll never say anything I don't mean again. (*turning to the* MAGUS) And now you owe me three wishes.
MAGUS	Double darn drat! Well, what do you want?
MANDY	First, I want Max to be free to be whatever he wants.
MAX	Are you sure you want to spend a whole wish on me?
MANDY	Yes, my dear friend. I want you to be free to go where ever you want and do whatever you want.
MAX	It's kind of scary being free.
MANDY	I know you'll like it. But I'm going to miss not having you as my doll. (*embracing* MAX) You are my very best friend.
MAX	Thank you Mandy. I'm going to miss you too.

MANDY   (*to* MAGUS) Next, I want you put somewhere where you will never bother anybody again.

MAGUS   And where's that?

MANDY   You'll see. And for my last wish, I want with all my heart for Michael and I to be home.

> *The lights dim and the wind howls. The thunder crashes and the lightning flashes. The Valley Of Dark Things is quickly turned back to* MANDY's *bedroom. The lights restore to find* MANDY *alone lying on the bed. A thunder crash causes* MANDY *to sit bolt up in the bed.*

                    ***

Scene Three

MANDY   Oh!...What a dream. Or was it? I can't remember
if it was or not. (*looking around the room*) Mr.
Davenport!?... Max where are you?...He's gone.
Then it wasn't a dream. It all really happened. I
wonder where Max went. I am going to miss
him so much.

SONG: "WHEN YOU GROW UP"

MANDY   When you grow up, you let things go
When you don't need them anymore.
Where is the donkey that I had when I was
four?
He's gone far away with my doll and my
sleigh,
To a land where they'll never grow old.

With my blocks and my bricks I could do
wonderous tricks,
And I'd play with my wagon all day.
They all seemed to know when it's time to
go.
And they all fly so gently away.

I hope they'll be carefree wherever they are.
And though I can't see them I know,
They'll remember me well and happily dwell
In a land where the days are pure gold.
In a land where they'll never grow old.

MOTHER *enters all smiles.*

MOTHER There you are Mandy. Happy birthday.

MANDY (*giving* MOTHER *a big hug*) Oh thank you Mom. I'm so sorry for all the trouble I've been.

MOTHER Don't be silly Mandy. You are no trouble. You are just a little girl who's growing up.

MANDY Mom, have you seen my doll, Mr. Davenport?

MOTHER I don't think you have a doll by that name Mandy.

MANDY Sure I have. Remember? He is all dressed in red with a funny little hat.

MOTHER Well it doesn't sound like any doll I have ever seen.

MICHAEL *enters.*

MICHAEL Well are we going to the zoo or not?

MANDY Michael! Are you all right?

MICHAEL (*looking at her as if she is from another planet*) Of course I'm all right. Were you hoping I wasn't?

MANDY (*giving* MICHAEL *a big hug*) I'm just so glad to see you.

MICHAEL Boy! Sisters are crazy. One minute they hate your guts and the next they get all mushy.

MANDY I'll never hate you again.

MICHAEL Great. Now can we go to the zoo?

FATHER (*off*) I'm home! Hey, where is everybody!?

MOTHER Your father is home. (*calling*) We're all up stairs!

FATHER *enters. He has the same look and mannerisms as* MAX *although the red suit has been replaced with a red sweater, white shirt and grey slacks. He has a big white box under his arm.*

FATHER So here's my birthday girl! (*crossing to* MANDY *and giving her a big hug*) Did you miss me today?

MANDY You are here! I can't believe it!

FATHER (*looking a bit oddly at* MANDY *then over to* MOTHER) I wouldn't miss your birthday for all the world. I couldn't wish to be any other place. (*handing her the white box*) Here, this is for you. Happy birthday.

MANDY *takes the box and opens it. Inside is an exact replica of the* MAGUS *as a doll.*

FATHER I hope you like it. It's supposed to be a wizard or something.

MICHAEL It's a Magus.

MOTHER A what?

MICHAEL A Magus. A spinner of magic from the olden days. I saw it on TV. They're really neat.

MANDY It's beautiful Dad. Thank you very much.

MANDY *gives* FATHER *a kiss.*

FATHER Thank you sweetheart.

MANDY And nothing would make me happier on my birthday than to *give* a present.

MANDY *hands the doll to* MICHAEL.

MANDY Here Michael, I want you to have this.

MICHAEL (*hardly believing his good fortune*) Do you mean it!?

MANDY It would make me very happy.

MICHAEL (*taking the doll with great joy*) Thanks Mandy. Wow! My very own Magus. (*talking to the doll*) Come with me slave and you shall do my bidding. (*flying the doll around the room*)

SONG: "WHEN YOU GROW UP"

ALL When you grow up, you let things go
When you don't need them anymore.
But there are some things you will
Need your whole life long.

MANDY & MICHAEL You may outgrow your toys
As do little girls and boys

ALL But you'll never out grow the beauty of a song.

MANDY & FATHER You'll always need a friend
A buddy to the end.

MOTHER A smile can really go a long long way.

ALL So enjoy the things you do
As long as you want to.
And may you never grow too old to play
And may you never grow too old to play.

Bye!

ALL *exit.*

The End.

Love and Work Enough

Collectively Created by:

Cynthia Grant, Kate Lazier, Anne Lederman, Eva Mackey,
Marilyn Norry, Peggy Sample, Heather D. Swain,
Mary Vingoe, and Cathy Wendt

Conceived and edited by Peggy Sample.

The Love and Work Enough Collective

Cynthia Grant is a founding Artistic Director of Nightwood Theatre, and co-founder and present Artistic Director of the Company of Sirens. Educator and feminist activist, she is also involved in developing and directing many new plays each year, for adult and youth audiences, including *Whenever I Feel Afraid* and *Shelter from Assault.*

Kate Lazier has abandoned the world of theatre for the world of politics, but sometimes wonders if there is much difference between them.

Anne Lederman, musician and composer, performs and researches music based on folk traditions in Canada. She has contributed both traditional and original music to many theatre productions and films, including the CBC series *Road to Avonlea*, and for the Blyth Summer Festival, Tarragon Theatre, and Theatre Passe Muraille.

Eva Mackay lives and works in Toronto. Since working on *Love and Work Enough*, she has pursued feminist academic studies in England, Spain, and Canada.

Marilyn Norrie is an actor and writer now living in Vancouver where she continues to write plays and screenplays.

Peggy Sample is a co-founder of the Company of Sirens, and continues to work as an actor, playwright, and director. Her scripts include *Peace & Plenty* written with Lib Spry, and a musical about Canadian farm women, *Harvest Moon Rising*, with music by Leslie Arden.

Heather D. Swain started her acting career with this project. It has been a wonderful journey where she now finds herself living 'happily' in Edmonton, still pursuing 'love' and searching for "enough work" in the theatre.

Mary Vingoe is a co-founder and past Artistic Co-ordinator of Nightwood Theatre. She is also co-founder of The Ship's Company theatre in Nova Scotia. She has directed for theatres across the country and written for stage, television, and radio.

Cathy Wendt, not unlike her foremothers, is currently looking West in the hope of rediscovering fame, fortune, and adventure.

Authors' Notes

Love & Work Enough began as an idea to create a play celebrating the role of Canada's pioneer women. Cynthia Grant (then artistic director of Nightwood Theatre) was very interested when, in the fall of 1983, Peggy Sample approached her with the idea and some research. The two women set about gathering funding — from the Summer Canada Works Employment program, Theatre Ontario's Youth Theatre Training Program, and the Ontario Secretary of State's Bicentennial Committee. The creative process began in the summer of 1984. For five weeks, eight women researched, improvised scenes, and created the first version of *Love & Work Enough* which then toured Ontario parks, libraries and senior citizens' homes. It was also presented by Nightwood Theatre at The Theatre Centre, Toronto. Having watched the play develop, Theatre Direct Canada decided to include the show in its fall schedule. The script was edited to suit four actors instead of five, and was then workshopped, with a new actor bringing new scene ideas and energy to the collective. *Love & Work Enough* toured schools throughout southern Ontario, playing to audiences of Grades 6 to 13. On the basis of this tour, it was awarded the Dora Mavor Moore Award for Outstanding Children's Theatre.

Acknowledgements

The collective members would like to thank:

Clara Thomas, whose biography of Anna Brownwell Jameson not only gave us our title, but which also, along with Marian Fowler's *The Embroidered Tent*, and Eve Zaremba's *Privilege of Sex*, was instrumental in the conception of the play. Her enthusiasm and support have been very much appreciated.

Ken Cruikshank, who believed in the project from the beginning, and who provided emotional support and historical information and references throughout...

Michael Fuller, whose tales of homesteading helped us to visualize, among other things, sticking a pig...

Shawna Dempsey, who stage-managed and mediated with grace and good humour, and who booked and managed the summer tour...

Jodi Segal, who saved everyone's sanity...

Rosemary Sullivan, Sabrina Reid, Lee Davis Creal, Madelaine Horton, Alan Risdell, Annie Skinner, Maureen White, John Glossop, Susan Serran, and, of course, Nightwood Theatre and Theatre Direct Canada.

Love and Work Enough was first produced, Summer, 1984 with the following cast: *Kate Lazier, Eva Mackey, Peggy Sample, Heather D. Swain, Cathy Wendt.*

Directed by Mary Vingoe, with Cynthia Grant.
Musical Director: Anne Lederman.
Stage Manager: Shawna Dempsey.
Administrator/Publicist: Shawna Dempsey.
Producers: Cynthia Grant and Peggy Sample.
Designer: Maya Duncan.
Costumes: Ronalda Jones.
Set Construction: Alistair Martin-Smith.
Step-Dancing Instruction and Choreography: Maureen Mulvey.

This published version of *Love & Work Enough* first toured in the fall of 1984 as a co-production of Nightwood Theatre and Theatre Direct Canada, with the following cast: *Marilyn Norry, Peggy Sample, Heather D. Swain, Cathy Wendt.*

Directed by Cynthia Grant and Mary Vingoe.
Musical Director: Anne Lederman.
Stage Manager: Victoria Vasileski.
Quilt created by Donna Bothen.
Production Manager: Bonnie Armstrong.
Step-Dance Coach and Choreography: Carmel Gaffney.
Tour Director: Kay Coughlan.

Casting Notes

Love & Work Enough is designed to be played by as few as four actors, or by as many as you want to put on the stage. Part of our fun was the quick changes of character and costume pieces — Our costume skirts were designed to close with Velcro, and we lost them more than once during the play's more vigorous moments! — but the fun of a large cast would certainly compensate. We are sure that there are many successful ways of dividing the roles, but we are including our division for reference.

Marilyn Norry played: Flora, Meg the horse, Ephraim, Cow 3, Loyalist Mother, Lady Frances, Corpse, Townsfolk 2, Wife Advisor 3, Vision Wife 1, Woman with quilt baby.

Peggy Sample played: Bridgit, Polly, Cow 1, Loyalist Big Sister, Catharine Parr Traill, Wife Advisor 4, Young Man in buggy, Jessie, Jennifer, Woman with baby clothes, Speaker 1.

Heather Swain played: Margaret, Buggy Driver, Henry, Susanna Moodie, Guide, Woodcutter, Border Guard, Woman with babe-in-arms, Townsfolk 1, Wife Advisor 1, Vision Wife 2.

Cathy Wendt played: Anna Jameson, Cow 2, Loyalist Little Sister, Circuit Preacher, Townsfolk 3, Wife Advisor 2, Betty, Diary Reader, Speaker 2.

NOTE: All of the music in *Love and Work Enough* is traditional. Copies of the music may be obtained from Playwrights Union of Canada. In addition, you may wish to obtain the album or tape "Scatter the Ashes", by Muddy York, which includes many of the tunes.

Scene One

Rise and Come Along: ANNA
JAMESON, MARGARET, *a midwife,*
BRIDGIT, *a young Irish woman,*
FLORA, *a young Scottish woman, all
enter, singing and step-dancing. Each
actor steps forward to sing her verse
while the others continue dancing. The
dance stops while monologues are
delivered.*

ALL   (*chorus*)
Rise and come along
Oh arise and come along
Rise and rise and come along
Bid welcome here to Canada.

ANNA   (*singing*) Come and follow me
We're heading 'cross the sea
If God above will show his love
We'll make it just in time for tea.

(*spoken*) I made my final farewells. The
Captain of the ship showed me to my quarters
and advised me that we would be leaving a bit
later. Eventually the rocking of the ocean lulled
me to sleep. The next morning I spotted land.
"Canada!" I cried. The Captain only laughed —
we hadn't even left England.

ALL   Dance & Chorus.

MARGARET   (*singing*)
                       I left the land I loved
                       For a land I didn't know
                       And hoped my life would start anew
                       When I arrived in Canada.

                       (*spoken*) We spent forty days on the ship that
                       brought me over here, but I was kept quite busy
                       — I helped to bring eight new babies into this
                       world. Well, five really. You can't count the
                       triplets I helped to deliver — they were puppies.

ALL   Dance & Chorus.

BRIDGIT   (*singing*)
                       Seasick for two months
                       As we crossed the ocean wide
                       My feet at last on solid ground
                       Bid welcome here to Canada

                       (*spoken*) It's what they call goin' into service.
                       You see, my parents didn't have enough money
                       to keep me, so they signed me over to this lady
                       in Canada to be her maid servant. It's not all that
                       bad though, for when I turn eighteen, I get me
                       own cow.

ALL   Dance & Chorus.

FLORA   (*singing*)
                       I think about my home
                       And the friends I left behind
                       My husband's here, and so I came
                       To build a life in Canada.

                       (*spoken*) After surviving the week in quarantine,
                       I finally made it to the docks of Montreal. I
                       couldn't find my husband anywhere. I was
                       thinking of how I'd get back home, when this
                       fine young gentleman came up to me and said,

FLORA	"Excuse me Miss, are you having a bit of trouble?" It was my husband, John. He'd grown a beard.
ALL	Dance & Chorus.
MARGARET	Look!
ANNA	Is it a whale?
BRIDGIT	An iceberg!
MARGARET	Canada.
FLORA	Rocks.

***

Scene Two

Buggy Scene: ANNA JAMESON,
BRIDGIT, THE DRIVER, *and* MEG,
*the horse (which was played by the actor
trotting as a horse and holding a small,
hand-made horse)— a bench and two
stools to make a buggy.*

BRIDGIT   *(lilting a reel or a jig)*

ANNA   Young woman.

BRIDGIT   Yes?

ANNA   *(introducing herself)* Anna Jameson.

BRIDGIT   Bridgit O'Shaugnessey.

ANNA   Where do we catch the carriage?

BRIDGIT   *(to the* DRIVER) Is this the the carriage to York, then?

DRIVER   Carriage? This ain't no carriage, lady, it's a buggy. You want a carriage, you'll have to go back to England. Climb aboard ladies. Come on Meg, let's get hitched up.

> MEG *enters, they arrange themselves on*
> *buggy and on* DRIVER'S *verbal signal*
> *i.e.. "gee up" They start bouncing as if*
> *riding in a buggy.*

BRIDGIT I was very excited to be taking my first journey on a buggy. The horse seemed a bit small for the load she was pulling, but she went on stoutly, the brave little horse!

DRIVER Duck!

> *All duck as they pass a low-hanging tree*
> *branch*

DRIVER I knew a lady who didn't duck once, and now she's got nothing to put her hat on.

BRIDGIT Our driver told the most interesting ancedotes. I was travellin' to join my new mistress, Lady Frances, and her husband in Upper Canada. The other passenger was an English lady wearin' a lovely hat, who kept writin' things down in a notebook.

ANNA The road is scarcely passable. There are no longer cheerful farms and clearings; only the dark pine forest and rank swamp. There are deep holes and pools of rotted vegetable matter. The very horses on the brink of some of these mud gulfs seem to pause...

> MEG *hesitates, they seem suspended*
> *as...*

DRIVER Come on, Meg, go!

> MEG *takes the plunge.*

ANNA ...ere they make their plunge. I set my teeth, grab on tight to my seat, and commend myself to heaven. Driver, will we be stopping soon?

DRIVER	We'll be stopping up the road at a great little inn. I highly recommend it. Besides, it's the only one. Whoa, Meg. This is it.

DRIVER *and* MEG *exit.*

ANNA	Young woman...
BRIDGIT	Bridgit.
ANNA	Ah yes, Bridgit. Where is the inn?
BRIDGIT	Well, I guess he means that little shack over there. I'll go look! (*exiting*)
ANNA	Ah, young woman...(*exiting in a most diginified manner*)

***

Scene Three

The Dirty Inn: HENRY, *the innkeeper,* EPHRAIM, *the simple lad,* POLLY, *the innkeeper's wife,* ANNA JAMESON.

HENRY, *carrying a jug, and* EPHRAIM *enter, both carrying a quilt which at the end of the song will be unrolled to represent a "vertical bed".*

**HENRY &
EPHRAIM**

(*singing*)
Our fathers of old were robust, stout and
strong,   And
kept open house with good cheer all day
long,
Which made their plump tenants rejoice in
this song

& POLLY

(*off*) Oh! the roast beef of old England,
And Oh! the old English roast beef.

POLLY *enters singing on the last two lines (the chorus). As song ends ,they unroll quilt and fall asleep.*

ANNA

(*entering*) One of my most memorable
experiences during my early days in Canada was

my first stay at a country inn. I recall finding myself alone, late at night, knocking at a strange door. (*knocking as* EPHRAIM *wakes up and goes to door*) It seemed that I was knocking for an extraordinarily long time. (EPHRAIM *opens door*) Hello. Do you have a room?... Do you have a room? The strange young man disappeared into the shadows. (EPHRAIM *goes and wakes* POLLY.) I took the liberty of entering.

POLLY (*getting out of bed*) Ephraim, what're you doing waking me up?

EPHRAIM *points towards* ANNA.

ANNA Is this an inn?

POLLY Yeah.

ANNA Do you have a room?

POLLY Henry, we have a guest.

HENRY (*dropping quilt*) Ooooh, yes we do. 'Ello,'ello,'ello.

POLLY Henry, love, why don't you get this lady some soup!

HENRY Alright. (*exiting*)

ANNA I gathered that I was about to taste my first authentic Canadian cuisine.

HENRY (*entering with iron soup pot*) Here's your soup, then.

ANNA What kind of soup is it?

HENRY Brown. That'll be brown soup.

ANNA Perhaps I'll have some tomorrow.

HENRY	Tomorrow it'll be green soup.
ANNA	I suddenly discovered that I had lost my appetite altogether. (*to* POLLY) It seems that I've lost my appetite altogether.
POLLY	I don't blame you dear; Henry is a terrible cook.
HENRY	Who're you calling a terrible cook, love?
POLLY	I'm calling you a terrible cook, love.
HENRY	At least I cook, love. (*exiting with soup pot*)
POLLY	You call what you do cooking? Why, he doesn't even know what vegetables is. The other day he...
ANNA	I've had a rather trying day. Would you be so kind as to show me to my room?
POLLY	Ephraim, show the nice lady where to sleep, love.
	EPHRAIM *points to the quilt on the floor.*
POLLY	Nighty-night.
ANNA	(*getting into bed*) The bedclothes smelled atrocious, but I had not the energy to rebel. Soon I found myself quite asleep.
HENRY	(*entering*) Alright, Ephraim, go blow out the light.
POLLY	Ooh, yeah, we don't want any more guests tonight.
HENRY	No, it doesn't pay to advertise.
POLLY	Back to bed, then. POLLY, HENRY *and* EPHRAIM *join* ANNA *in bed.*

ANNA   Suddenly I awakened and realized that I was not
                       alone. Another quaint Canadian custom...one to
                       which I never did become accustomed.

                              ANNA *screams, and runs off.*

                              EPHRAIM, HENRY, *and* POLLY *clear
                              the stage and exit, singing...*

                       Oh! the roast beef of old England,
                       And oh! the old English roast beef.

                              Bridge to Scene Four.

ANNA   (*entering*) I had many such experiences on my
                       travels throughout the Canadian wilderness —
                       and I believe the manners of the country inn-
                       keepers to be worse than anything anyone could
                       ever imagine. If one were to label these
                       experiences, perhaps they would be called Terror
                       in the Trees...ehm...Hard Times in the
                       Forest...no, no... Ah! Roughing it in the Bush!
                       (*exiting*) Yes, I like that one.

                                   ***

Scene Four

Susanna and the Cows :
SUSANNA MOODIE, THREE COWS
*The actors play the cows in their basic
costumes, bending forward at the waist,
using an arm as a tail. If play is cast
with more than four actors, the number
of cows could be increased to four or
five.*

SUSANNA   (*entering*) "Roughing it in the Bush" By
           Susanna Moodie — that's me. Chapter One
           "My Arrival in Upper Canada". I will not soon
           forget my arrival at my new home.

           *Others have entered and stand facing
           upstage in front of backdrop.*

SUSANNA   I expected to find a quaint, charming little estate
           in the midst of the picturesque Canadian forest.
           Unfortunately, all that I found was a dilapidated
           shed. It had no windows, not even a front door.
           As I came upon my doorway, though, I found
           that...

COWS   Mooo (*the actors act as cows*)

SUSANNA   ...my home was inhabited by three rather large
           cows. It was quite obvious that they had made
           my home their home. The sight and smell of
           three cows in a confined space is something for
           which a refined Englishwoman is not properly
           prepared. I decided something had to be done. I
           remembered that I was carrying some sugar...

SUSANNA	for my tea, of course. I thought that if I could lure one cow away, the others might follow.
COW 1	Hey, that looks like salt!
SUSANNA	They seemed quite intrigued. One cow who had an amazingly long tongue came closer and...
COW 2	Don't!
SUSANNA	...rolled out her tongue, sucked it up...and spit it out.

COW 3 *has been doing so as* SUSANNA *descibes the action.*

COW 2	Told you so.
SUSANNA	I guess cows just don't have the same good taste as a refined Englishwoman. You know, it's quite fascinating really, how cows can remind you of people you might know. Hello.
COW 1	Doesn't she look like Mabel?
COW3	No. More like Mother.

COWS *crowd* Susanna, *their backs to the audience.*

SUSANNA	I soon found myself being penned up against the back wall. A terrible thought flashed across my mind...I could die. To think that my obituary would read "Susanna Moodie, found dead in a shed with three cows!" No thank you. Excuse me. (*exiting*)

COWS *spin around and play end of scene to audience.*

COW 1	Hey, where did she go?
COW 2	Oh Susanna!

ALL   (*singing*)
           O Susanna, oh don't you cry for me-ooo (*as
           they tap dance and exit*)

                    ***

Scene Five

> *Pail of Lard:* MOTHER, BIG
> SISTER, LITTLE SISTER, NATIVE
> GUIDE, FRENCH CANADIAN
> WOODCUTTER, AMERICAN
> BORDER GUARD. *The scene can be
> performed using only the following
> props: a wooden bucket, a silver spoon,
> two sacks, a "baby", and an ax handle
> which was used as a paddle and gun.*

MOTHER   This is a pail my mother brought to Canada
during the American Revolution. My father was
a Tory...

(offstage, sung)
I'll be a Tory, I'll be a Tory
I'll be a Tory in Upper Canada.

MOTHER   ...what we now call a United Empire Loyalist.
He was a member of the Royal Yorkers
regiment, and as the local Sons of Liberty knew
this, they confiscated all of our property. So, in
the middle of the night, we set off to meet him
in Montreal. As my mother and sisters told me
later — I was only a baby at the time — we
packed up all of our belongings, and snuck away
in the dark. (BIG SIS *and* LITTLE SIS *enter,
one hands* MOTHER *the baby*) This is me.

BIG SIS   We had to walk very quietly, because if anyone
                 heard us they would take away all of our
                 belongings. And we couldn't use the roads, so
                 we had to walk along deer paths through the
                 forest. And my mother made me carry all sorts
                 of things, including this really heavy pail of lard,
                 and it hurt my hand.

LITTLE SIS   We all carried as much as we could and left the
                 rest of our things behind. I carried a silver spoon
                 my grandma gave me 'cause I could. So we
                 walked and walked through the wilderness...

BIG SIS   ...heading North.

                 FRENCH CANADIAN
                 WOODCUTTER *enters and freezes
                 upstage.*

BIG SIS   And we had to hide from any people we saw or
                 heard, since we couldn't tell who was a friend and
                 who was an enemy.

                 WOODCUTTER *makes a loud sound,
                 everyone drops to floor and waits*

WOODCUTTER   Madame?

BIG SIS   He spoke French — a friend!

                 They all stand up.

WOODCUTTER   I was chopping down de tree in de forest, you
                 know, when all of a sudden dis lady and her
                 babies went by. I asked if dey wanted to share
                 some bean wit me...

BIG &
LITTLE SIS   Yeah!

MOTHER   No.

WOODCUTTER ...but she say no, she just wanted to know where "Lake Champlain" was. Lac Champlain is right dere, lady.

MOTHER Merci.

> WOODCUTTER *changes into* NATIVE GUIDE.

BIG SIS So we looked for an Indian, because somebody had told us that they would take us across the lake. (*seeing* GUIDE *sitting as in a canoe*)...and there one was. So we got into his canoe, and he started paddling us across.

NATIVE (*singing traditional song underneath*)
Yo ho, way dee yah, ho dee yay yay ya,
Way dee yay, ho dee yay yay ya.
Way doe yay, ho dee yay yay ya,
Yo ho.

BIG SIS But the sky grew dark, and the wind started blowing, and the waves grew higher and the canoe sank lower because it was too full.

> *During this, the actors slowly sway down into crouch position in canoe, then sway up again as they toss out mimed objects.*

LITTLE SIS So we threw out all of our clothes, and the tent, and the kitchen box my father made...

BIG SIS And we threw out the heavy pail...

MOTHER (*grabbing pail*) NO! Not the pail of lard.

BIG SIS Finally...

> *They run aground and get out of canoe.*
> NATIVE GUIDE *becomes* BORDER GUARD.

BIG SIS	We reached the end of Lake Champlain and we were within a few miles of the British land of Canada.
ALL	Yea!
LITTLE SIS	(*seeing* BORDER GUARD) But we were caught...
BIG SIS	...by some Sons of Liberty.
GUARD	Out on a Sunday stroll, are we? You could be tarred and feathered for this, you'd serve as an example to all of those other Tory crown kissers. Or I suppose I could shoot you right here. But let's just say you give me half of what you've got as a kind of duty payment.
MOTHER	So we gave him our cooking pot, and all of the flour, and the rest of our meat.
GUARD	Little girl! Step out here. What's that behind your back, girl?
LITTLE SIS	Nothing.
GUARD	A silver spoon! Got any more gold or silver?
MOTHER	That's all, you've taken everything.
GUARD	What's that?
MOTHER	A pail of lard. It's the only thing I have left to feed the children with.
BIG SIS	Disgusting! He stuck his hand right in the lard!
GUARD	Well, I gues you can go, but I don't want to see you around here anymore!
LITTLE SIS	Don't worry.

GUARD *exits.*

BIG SIS	We ran those last few miles into Canada, and just outside Montreal...
LITTLE SIS	Mother, I'm hungry.
MOTHER	Well, I guess we can eat something now. (*to* BIG SIS) Go build us a fire.
LITTLE SIS	So we did. And Mom put the pail of lard on the fire.
BIG SIS	Lard soup.
LITTLE SIS	And then the lard started melting, and it got clear...and in the bottom we could see...

The two sisters freeze after MOTHER *hands the baby to* BIG SISTER.

MOTHER	And this is the pail my mother brought with her. And in the bottom of the pail, under the lard, she had hidden 54 gold pieces, 78 silver pieces, an emerald and diamond brooch, and her wedding ring.

BIG SISTER *and* MOTHER *exit,*
singing chorus of "I'll be a Tory".

***

Scene Six

Schizophrenia : SUSANNA
MOODIE *and* CATHARINE PARR
TRAILL.

LITTLE SIS   In the 1830's, two of the Strickland sisters came over to Upper Canada from England. They both took to writing books in the little spare time they had, and they were read by nearly everyone. Both of them were married, so they had different last names. One was called...

SUSANNA   Susanna Moodie

LITTLE SIS   ...and the other...(*exiting*)

CATHARINE   Catharine Parr Traill. Today we moved from our shanty to our new log house. It is a marvel of comfort compared to what we have endured so bravely for the last six months. Two windows, a front door, a chimney, and one of the windows even has glass!

SUSANNA   I saw our new home today. My husband is very proud of it, as I pretended to be, but my heart sank. It has a distressing air of permanence to it.

CATHARINE   There is nothing so exhilarating as a Canadian winter. Although my wardrobe is not as practical as I had hoped, I find that the chill keeps me alert.

SUSANNA   If the fire goes out, we freeze to death.

CATHARINE	When one of our neighbour's barns burnt down, the entire community gathered to rebuild it within a week. And then everyone brought some hay or grain to replace what had been lost.
SUSANNA	Our neighbours here seem to practise a rather strange custom, that of borrowing whatever they need and never returning it. Residing in such a remote place, surrounded by such savages, I am rather afraid to request their return.
CATHARINE	The flying squirrel is a native of our woods, and I was agreeably surprised by the appearance of the little creature.
SUSANNA	Have you ever eaten squirrel?
CATHARINE	Its colour is the softest, most delicate shade of grey, the fur thick and short, and the eyes are so tiny and bright.
SUSANNA	Bones! They're just all bones and gristle, no matter how you cook them.

The other two actors enter. The following "Cold Chorale" is to be spoken as a round.

ALL The cold is at this time so intense, that the ink freezes while I write, and my fingers stiffen 'round the pen. A glass of water by my bedside, within a few feet of the hearth, heaped with logs of oak and maple kept burning all night long, is a solid mass of ice in the morning. God help the poor immigrants who are yet unprepared against the rigour of the season.

All exit except the actor who becomes LADY FRANCES, who begins sketching.

***

Scene Seven

Bridgit and Lady Frances :
BRIDGIT *and* LADY FRANCES.
*During this scene the barrel which we
had onstage became a butter churn when
BRIDGIT enters with a piece of
doweling which is used as the handle —
a broomstick works well, also.*

FRANCES   When my husband and I first came to Upper
            Canada, I knew something of what to expect of
            the life here. The most distressing thing I
            discovered was the serious lack of good domestic
            help. You simply cannot find good help these
            days. We had to send away to Ireland for ours....

BRIDGIT   *(enters singing)*
            Oh whistle and I'll come to ye me lad,

FRANCES   ...and then we had to put up with what we got.

BRIDGIT   *(singing)*
            Oh whistle and I'll come to ye me lad,
            Thae father and mother and ae' shoud gae
            mad
            Oh whistle and I'll come to ye me lad.
            At kirk or at market whene'er ye see me,
            Gang by me as thae that ye cared na' a flea,
            But steal me a wink of your bonnie black e'e
            Thae look as ye were not lookin' at me.
            Look as ye were not lookin' at me.

> *As* BRIDGIT *sings, she dances at the churn until at some point in the song as she gets a bit carried away.*

FRANCES   Bridgit.

BRIDGIT   Oh! Lady Frances.

FRANCES   Bridgit, must you be quite so vigorous?

BRIDGIT   Well, if you want the butter to be butter.

FRANCES   Yes, but how can I sketch you if you won't stay still?

BRIDGIT   Well...Open your eyes when I'm like this, close 'em when I'm like this, keep on blinking your eyes, and it'll look like I'm not movin' at all!

FRANCES   Bridgit, it is four o'clock.

BRIDGIT   Is it?

FRANCES   Where is the tea?

BRIDGIT   Last time I checked, it was in the tin, same as it always is.

FRANCES   It is four o'clock, and all over the world civilized people are sitting down to their cup of tea.

BRIDGIT   And here we are churning butter and painting pretty pictures!

FRANCES   Queen Victoria is having her tea and I want mine.

BRIDGIT   And you shall have it...just as soon as this butter you've been achin' for is ready. Think of it now, meltin' on your scones.

FRANCES   Bridgit, Bridgit. What will you do when I can no longer suffer your impudence? You'll be lost on a corner in the cold, wearing a red petticoat.

BRIDGIT	Actually, I'll be on the arm of a man in a red great coat.
FRANCES	Bridgit?
BRIDGIT	Oh, Lady Frances, I've been wantin' to tell you all day. Last night Captain Merrick asked me to marry him...and I said yes.
FRANCES	But Bridgit, he is a captain.
BRIDGIT	Oh, yes, and a handsome captain, too.
FRANCES	But you are only a serving girl.
BRIDGIT	That might matter in England — but this is Canada — things are quite a bit different here.
FRANCES	Yes, as in no tea at four o'clock. Oh, Bridgit, this is all so sudden! I suppose you are planning to run off with your captain this very afternoon.
BRIDGIT	Lady Frances, I would never do such a thing! Why, I've even told Tom — Captain Merrick — that I want to stay close enough to you so's I can still bake you your special cakes every second Saturday of the month.
FRANCES	(*sniffing*) But Bridgit, weddings must be planned carefully.
BRIDGIT	I've always admired how you know the proper way of doing everythin', and I was hopin', since I've no mother or sister here, that you would help me plan my weddin'. You'd not have to work at all, mind, just help plan.
FRANCES	Well, weddings are important events...I would be pleased to advise you. Oh dear, we have so much to do. (*exiting*) I do love planning!

Scene Eight

The Circuit Preacher.
BRIDGIT, WOMAN WITH BABE IN
ARMS, CORPSE, CIRCUIT
PREACHER, TOM *who is played by a
broomstick.*

BRIDGIT   So Lady Frances planned to her heart's content;
and it was a lovely day in my life.

FRANCES *enters with broom which
she hands to* BRIDGIT, *places veil on
her head and top hat on broom — which
has a moustache on it — at the
appropriate times in* BRIDGIT's *lines.*
FRANCES *exits.*

BRIDGIT   She even let me wear her very own weddin' veil,
and not only that, she also presented Tom with a
top hat for the occasion! So we were all set to
be married — but for one thing. You see there
was no church in our community, so we had to
wait for the circuit minister to come ridin' by.
So Tom and I waited one week...and we waited
two weeks...

WOMAN *with baby enters.*

BRIDGIT   ...and we waited three weeks...

CORPSE *enters.*

BRIDGIT ...and then finally we heard him comin' down the road. And we weren't the only ones waitin', neither. There were some wee babies waitin' to be christened, and a couple of dead souls waitin' to be sent on their way to heaven...(*the* CORPSE *smells bad, and* MOTHER *and* BRIDGIT *edge away*)...We let them go first.

PREACHER (*appears riding in on hobby horse*)
Whoa!
Ashes to ashes, as God had intended,
I baptise this baby, your sins are amended,
And now man and wife, to all I have tended,
So now I must go to where I am sended.

ALL (*singing*) Amen.

All but BRIDGIT *and* "TOM" *exit.*

BRIDGIT After that lovely ceremony, we had some dancin'. Then Tom and I went off to our new home to spend a quiet, romantic evenin' together, when all of a sudden a wailin' like a pack of banshees surrounded our house...

Whooping offstage.

BRIDGIT ...and I knew that we were to be the victims of a charivaree! (*exiting*).

***

Scene Nine

Charivaree : Pronounced 'shivaree'.
BRIDGIT, *and three* TOWNSFOLK
who perform a play in which appear 2
horses named LADY *and* WILLIAM,
SIR REGINALD, JANE SMITH.

Note: Charivarees were often quite lewd.
This scene can be played quite broadly.

TOWNSFOLK *enter singing, banging*
pots and spoons, etc.

ALL

(*chorus*)
To me right spit polish up and buff my boot,
To me right spit polish up and buff my boot,
Too ra loo ra loo ra loot,
To me right spit polish up and buff my boot.

1.

A captain brave rode out one day,
He spied a damsel in dismay,
Standing 'neath the sky so blue,
And under her skirt she wore a dirty shoe.

2.

She said, "Young man what trade do you bear?"
He said, " I am a captain I do declare,
I ride my horse and I give commands,
And when I salute I use both hands."

	BRIDGIT *appears looking over backdrop, as if out of a bedroom window.*
3.	She said, " Your boots are polished bright, They shine like the stars on a moonlit night, Mine are a trifle soiled, you see, Kind sir, won't you polish up my boots for me?"
ALL	To my right spit polish up and buff my boot, To me right spit polish up and buff my boot...
BRIDGIT	What's all this racket about, then?
3	Bridgit, what are you doing up there with a husband as old as your grandfather?
2	Come on down here and we'll show you how it's done for real!
3	Yeah, we come to entertain you, Bridgit.
BRIDGIT	Well, I don't need any entertainin' tonight, boys.
3	I guess that means the charivaree is over, and we'll be collecting some money for a few drinks, then.
BRIDGIT	You want money for that singin'?
2	Oh, she doesn't like our singing?
BRIDGIT	Not particularly.
2	Maybe she'll like our acting!
BRIDGIT	I strongly doubt it.

At this point "the play "begins. 1 becomes the two Horses, 2 becomes SIR REGINALD, and 3 becomes JANE SMITH.

HORSE	Once upon a time there was a fair young maid riding through the park on her faithful horse, Lady. This is your fair young maid.
JANE	And this is me faithful horse, Lady.
HORSE	They stopped in a sunny clearing to enjoy the beauty of the day. Whereupon they heard the sound of approaching hooves, and to their amazement appeared a handsome young officer on his faithful horse, William. The handsome young officer introduced himself as Sir Reginald Roncesvalles Roquefort Sir.
SIR REG	I am Sir Reginald Roncesvalles Roquefort Sir.
HORSE	And the fair young maid introduced herself as...
JANE	Jane Smith.
HORSE	The horses were tired, seeing as I'm playing both parts, so they decided to have a bit of a rest over here, while Sir Reggie and Jane indulged in idle conversation...And they fell in love...And he polished her boot!
SIR REG	(*singing*) So he polished her boot with his polish black, He rubbed them front and he rubbed them back, He buffed them up and he buffed them down, And then he shone them all around.
1	What do you think of that, Bridgit?
BRIDGIT	I knew I wouldn't like it.
3	Will you give us some money then?
BRIDGIT	No!
2	Well, we'll give her more, then!

BRIDGIT   Wrong choice.

HORSE   Just as Sir Reggie was putting on the finishing
                 touches — and Jane seemed to be enjoying
                 herself just a bit too much — the faithful horse
                 Lady, that's me, decided to save me Lady's
                 honour by "accidentally" kicking Sir Reggie!

                 Song continues.

HORSE   The hero of the story is the horse you see,

SIR REG   Lady kicked the captain just above the knee,

JANE   I tried to revive him with a kiss,

                 *JANE kisses him, the false moustache
                 SIR REGGIE has been wearing transfers
                 to her face.*

ALL   And she found not a mister, but a MISS!

                 *The three sing chorus as BRIDGIT ad
                 libs "All right, I'll pay you, Leave us
                 in peace, away with yez all, etc."*

ALL   To me right spit polish up and buff my boot,
                 To me right spit polish up and buff my boot,
                 Too ra loo ra loo ra loot!

                 ALL freeze.

                 ***

Scene Ten

Advice to Wives:The actors play this straight, in neutral character. Each actor breaks the freeze on her line.

1   The Niagara Herald, May 22, 1828 Advice to wives. Avoid contradicting your husband.

2   All men are vain, never wound his vanity.

3   If he is abusive, never retort.

4   Never forget that a wife owes all of her importance to that of her husband.

ALL   And above all, *(with feeling)* Pray to God for guidance.

Song divide the parts to suit your production.

Obey, Obey!

BRIDGIT   A maid there was who did declare, *(descending below backdrop)*

ALL   That if she ever married were,
No power on earth should make her say,
Amongst the rites, the word OBEY.

ANNA JAMESON *exits.*
BRIDGIT   *(entering)*

When this she at the church confessed,
And when she saw the angry priest,
Shut up his book to go away,
She curtsying cried Obey, Obey. *(exiting)*

2   *(onstage)*
A maid there was who did declare,
That if she ever married were,
No power on earth should make her say,
Amongst the rites the word Obey. *(exiting)*

***

Scene Eleven

Visions : ANNA JAMESON, YOUNG
MAN, 3 DREAM VISION WIVES
*The two actors playing the wives can
have either the first or second vision as
her character, and each performance they
would play "Rocks, Scissors, Paper" on
stage to determine which one would
portray the third "perfect" vision. A
lace tablecloth can be the gown, and the
third wife throws it over her head.*

ANNA *enters humming "Pomp and
Circumstance" — sits on bench. The*
YOUNG MAN *enters, sees her and
approaches her.*

YOUNG MAN   May I?

ANNA *nods affirmatively, he joins her
on the bench. Suddenly they jolt and
start bouncing as though they are riding
in a buggy. The* YOUNG MAN *has
fallen immediately to sleep.*

ANNA   Continuing on my westward journey from
Toronto to London, I found myself in the
company of a young man. He was pale and
drawn, and occasionally nodded off to sleep,
moaning and sighing.

The YOUNG MAN *moans.*

ANNA	I finally attempted to engage him in conversation. (*as the* YOUNG MAN *abruptly awakens*) Are you all right?
YOUNG MAN	Yes.
ANNA	You look tired.
YOUNG MAN	I am.
ANNA	Did you not sleep well last night?
YOUNG MAN	No, I do not sleep well at night.
ANNA	Why is that?
YOUNG MAN	Madam, I suffer from terrible dreams.
ANNA	Intrigued, I questioned further. Perhaps talking about them, they might go away.
YOUNG MAN	Possibly.
ANNA	Perhaps talking to me about them...
YOUNG MAN	AH! It begins in a drawing room in Buckingham Palace. There is a ball going on.

The actors who play the VISION WIVES *sing Bach's "Minuet in G".*

YOUNG MAN	I am struck by a vision of loveliness, a woman in a white lace gown. I ask her to dance. We dance. By dawn...

Singing stops.

YOUNG MAN	...we are in love. I propose to her.

WIFE 1 *has entered on "vision of Loveliness" and mimes scene through to collapsing in death.*

ANNA	She accepts?

YOUNG MAN   Of course. I take my bride to our home in
                  Canada. It is winter. It is cold. She cannot take
                  the cold. She cannot take the hard work. She
                  does take sick. She dies.

ANNA   Oh, how frightful! But surely this dream does
                  not last the whole night.

YOUNG MAN   No.

ANNA   Ah, you have a second dream?

YOUNG MAN   I do. It begins in a drawing room near Fort
                  York. There is a ball going on.

                        The VISION WIVES *again sing the*
                        Minuet — WIFE 1 *from her position of*
                        the floor, dead.

YOUNG MAN   I spill wine on my trousers and hurry off to the
                  kitchen (*as singing stops*) to remedy the
                  situation. There I am struck by a vision of
                  loveliness...

                        WIFE 2 *enters.*

YOUNG MAN   ...a woman in a white apron. She is scrubbing
                  the floor, stoking the fire, making candles,
                  baking bread, spinning, and soothing two tiny
                  children. I am so impressed that I fall
                  immediately in love and ask her to marry me.

                        WIFE 2 *is miming all of this and*
                        subsequently described action.

ANNA   She accepts?

YOUNG MAN   Of course.

ANNA   Well, that doesn't sound so terrible.

YOUNG MAN	Ah, but the dream is not yet finished. I take my new bride to our home in the bushlands of Canada. My wife clears the land, burns the stumps, sows the seeds, builds the cabin, and makes the dinner in the time it takes me to walk from the wagon to the front stoop which is now constructed.
ANNA	How industrious!
YOUNG MAN	Then after dinner I present my wife with my late mother's harp. My wife places the harp in front of the fire, and hangs my socks upon it to dry.
ANNA	How quaint.
YOUNG MAN	I did not find it so. Such a woman could never fulfill my spiritual needs. Inconceivably, she knew neither Shakespeare, nor Aristotle.

WIFE 2 *is crestfallen.*

ANNA	How sad for you. But surely even these two dreams cannot take you to dawn.
YOUNG MAN	Alas!
ANNA & YOUNG MAN	There is a third dream.

WIVES 1 *and* 2 *rush together to decide who is to be* WIFE 3.

YOUNG MAN	It begins in a drawing room. There is a ball going on. I am struck by a vision of loveliness, a woman in white lace.

WIFE 3 *throws the tablecloth over her head and mimes.*

YOUNG MAN	She is scrubbing the floor, stoking the fire, and dancing the minuet!
ANNA	You fall in love?

YOUNG MAN   I propose.

ANNA   She accepts?

YOUNG MAN   Of course.

ANNA   The girl of your dreams. And this time you live happily ever after?

YOUNG MAN   No. This time... I wake up.

> *The* VISION WIVES *exit, and the* YOUNG MAN *falls asleep.*

ANNA   He quickly fell back asleep, once more in search of the girl of his dreams.

YOUNG MAN   (*standing, asleep and exiting on*) Where are you?

ANNA   Alas, she may never be found. These days a woman is either artistically educated or domestically trained. It is all nonsense. The true purpose of education is to develop all the capacities with which God has endowed us. Then we shall be ready for all circumstances.

> ANNA *exits, picking up the bench at "endowed us" and demonstrating one of her capacities by clearing it upstage.*

***

Scene Twelve

How to Stick a Pig: FLORA, *the Scottish Woman, and* JESSIE.

These are basically two intercut monlogues. FLORA *is unaware of* JESSIE *throughout, but* JESSIE *takes note of* FLORA *from time to time.*

FLORA   (*entering*) In the spring of my first year in Upper Canada we purchased a piglet and watched it grow through the summer. It was almost a pet to us, and reminded me greatly of the dog we'd left behind in Scotland. Then one sunny day in autumn, we gathered together with some neighbours to "stick" the pig.

JESSIE *enters. She knits throughout the scene.*

FLORA   First my husband took Violet — our pig — by the snout and looped a rope in a kind of a noose around the upper jaw. He tightened the rope and pulled her head way back. Then he kicked out one of her back legs as the neighbour man drove the knife into the base of her throat, flicked his wrist, and pulled it back out again.

JESSIE   Pig's blood makes blood pudding.

FLORA	The neighbour's wife was right there with a bucket to catch the blood that sprayed out over the four of us. She seemed oblivious to the pig's squeals...screams, actually....
JESSIE	The bristles are collected and made into brushes.
FLORA	Then one of the men slid a stick through the slits that he had carved into the pig's hocks. They flipped and hoisted her upside down into the air, and the blood poured into the neighbour's bucket below....
JESSIE	The intestines become sausage casings.
FLORA	Then the carcass was lowered into a huge cauldron of boiling water, lifted back out again, and scraped all over with a flat piece of metal...
JESSIE	Pork chops and roasts are eaten immediately or stored in brine for winter meals.
FLORA	The children scurried around, pulling away the strips of skin and amassing little piles of the pig's bristles....
JESSIE	Smoking preserves hams and bacon.
FLORA	Meanwhile, the knife was again used to slit...
JESSIE	The lard is used in ointments, soap and candles, for cooking and baking.
FLORA	...from the back legs down to the front legs, across the stomach, and all of the insides and entrails came rushing out in a heap.
JESSIE	The liver, heart and kidneys are extremely nutritious.
FLORA	And everyone had a job to do what with the wielding of saws and the cutting of hams...
JESSIE	The bones are ground up and used as fertilizer.

FLORA   ...so they did not notice my leaving.

JESSIE   Pickled pig's feet and tails are a midwinter
               delicacy.

FLORA   When I returned to the barn there was no sign of
               any part of my pig.

JESSIE   Head cheese is made by boiling down the entire
               head skin, bones, brains, eyes and tongue.

FLORA   Every part of that pig had to be used for
               something.

JESSIE   Thus, a good butcher uses every part of the pig
               but its oink.

               JESSIE *exits,* FLORA *stays and gets*
               ready for the Bee.

                    ***

Scene Thirteen

The Bee : FLORA, MARGARET, *the
midwife,* BETTY, *a Cockney servant,
and* JENNIFER *who is in late
pregnancy.*

MARGARET *and* BETTY *enter singing
"E Mo Leannan" and join* FLORA *in
preparation — doing dishes, cutting
vegetables, kneading bread, etc. The
chorus is sung softly under the spoken
lines.*

ALL   E mo leannan, o mo leannan,
'Se mo leannan am fear ur,
E mo leannan, o mo leannan.

*This song is Gaelic and is pronounced:
Eh mo lennan o mo lennan, Shay mo
lennan ahm fair uhr, Eh mo lennan o
mo lennan.*

JENNIFER   *(entering singing)*
I rose early in the morning,
Everyone was here by nine.

MARGARET   So here I am at another bee in a brand new
community. It seems I just get to know
everyone and my husband decides it's time to
move on.

FLORA   Do you think there'll be dancing tonight?

BETTY	Providin' the fiddler doesn't get too drunk.
FLORA	At the McCarthy's bee I danced so much my feet were too swollen to get my boots on.
FLORA	(*singing*) All the morning we've been cooking While the men are working hard.
MARGARET	You see he loves the wilderness — I have to admit that I do, too. So that's the way it's been for the last thirty-five years. We buy a plot of land, clear it, build a house, and move on.
JENNIFER	I'm going to look out on the children.
BETTY	(*singing*) Tables full of hungry workers, At this rate they'll eat their plates! (*cutting her hand*)...OW!
MARGARET	I've picked up quite a few things over the years, though. For one thing, the Indians have taught me natural cures using local herbs and plants. Leave this on 'til morning and you'll be fine.
JENNIFER	(*enters singing*) Food and cider fill their bellies, Satisfied their work is done. (*spoken*) The frame is up!
FLORA	It'll be a fine barn for the winter.
BETTY	(*singing*) All that's left are dirty dishes, Never will our work be done.
ALL	(*singing*) E mo leannan, o mo leannan, 'Se mo leannan am fear ur, E mo leannan, o mo leannan.

> MARGARET *helps* JENNIFER *to sit down on the barrel.*

JENNIFER   I tried your suggestion of putting a pillow under my stomach when I sleep — it really helps.

MARGARET   I love to pass on what I know, so at least when the time comes for me to move on, maybe you'll know as much as I do.

> FLORA *exits.*

BETTY   What is this stuff?

MARGARET   It's an herb called comfrey, and it helps stop bleeding. And you should be drinking raspberry tea.

JENNIFER   Raspberry tea?

MARGARET   It's good for a woman in your condition.

> FLORA *enters with catalogue.* FLORA *and* MARGARET *converse at the same time as* BETTY *and* JENNIFER. FLORA *and* MARGARET *have vocal focus,* BETTY *and* JENNIFER *have visual focus as they quietly ad lib as* BETTY *feels the baby kicking.*

BETTY   Would you like me to make you some tea?

FLORA   Mrs. Grant wanted me to ask you what the remedy for lice is. Her son, Thomas has picked some up from I don't know where.

MARGARET   All you do is shave off all the hair, scrub the head down with lye, rub it down with turpentine, and if eggs don't form, it should clear in about two weeks.

FLORA   Turpentine!

> BETTY *has exited by this point.*

MARGARET	Yes.
JENNIFER	That sounds terrible!
BETTY	(*off*) I'll have your tea in just a minute.
JENNIFER	Thank you.
MARGARET	You're near your time. Will it be a boy, or will it be a girl?
JENNIFER	I'm not sure.
MARGARET	If you give me your wedding ring, I can tell you.
JENNIFER	How?
MARGARET	It's very simple. Just put a thread through the ring and hold it over the tummy — back and forth means a boy, a circle means a girl.
FLORA	Get on with you!
MARGARET	Wait to see...something's coming...
	The ring swings back and forth in a larger and larger arc.
FLORA	It's a boy, she's going to have a boy. Look at the size of that baby!
BETTY	(*entering with cup of tea which she gives to* JENNIFER) There you go — careful, it's hot.
FLORA	Look what my sister sent me from Niagara, a catalogue of the latest fashions from Boston. This one is my favorite — look at those pleats!
MARGARET	It may be your favourite, but you can't milk a cow in it.
BETTY	The cow would like it though. She'd say, "Oh, moo, what a lovely dress!"

FLORA	But for a dance...Betty, do you think you could make over one of my dresses to look like that?
BETTY	Oh no, I don't think I could do that.
FLORA	Betty is such a marvelous seamstress.
JENNIFER	You have the smallest stitches of any of us.
FLORA	Look at the new things she's put on the quilt.

> *Quietly ad libbing conversations as JENNIFER begins talking to audience. They are silent at "community quilt".*

JENNIFER You see, this is what we call a community quilt. Everyone saved their scraps and pieces of material, and this winter we started making it together. That green is from Mr. Graham's old pair of breeches, and the blue is from a shawl that my mother brought with her all the way from Germany. When we were little she used to wrap us up in it, and then she'd sing us to sleep.

> *One of the women has brought out a blue quilt, and as they sing "Das Tanzen" — it is sung as a round — they ceremoniously fold the quilt in a dance-like manner. The quilt becomes a baby that one of the actors is singing to sleep. JENNIFER begins the song.*

ALL Das tanzen is aus,
Und wir gehen nach haus,
Gude nacht auch, gude nacht auch,
Gude nacht, gude nacht.

***

Scene Fourteen

Mrs. Crawley's Children:
Three actors perform this scene. "Das
Tanzen" is sung softly beneath the scene
by the woman who cradles the quilt-
baby. One woman uses a basket of baby
clothes or plums and gourds to
symbolise the births and deaths of the
children — we had her placing them on
the basket at birth and replacing them in
her basket at death. The third woman
reads from a diary.

NOTE: It is not necessary for the
woman with the baby to exit. An
alternate choice is that she watches the
woman with the baby clothes, in which
case we found it best to stop the singing
at "died July 29, 1806".

READER   Crawley Family Documents, 1805 to 1855

April 20, 1805. I was married to my ever dear
and beloved T. Crawley, note, at age 25.

January, 1806. My son Thomas Crawley was
born on Friday, ten at night, and died July 29,
1806.

January, 1807. My second son Thomas Crawley
was born Monday night, ten o'clock, being Plow
Monday.

February 9, 1808. My son Applebee Crawley
was born Thursday morning...and died December
28, 1808.

January 5, 1809. My son Richard Crawley was
born Friday morn, five o'clock, being old
Christmas day.

July 24, 1810. My son Charles Crawley was
born Tuesday morn, eight o'clock, being
Midsummer day.

May 12, 1811. I was delivered of a Boy, dead.

May 16, 1812. My son Joseph Crawley was
born Sunday night twelve o'clock... and died
March 31, 1813.

April 20, 1813. My son James Crawley was
born...It is my eighth son, and my eighth
wedding anniversary...and he died August 21,
1813.

October 23, 1815. My daughter Anna Crawley
was born at four o'clock in the afternoon.

July 14, 1818. My daughter Eliza Crawley was
born...and died January 5, 1819 — found dead in
bed.

November 24, 1821. My son John Crawley was
born.

> WOMAN *singing to baby has exited by*
> *now. The singing has stopped*

26 October, 1837. Died, my-ever-beloved child
Anna Crawley at five o'clock in the
morning...and buried November 1, 1837, aged 22
years. Oh my darling child that I shall never
forget....Oh my child, my child.

*ANNA's gown is slowly re-placed in
basket.*

*The woman, or two women, enter from
offstage singing "Brave Wolfe", and the
other women already on-stage slowly
join in*

ALL

Come all ye young men all, let this delight
you.
Come all ye young women all, let nought
afright you.
Nor let your courage fail when comes the
trial,
And do not be dismayed at the first denial.

***

Scene Fifteen

The Accomplishment Reel :
Speeches can be assigned to various
characters from earlier in the play.
Scene can start with two actors step-
dancing rather badly, without music, ad
libbing that "something seems to be
missing", etc.

BETTY begins her monologue as they
listen with interest and the fourth actor
joins them in listening.

BETTY   When I came to Canada there wasn't much fiddle
music to dance to...mostly because there weren't
too many fiddles around. So I took it upon
myself to learn mouth fiddling, or lilting. What
I had to do was go into the next township to
listen to a particular old gentleman there who
would do this at bees and charivarees — things
like that. I listened for a long time, and I finally
learned a reel It's called The Accomplishment
Reel — and it will be a real accomplishment if I
can get through this.

BETTY begins to lilt, and everyone else
dances a 3-handed reel. The reel is
divided so that at the end of each section
the lilting and dancing stops, and one
person delivers her speech as all four
actors take part in acting out the story,

becoming trees, chickens, rocking
chairs, etc. as the story requires.
The storyteller plays herself. On the
final "chorus" of the reel, all the actors
joined in the lilting, and BETTY *joins*
the dance.

SUSANNA

I remember my first summer in Upper Canada. I
craved fresh tomatoes on my table. I took great
pride in planting each of my little tomato seeds.
I watered them every day, the sun beat down
upon them, the vines grew out of the ground, and
lovely little balls formed on them like glass
ornaments on a Christmas tree. How I loved to
see them grow plump and juicy and ripe.
Unfortunately, I was not the only one who loved
my tomatoes...the local chickens loved them,
too. Each day they would come by and peck at
my tomatoes — I'd push them away — and
they'd peck, and I'd push, and they'd peck, and in
the end my tomato plants were destroyed. So I
simply decided to boil some water, throw the
tomatoes in the hot water — with the chickens
— and make a lovely soup.

ALL

Lilting and dancing.

MOTHER

The first time I made maple syrup, I was so
proud. I had watched someone else make it and I
thought I knew everything. The first thing I had
to do was to find a forest of maple trees. Then I
took the spiles — those little wooden tubes —
and I drove them into the maple trees. I only hit
one oak. (*to the tree*) Sorry. Then I waited
while the sap dripped into the buckets I had
placed on the ground below, and then I gathered
up the sap, took it into the house, and put it on
the stove where I had built a huge fire. The sap
started to bubble and boil, and it smelled so good
with the vapours going all over the house. After
a while things calmed down, and there it was —
maple syrup. It tasted so good — I was going to
use it in all of my cooking. I was feeling rather

MOTHER	tired, so I leaned against the wall to catch my breath...and the vapours had stuck themselves to all of my walls. That's when I learned that you make maple syrup outside the house.
ALL	Lilting and dancing.
JENNIFER	What I remember best is the first time that I gave birth. It was a hot, sunny day, and my husband and I were out in the fields bringing in the crops. He was cutting the hay with a scythe, and I was gathering it into bundles when...The pains began around noon. I sent my husband off to get the midwife, while I went into the house to sit in my rocking chair and wait to see who would arrive first...the midwife...or my baby. My breathing started changing, my rocking chair's breathing started changing...and the next thing that I knew — My daughter was born!

To give birth, JENNIIFER can sit in the arms of two women who were the rocking chair - they rock back and forth with more and more energy until JENNIFER is lifted up and the fourth woman catapulted herself out from behind, rolling along the floor, crying, at "I knew".

ALL	Lilting and dancing. (*all joining in both activies*)

The dance ends and two actors speak the last two lines, each taking one sentence. The woman who has played ANNA JAMESON can speak the second line, as "love and work enough" was coined by her.

1	You know, it might have been the men who discovered this country — but it was the women who made it our home.

2   So with our hearts full and our hands busy,
           we have love and work enough to last the
           rest of our lives.

                    Chorus of "Rise and Come Along" is
                    sung through once slowly, with actors
                    joining in and building the sound, and
                    then a second time in a very rousing
                    fashion.

ALL   Rise and come along,
            Oh, arise and come along,
            Rise and rise and come along,
            Bid welcome here to Canada.

            Rise and come along,
            Oh, arise and come along,
            Rise and rise and come along,
            Bid welcome here to Canada!

                 The End.

Beware the Quickly Who
by Eric Nicol

Eric Nicol was born in 1919, in Kingston, Ontario. He moved early to Vancouver and attended the University of British Columbia — B.A., 1941. After three years service with the RCAF ground crew, he received an M.A. in French from U.B.C., in 1948. After a year at the Sorbonne, he moved to London and wrote for the B.B.C. His first book, *Sense and Nonsense* was published in 1948. He returned to Vancouver in 1951 to be columnist for *The Province*. His books are numerous and include *The Roving I* and *Girdle Me a Globe* — both Stephen Leacock Humour Medal winners. His plays include *The Clam Who Made a Face* and *The Fourth Monkey*, among many others.

Beware the Quickly Who was first produced at the Holiday Theatre in Vancouver in 1967, with the assistance of the Centennial Commission.

The Characters

THE WHO, who also appears as **DR. WHITE** and **SNIDDELEY**.

JOHNNY

SCENERY

TWO HOODS, who also appear as **SNEER** and **SNORT**.

THE LION — British, Mod.

THE BEAVER

THE GIANT

JOY DE VIVRE

JACQUES

Several of the other roles may be doubled.

Act One

The stage is bare. The lights go out. The voice of THE WHO *is projected over a loudspeaker, from a height upstage. It is a loud and sexless voice, authoritarian yet blustering — the voice of the shrewish schoolmaster.*

WHO Silence! Silence, I say! Silence! *(once silence is established)* Come up — that boy! That boy in the front row, come up at once. Come up here! Yes, you! Quickly! Come! Quickly, quickly!

JOHNNY leaves his seat in the front row of the audience, picked out by a spotlight, and reluctantly goes up on the stage. He is a young man dressed in a little boy's outfit: a red toque, white shirt and blue short pants, which have a maple leaf on the seat. His socks, pea-soup green with clocks of white lilies, don't blend with the rest of the costume. In moments of stress he pulls them up, but they soon fall down again. He reaches the middle of the stage, bewildered and frightened.

WHO Stand right there! Not a move!

> *The spotlight tightens on* JOHNNY's *face. At the same time a luminescent "black light" mask appears on the back curtain, at some height above the stage. The mask, mildly horrifying, is a caricature of errant curiosity, the ultimate nosey parker.*

JOHNNY   Oh!

WHO   Silence! I make all the exclamation marks here.

JOHNNY   But who?—

WHO   And the question marks. Understand? When you speak, end with a period. Do you get the point?

JOHNNY   Yes, sir.

WHO   Good. Quickly, who are you?

JOHNNY   Who, me?

WHO   I said no question marks! One more and you will be held for interrogation. Quickly, now, who are you?

JOHNNY   Why, I'm...I'm...I'm...

WHO   *(mimicking)* "I'm...I'm...I'm..." You sound like a squeaky clothesline. Answer! Or don't you know?

JOHNNY   Yes, I know who I am. I know it as well as I know my own name...John! That's who I am. Most people call me Johnn—

WHO   *(butting in)* John! *(derisive cackle)* John! "John", he says. Do you know how many Johns there are in the world? Johns, Juans, Jons and Johans?

JOHNNY   No, sir.

WHO	Two hundred and sixty-five million, four hundred and eighty-nine thousand, seven hundred and three—not counting the Chinese "Chong".
JOHNNY	*(trying again)* Most people call me Johnn—
WHO	*(savagely)* Most people don't even know you're alive, sonny boy. What I want to know is your identity.
JOHNNY	My identity? What's that?
WHO	Your identity is what makes you special. Quickly, what's your identity?
JOHNNY	*(retreating)* My identity? Maybe I could find it if I went back to my—*(turning to bolt)*
WHO	Stay where you are! *(JOHNNY does)* Trying to end up your sentence with a dash, eh? Turn around! Stand up straight! You have exactly five minutes in which to state your identity.
JOHNNY	Five minutes! I don't even have a watch!
WHO	We shall use my clock. *(projecting)* Bring in the clock!
	The two HOODS, *figures completely cloaked in black, carry in a large, grotesque, coffin-shaped clock. The hands, taped or painted to show up in ultraviolet light, are turning at a brisk pace.*
WHO	Wind it up! It is running slow. Wind it!
	The HOODS *crank up the ratchety mechanism, accelerating the hands.*
JOHNNY	Wait! It runs so fast. What kind of clock is—

WHO	This is a Special Occasions clock. It tells the time for birthday parties, Christmas morning, summer holidays — any occasion when the hours pass like minutes, and the minutes pass like seconds, and, as for seconds...

> *The clock buzzes harshly. The hands stop.*

WHO	There, time's up. You failed. It is my unpleasant duty...tee hee...to sentence you to —
JOHNNY	Wait! I wasn't ready. That clock is mean.
WHO	*(strident)* Of course it is mean. It's on Greenwich Mean Time, only meaner, numbskull. I sentence you to be a nonentity. To live in oblivion. To die a big nobody, a name written on water, a —
JOHNNY	Please! Please, give me another chance. I know I must be somebody. Just give me another chance to remember.
WHO	Very well. Never let it be said that the Quickly Who was not sporting enough to prolong the agony. Ha-ha! You have another five minutes in which to learn who you are. Clock, start !

> *The clock hands start moving again.*

JOHNNY	*(to himself)* I must remember who I am! I will!

> *With this assertion, the lights go up a little on stage. The mask withdraws.*

WHO	*(off)* Too light, too light! Who turned up the lights?

> *SCENERY enters, behind JOHNNY, who does not at first notice him. SCENERY is a twiggy apparition who does not believe in hurrying.*

JOHNNY   I'll find out who I am if I have to search up mountain and down valley. Over lake and stream. Through forest and meadow. Up...

SCENERY   Hold on. Hold on, there.

JOHNNY   Who are you?

SCENERY   I'm the scenery in this play. Within bounds, that is. "Up mountain and down valley. Over lake and stream." *(shaking his head)* You'd better narrow it down a little, son. I don't have help.

JOHNNY   *(grabbing him)* You've got to help *me*. I've only got five minutes. And that clock goes so fast...

SCENERY   The clock? Oh, yes. Leave it to me. I'll slow it down. *(going to the clock)* Clock, the scene is changed from Newfoundland to Nova Scotia—you lose half an hour.

> *The clock brakes violently, with a ratchety noise. And the hands spin backwards.*

SCENERY   *(rapidly)* The scene changes from Nova Scotia to Ontario, you lose another hour. From Ontario to Manitoba, you lose another hour. From Manitoba to Alberta, you lose another hour. From Alberta to British Columbia, you lose another hour.

> *The clock, badly frazzled, has one hand running one way, the other hand running the other.*

SCENERY   *(rejoining JOHNNY)* There, that should keep his hands busy for awhile.

JOHNNY   You've got to help me.

SCENERY   Do what?

JOHNNY   Find my identity.

SCENERY	Yeah? Where did you lose it?
JOHNNY	I don't know. Oh, I've got to find it. Please help me. The Quickly Who is going to make me into a nonentity, and I'll have to live in oblivion.
SCENERY	Oblivion? Oblivion, Saskatchewan, or Oblivion, New Brunswick?
JOHNNY	I don't know. All I know is one big question. *(singing to a melody approximating "O Canada")*

Who can I be?
I wish I knew who I'm.
Help, Scenery!
While I have still got time.

I must be someone,
To learn who,
is what I've got to do.
I don't care who.
I could be you.
But tell me,
tell me what is true.

Who can I be?
He, it or she?
Animal, veg or mineral,
or gee! all three!
Who can I be?
Won't someone please tell me?

SCENERY	Okay, okay. So you want to find out who you are. The best place to find that out is where you live. Where's your home? *(as JOHNNY stares at him)* You do have a home, don't you?
JOHNNY	Everybody has a home.
SCENERY	No, everybody hasn't got a home, but most people have a home, and you look like most people, so where's yours?

JOHNNY	...I don't remember. I'm so mixed up I can't even remember my address.
SCENERY	What about your parents?
JOHNNY	Parents? Ohh! *(biting his knuckle in frustration)* I know I had them when I came in here.
SCENERY	Surely you remember something about them? What's that crest on your shirt?
JOHNNY	*(looking at it)* It's a lion and a unicorn. A lion! That rings a bell.
SCENERY	You live with a lion that rings bells?
JOHNNY	No. My parents. I have a feeling that one of them was a lion.
SCENERY	Well, having a lion for a parent would give you an identity, all right. The lion is brave, and strong, and nobody messes with his cubs.
JOHNNY	Yes! That would make me special. Quick, how can I find him?
SCENERY	The lion?
JOHNNY	Yes, yes!

The LION *enters.*

LION	*(leaning against something)* Where's the action, luv?
JOHNNY	You're the Lion?
LION	*(holding up two fingers in a "Peace" sign)* Non-violent.
JOHNNY	Don't you recognize me...Daddy?
LION	Daddy? Did you call me "Daddy", dearie?

JOHNNY	Yes! See the crest on my shirt. It's a lion, isn't it?
LION	Establishment lion. One of the real Trafalgar Squares. Dig that freaky horse he's trying to groove with.
SCENERY	That's not a horse. That's a unicorn.
LION	It's *all* corn.
JOHNNY	You mean you're not my father?
LION	No offence, duck. Lots of people don't have me for their father. Farsends. *(meaning 'thousands')*
JOHNNY	Heck! I was hoping to be related to the King of the Beasts. Then I'd be special.
LION	Look, man, you don't have to be King of the Beasts to be special. I'm special, and I haven't been King of the Beasts for, blimey, months now.
JOHNNY	You're not? Who is?
LION	Oh, eagle, bear, dragon — who cares? I've had bags more jollies since I became the Jack of Beasts.
JOHNNY	The Jack of Beasts?
LION	The I'm-all-right-Jack. The lion of least resistance. Life's a giggle, luv.
JOHNNY	You still have an identity. You're Lord of the Jungle.
LION	Dirty word.
JOHNNY	Pardon?
LION	Jungle. Dirty word. Bad vibes, man. Survival of the fittest. Eating meat. Yech!
JOHNNY	You don't eat meat?

LION	Please. You are talking to a health food nut. Strictly vegetarian. Have an organically-grown prune?
JOHNNY	No, thanks. Gee whiz, why couldn't you have been my father?
LION	Look, luv, if you want me to be your father, I'm game. In the protected sense of the word.
JOHNNY	Really?
LION	Course. I've had dozens of cubs in my time.
JOHNNY	Wow! What do cubs grow up to be?
LION	Scouts.

Loud chomping backstage.

JOHNNY	Ssh! Did you hear anything?
LION	Like what?
JOHNNY	Like...

Chomping, off

JOHNNY	That!
BEAVER	(*off*) Timber! Tim-ber!

Snapping of branches. Thud of tree hitting ground. BEAVER pops his head up over a log. He uears a hard hat.

BEAVER	Hi.
JOHNNY	Yike!
BEAVER	Sorry. Felling trees. Didn't mean to butt in. Ha, ha. Felling trees, butt in...get it? You don't get it.
JOHNNY	Who...who...

BEAVER	Am I? Castor Beaver, your friendly symbol of industry. Trees felled promptly. Two teeth, no waiting. Who are you?
JOHNNY	I'm a lion cub. This is my Daddy Lion.
BEAVER	Your dandelion? What's a nice lad like you doing with a weed like that?
LION	Fascist!
JOHNNY	If I'm not a lion cub, what am I?
BEAVER	You? It's perfectly clear what you are.
JOHNNY	It is?
BEAVER	Certainly. You're a giant.
JOHNNY	A giant!
BEAVER	What else? You're at least ten times bigger than I am. That makes you a giant.
JOHNNY	A giant! Golly! I don't want to be a giant. Giants are always stupid and cruel, and they get killed in awful ways.
BEAVER	*(shrugging)* Nobody's perfect. Look at me. Braces on my teeth. You learn to live with it. You're a giant, all right.
JOHNNY	But if I were a giant I'd have lots of gold. My pockets would be full of gold...Oh, no!...No!

> JOHNNY *plunges his hands into his pockets. They come out bulging and dripping with gold coins. He bends down to pick up some and his toque falls off. It spills more bullion. He miserably refills the cap and his pockets.*

BEAVER   Yep, you're a giant. A typical giant-size that saves money. Gold always goes to their head.

                LION *has pussyfooted back downstage, attracted by the gold.*

LION   Can't stand litter. Shame on you for polluting the environ-ment.

JOHNNY   *(wearily)* What difference does it make?

LION   What difference! You've heard of Richard the Lion-Hearted?

JOHNNY   Yes.

LION   Well, you're looking at Lion the Rich-Hearted. Mm, love that lolly !

JOHNNY   I don't understand. I don't remember having all this gold.

BEAVER   Your golden hen filled your pockets while you were snoring after gorging yourself on your dinner in your castle.

JOHNNY   *(hurt) I* don't snore.

BEAVER   Nonsense. All giants snore. You also stamp around singing Fee, fie, foe, fum, I smell the blood of an Englishman!

LION   *(alarmed)* You smell what?

JOHNNY   I can't stand the sight of blood.

LION   Me either. Especially mine.

BEAVER   Never say "can't". You're going to have to try harder, Mr. Giant. At the moment you are a D-minus monster. Let's try to bring up your music grade a little, shall we? Together now, Fee, fie, foe, fum, I...Come on! Think big! Fee, fie, foe, fum, I smell the blood of an Englishman!

JOHNNY	*(joining in)* ...fie, foe, fum, I smell the blood of an Englishman!
BEAVER	Good! Again!
JOHNNY	*(putting out)* Fee, fie, foe, fum, I smell the blood of an Englishman.

> JOHNNY *stamps around the stage. His steps are amplified by those of a much heavier body, offstage, and a very deep voice chimes in from the loudspeaker.*

BEAVER	By George, I think he's got it! Johnny Fee, fie, foe, fum...

> JOHNNY *breaks off and the* GIANT *carries on alone.*

GIANT	...I smell the blood of an Englishman!
JOHNNY	Was that an echo?

> *Backdrop is rolled up to reveal a* GIANT *football player— a flat with a hole for the actor's head.*

BEAVER	*(impressed)* Not unless...it was a very *tall* echo. It's a Giant!
LION	*(backing off)* You and your singalongs!
JOHNNY	A Giant? *(staring upward)* But if that's a Giant?, what am I?
BEAVER	I don't know, boobie, but if you take my advice, you won't be an Englishman. Ciao! *(exiting)*

> JOHNNY *is left alone, downstage, facing the* GIANT, *deflated and scared.*

GIANT	Hi y'all.
JOHNNY	You're...a real Giant.

GIANT	An' the coach says ah'm still growin'.
JOHNNY	Are you going to eat me?
GIANT	That depends. Are you clean?
JOHNNY	Yes.
GIANT	Are you wholesome?
JOHNNY	Very wholesome.
GIANT	Are you ranch-fresh, vitamin-enriched, and finger-lickin' good?
JOHNNY	Yes! Yes! Yes!
GIANT	You've sold me. I'll eat you.
JOHNNY	No! You can't eat me. I don't want to be eaten.
GIANT	Ho, come now. I'm your friend. I'm everybody's friend.
JOHNNY	How can you be my friend when you're going to eat me?
GIANT	I have a very friendly appetite. It doesn't matter *who* you are. You go down well with me.
JOHNNY	I don't want to go down well with you. I'll give you indigestion.
GIANT	Ho, spunky fella, ain't yuh?
JOHNNY	I have to find out who I am, my identity, and I'll *never* do that if you eat me.
GIANT	Ho, don't worry, bite-size. You're not worth the chewin', a dwarf like you.
JOHNNY	*(a blow)* A dwarf!

GIANT	Sure. You're at least ten times smaller than I am, that makes you a dwarf. Go stand under a toadstool. *(going off)* Fee, fie, foe, fum, I smell the blood of a leprechaun! Ho, ho, ho...
JOHNNY	A dwarf!
LION	*(emerging)* Has he gone?
JOHNNY	Scenery! I'm a dwarf. He told me to go stand under a toadstool.
SCENERY	A toadstool. Poisonous or non-poisonous?
JOHNNY	What difference does it make. I'm the one that isn't worth eating.
LION	Well, he seemed to take a fancy to me. Thanks, mate. You may be square, but you're spunky. *(guiltily)* Here, you dropped this.
	LION *holds out a gold coin he picked up earlier.* JOHNNY *waves it off.*
JOHNNY	Keep it. What good is gold if you're a dwarf?
LION	*(his jaunty self)* It's better to be an elf with pelf than a troll on the dole. Maybe you'll meet Snow White. *(singing)* Hi ho, hi ho
WHO	*(off and owlish)* Who! Who! Who!
JOHNNY	What was that?
LION	Sounded like an owl.
	The clock has started to gain time again.
JOHNNY	The clock! It's running again! Scenery, do something! If I'm a dwarf, maybe Snow White can help me.

SCENERY	For gosh sake...All right, you want to meet Snow White, we'll be in a place that's timeless — fairy-tale land.
JOHNNY	Fairy-tale land?
LION	*(alarmed)* No! Not that! I'll get...

> LION *is interrupted by the lights and music that create fairytale land, as* SCENERY *provides an enchanted forest. The clock has a fit, reeling offstage.* LION *hops about in pain, clutching a hind paw.*

LION	...that darn thorn in my foot again. Ooh! Ouch! That smarts! You and your fairy-tale land! Ouch! *(hopping offstage)* You sure know how to hurt a feline. *(projecting)* Androcles! They've done it again.

> *From the opposite wing there emerges, flapping, a figure wearing a dirty white academic gown and an outlandish mortar board. A vaguely male yet witch-like apparition, whose manner is very solicitous.*

WHITE	Snow White! Who called for Snow White?
JOHNNY	Oh! I did, ma'am.
WHITE	Sir!
JOHNNY	Sir?
WHITE	You called for Snow White. Lucky you! I heard you, and here I am
JOHNNY	*You're* Snow White?
WHITE	No, no, no, no, no. I'm not Snow White. I am her older brother — Slush White. *Dr.* Slush White. You may call me "Doctor".

JOHNNY   Doctor? Golly, maybe you can help me, Doctor, I'm trying to find out who I...

WHITE   Say no more ! That is exactly the kind of doctor I am — Doctor of Knowing Everything.

JOHNNY   You mean...you know, for sure, whether I'm a dwarf?

WHITE   A dwarf? You? Oh, tch, tch, tch. And tsk, tsk, tsk. Didn't I hear you say you had more gold than you know what to do with?

JOHNNY   Yes, sir.

WHITE   Well! Nobody who is rich can be a dwarf. It simply isn't possible.

JOHNNY   It isn't?

WHITE   Never. You may be diminutive, stocky, small-boned, dainty, abbreviated, petite or piccolo...

JOHNNY   Piccolo?

WHITE   But a dwarf — never!

JOHNNY   Oh, thank you!

WHITE   You want to know what you are, you wealthy ignoramus?

JOHNNY   Oh, yes, please! Please tell me!

WHITE   You, my sweet, sugar-coated pal, are...a girl!

JOHNNY   A girl?

WHITE   Of course you are a girl. Who ever heard of a boy with naturally straight hair?

JOHNNY   Straight hair? *(pulling off his toque, discharging the gold once again, and quickly getting help in picking it up)*

WHITE   Here, here, let me assist you. My, you *do* need help, don't you? A nice young lady like you shouldn't have all this money on her mind.

JOHNNY   A girl! I never thought I might be a girl. Me, Johnny...

WHITE   Not Johnny, dear, Jo Annie.

JOHNNY   Jo Annie?

WHITE   You weren't pronouncing it quite right. Tell me, do you always carry your gold in your cap?

JOHNNY   All my clothes are full of gold...my cap, my pockets, even my shoes. *(demonstrating)*

WHITE   What a delightful wardrobe! A truly gorgeous bridal ensemble.

JOHNNY   Bridal! Me? A bride?

WHITE   My dear! We were destined to be wed, you and I. With all your worldly goods you me endow.

JOHNNY   But I can't be a girl. I don't look like a girl.

WHITE   Poor darling. Eyes still fogged by sleepy-sleeps, are they? Let me show you to you as you really look...in a nice clean mirror. Close your eyes.

                              The HOODS *produce a large oval mirror frame, without a glass, while* JOHNNY *closes his eyes.*

WHITE   No peeking, now! Keep them shut tight if you want to see the real you.

                              Music. HOODS *leave.* JOHNNY *puts his hands over his eyes, as* WHITE *leads forth a pretty young girl with long golden hair,* JOY, *who moves as in a trance. He whispers instructions in her*

> *ear and positions her behind the empty*
> *mirror frame.*

WHITE   *(to* JOHNNY*)* Rub all the sand out of your
             eyes...Get ready to switch your eyeballs to high
             beam...Now...look at yourself!

> JOHNNY *turns and sees the girl in a*
> *position identical to his own. She*
> *mouths his words.*

JOHNNY   Oh, no!

> *Experimentally,* JOHNNY *lifts an arm,*
> *shakes a leg, scratches himself; trying to*
> *catch his reflection out. The girl's*
> *movements are synchronized with his,*
> *to musical accompaniment. At last*
> JOHNNY's *shoulders slump in despair.*
> *Music out. The* HOOD's *remove* JOY.

JOHNNY   It's true. I *am* a girl.

WHITE   Of course you are. And a very *pretty* girl, what's
             more. *(As* JOHNNY *moves to touch the mirror)*
             Ah-ah. Mustn't touch. It's a very sensitive mirror,
             and we need it to frame other young ladies.

JOHNNY   *(turning away, disconsolate)* I'm a *girl.* If I'd
             known, I wouldn't have bothered to find out.

WHITE   Nonsense, my b...my beauteous damsel. A young
             lady like you shouldn't be encumbered with a lot
             of heavy bullion. *(taking the toque)* Let's get you
             out of those clothes and into a nice synthetic.

JOHNNY   Synthetic?
             WHITE *has removed* JOHNNY's *pants*
             and shoes, throwing them behind
             JOHNNY *to the* HOOD *waiting with a*
             set of chains.

WHITE   I have a very becoming frock for you. Wonderful
             material. Wears like iron. You see...

While the HOOD's *back is turned,* JOY
walks out with an air of being drawn to
JOHNNY *in spite of her bewitched state.*

JOHNNY   Hello. Who are you?

                  JOY *just stares at him.* HOOD *sulks.*

JOHNNY   *(to* WHITE*)* Say, she looks a lot like me.

WHITE   She does? Oh, why yes, I suppose she does, here
                  and there. In you go, my dear. Under a spell, poor
                  thing. Bewitched, till someone makes her laugh.
                  Go...

JOHNNY   Wait. What's her name?

WHITE   Um, Joy. Joy de Vivre. I took her under my wing,
                  poor creature, and have cared for her these many
                  years. After all, we can't let Joy be unconfined,
                  can we darling? *(pointing)* Inside, at once.

JOHNNY   Wait. She's beautiful.

WHITE   Oh, I dare say, in a flashy sort of way. But not
                  half so ravishing as you, my dear. *(fondling the*
                  toque) You positively drip charm. Shall we get on
                  with the wedding? Music—

JOHNNY   I'm sorry, Dr. White, but I don't think I want to
                  marry you.

                  Second HOOD *oozes on stage.*

WHITE   What's that? Don't want to marry me? Me? Dr.
                  Slush White? Poor boy, the excitement has addled
                  your—

JOHNNY   Poor *boy!* You said "poor *boy"!*

WHITE   A slip of the tongue. There's frost on the roof of
                  my mouth.

JOHNNY   *(throwing off mantle)* I *am* a boy! *(to* JOY*)* And
                    you're a girl.

WHITE   *(snarling)* Congratulations! You've narrowed it
                    down. *(to the* HOODS*)* Seize him!

                              The two heavies grab JOHNNY, *pinning
                              him with the chain of the iron ring.*

JOHNNY   Let go of me.

WHITE   There's more than one way to cook a goose.
                    You're not especially plump, but you will make
                    lovely gravy. Toss him in the dungeon.

JOHNNY   Wait! You can't do that to me. You don't know
                    who I am.

WHITE   Who are you?

JOHNNY   I don't know. But I could be somebody important.

WHITE   Right. *(to the* HOODS*)* Toss him in the
                    important dungeon.

                              *They are interrupted by the reappearance
                              of* LION, *gyrating wildly as he clutches
                              one foot and hops on the other. He
                              weaves among them, a dervish in agony,
                              running into* SCENERY.

LION   Ouch! Ootch! Oh, won't somebody get this thing
                    out of my foot? Ouch! Ootch! Fairy-tale land,
                    who needs it? Yow! Yipe!

                              *This apparition, which has merely stalled
                              the others, amuses* JOY. *Her face breaks
                              into a smile, then a grin, and at last she
                              laughs.*

JOHNNY   She laughed! The spell is broken. She's cured!

LION   She's cured! *(still hopping)* What about me?
                    What's so funny about—

WHITE	*(falling back in terror)* Stop that laughter! Stop it!
	JOHNNY *throws off the* HOODS, *who retreat behind their master.* LION *keeps hopping, though mystified.*
JOHNNY	You're afraid of laughter! That's what you're afraid of laughter. Ha, ha.
WHITE	Stop it, I say!
JOHNNY	Come on, Lion, laugh!
LION	Ha, ha! Ouch, ootch! Ha, ha! Ouch, ootch!
JOHNNY	See, Joy, they're afraid of laughter.
JOY	I'm free! At last, I'm free!
WHITE	*(falling back)* Not for long. You're mine, both of you—
SCENERY	*(to audience)* Come on, everybody, laugh!
	WHITE & C. *are gusted off the stage by laughter.*
JOHNNY	Hurrah! We drove them away. You were great, Lion
LION	*(sitting, nursing his foot)* Then do us a favour, mate. Get us out of this fairytale land.
JOHNNY	You've still got the thorn in your foot.
LION	The thorn's the least of it. There's an idiot running round trying a glass slipper on everybody's foot. Like to cripple me, he did.
JOY	Oh, thank you, both of you. It's like waking from a bad dream. How can I ever thank you?
LION	You could begin by...

VOICE	*(offstage)* Cinderella! Cinderella!
LION	Blimey! Here he comes again. Get us out of it.
JOHNNY	All right. Scenery, can you take us out of fairytale land to some place where Lion's feet won't hurt?
SCENERY	I wish you people would make up your minds. Where do you want to be?
LION	Home! My home! Lunnon town.
SCENERY	London? That's one of the largest cities in the world. All that traffic — cars, buses. *(to audience)* May I have some assistance with London traffic, please?

> *While the audience beeps and honks, SCENERY creates a bit of swinging London.*

LION	*(cured and galvanized)* That's it! Good old turned-on Lunnontown. *(to JOY)* Say, I know you. You're Joy de Vivre. We met during old Charles the Second, remember, bless his naughty nibs?
JOY	And I know you — the British Lion.
LION	Call me Brit!

> *LION swings JOY into a vigorous dance, part Morris, part Monkey. After a moment JOHNNY turns away, the wallflower, lonesome in his anonymity. The music stops. The dancers notice JOHNNY, and JOY goes to him.*

JOY	Who are you?

> *JOHNNY looks miserable.*

SCENERY	Here we go again.

JOHNNY	I don't really know who I am.
JOY	Oh. Well, it doesn't matter. Remember what Juliet said to Romeo "What's in a name?...a rose by any other name would smell as sweet."
JOHNNY	Yes, but I don't even know if I smell sweet. I'd give anything to be able to dance like that.
LION	Anyone can dance, luv. You must have some dance you call your own. Come on, have a go.
JOHNNY	No, I don't think so.
JOY	Oh, yes, do try. Dance *your* dance.
JOHNNY	I don't know any. Not really...

> *Music: a Scottish reel.* JOHNNY *reels a bit then peters out.*

LION	That's a Scottish reel. You must have a dance of your own.

> *Music: a Ukrainian folk-dance.* JOHNNY *squats and bounces awkwardly and abortively, finally falling on his behind. Music out.* LION *leaves.*

JOY	*(helping him up)* That's a Ukrainian folk-dance. Think! What *is* your dance?

> *After concentrating hard,* JOHNNY *does the Indian prairie-chicken dance, to a tom-tom. This too is a failure.*

SCENERY	That was the Indian prairie-chicken dance. You the Indian or the prairie-chicken?

> JOY *and* SCENERY *stand apart.*

JOHNNY	*(in despair) You* see? Even in dancing I'm nobody—nothing. *(sings to guitar)*

JOHNNY
I dreamed I was a great big maple tree,
standing way out. . . way, way out,
on the bald prairie.
My hair it touched the sky, oh, the blue, blue
sky,
and an itty-bitty bird came and sat in my eye.
Chugarum, chigaree,
won't you love this maple tree?

I dreamed that as I stood there,
lonesome as a skunk,
a man with a bucket came
and stuck it in my trunk.
My sap he tapped and took away,
and oh it's just too awful—
Stranger, that's me you are pouring on your
waffle.
Chugarum, chigaree,
nobody loves this maple tree.

WHO
(over loudspeaker) True, true, my young dance
dunce. Your Irish jig is up too. Only a couple
more minutes and you shall vanish from the earth
without a trace, the little man who was never
there. Ha, ha.

JOHNNY
I'm tired of trying to be somebody. I just want to
be anybody. I just want to drop out of the whole
world. Scenery!

SCENERY
To do that, you have to eat the magic mushroom.

JOHNNY
All right, I'll eat the magic mushroom. Lay it on
me, man.

SCENERY
(handing him the magic mushroom) And you have
to walk backwards, hitching a ride back to the
primitive.

JOHNNY
(eating and walking backwards) That's where I'm
headed, man. Back to Middle Earth. Back to the
beginning. Back to the garden.

LION, *nakedly lionish, enters.*

LION	Now see what you've done! I'm prehistoric. *(roaring)* There, you hear that? Roaring! *(roaring)* Oh, how embarrassing! First thing I know I'll be *(going down)* back on all fours. *(roaring)* Oh, this is a *beastly* situation. *(gallopping offstage, roaring)*
JOHNNY	Wait! Lion wait! He's gone.
JOY	Never mind. I'll stay with you. Do you feel any different?
JOHNNY	No. I guess I was pretty primitive to begin with. Scenery! Scenery, what are you doing down there?
SCENERY	*(prostrate)* I'm the primordial ooze.
JOHNNY	Whal kind of ooze?
SCENERY	Primordial. The beginning of all life. Don't step on me — I'm gucky.
	During this, an apple tree slides on stage behind JOY *and* JOHNNY. *It is an ostentatious, huckstering apple tree, heavy with apples of various hues. Entwined around the trunk is* MR. SNIDDELEY, *a serpentine personality whose face bears a family resemblance to both the* WHO *and* DR. WHITE.
JOHNNY	Gee, maybe we've gone back too far. Maybe there's nobody around yet at all.
SNIDDLEY	Never fear, Sniddeley's here! Do not be alarmed, my friends. Lucifer D. Sniddeley is at your service. *(tipping his straw hat)*
JOY	A snake!
SNIDDELEY	Don't say "snake", doll. It suggests a limbless reptile. As you can see, I have a whole tree full of limbs.

JOY	You remind me of somebody.
SNIDDELEY	That's what everybody says. I have that kind of face — familiar as an old shoe a sneaker. But I know who you two are.
JOY & **JOHNNY**	You do?
SNIDDELEY	The first boy and girl on this brand new world of ours? Who else would you be but Adam and Eve?
JOHNNY	Adam?
JOY	And Eve?
SNIDDELEY	Welcome to Paradise Gardens. A prestige home site, ideal for couples without children.
JOHNNY	I don't think I know what you're talking about.
SNIDDELEY	I'm glad you raised that point, Mr. A., I have here the answer to your ignorance — The Knowledge Tree.
JOHNNY	The Knowledge Tree?
SNIDDELEY	The Knowledge Tree.
JOY	It looks like an apple tree.
SNIDDELEY	A perceptive observation, Miss E. It is an apple tree, but an apple tree with a difference. Each and every one of the apples you see before you contains the solution to your special problem. No two apples alike. Arithmetic, spelling, geography, social studies...*(indicating an unusually large apple)* parents, all the problems.
JOY	How do you get so many apples to grow on one tree?
SNIDDELEY	Graft, girlie, graft. *(plucking a particularly bright red apple)* Gather 'round a little closer, folks.

(confidentially) This offer is not open to the hoi polloi. Here is the apple you need, Adam, baby. One bite of this and all becomes clear — who you are, where you came from, and where you're going. Especially where you're going. *(as* JOHNNY *hesitates)* You take it, sir.

> JOHNNY *takes it.*

SNIDDELEY   Go ahead, it won't bite you. You bite *it.* There's nothing I like better than the sound of good, strong, teeth biting into an apple. It's like the crack of...do have a bite, sir.

JOHNNY   It would be great to solve my problems.

SNIDDELEY   Wouldn't it? An apple a day keeps the doctor away.

JOY   *(reacting to the reminder of* DR. WHITE, *but not sure)* The doctor?. . .

SNIDDELEY   *(realizing he has made a gaffe, hastily recovering)* Quick, before all the goodness goes out of it. Bite! Once they're picked they leak information. Bite!

> JOHNNY *puts the apple to his mouth, but* JOY *rushes to him and seizes the apple.*

JOY   No! I'll try it first. *(taking a big bite of the apple)*

SNIDDELEY   *(voice reverting to the* WHO) No! Confound you, girl!

> JOY *totters and falls unconscious into* JOHNNY*'s arms.*

JOHNNY   Joy. What's the matter? *(to* SNIDDELEY) What was in that apple? What have you done to her?

SNIDDELEY   Bah! Foiled again.

JOHNNY	You poisoned her. You're the Who! Joy! Speak to me!
SNIDDELEY	She won't speak to you, ever! I fixed her and I'll fix you too, Mr. Lummox.
	JOHNNY is incensed and suddenly emboldened by what has happened to JOY.
JOHNNY	Get out of here! Leave us alone! Get out!
	JOHNNY lobs apples at SNIDDELEY, who retreats from the sheer fury of the barrage, behind and with the tree.
SNIDDELEY	Hey, stop that! Ouch! You're picking on my tree. Ouch! Stop! You're picking on me! Ouch! Ouch!
JOHNNY	Oh, Joy, come back to me. Please come back to me. Scenery, is she dead?
SCENERY	I don't think so. She's not breathing, and I can't feel any pulse, but she's very warm.
JOHNNY	She can't die! She's all I've got in the world—in the universe.
SCENERY	For Pete's sake, boy, stop thinking of yourself all the time.
JOHNNY	Pardon?
SCENERY	You heard me. All you care about is you, you, you.
JOHNNY	*(the scales are falling from his eyes)* You're right, I have been thinking only of myself.
SCENERY	The best way to find out who you are is to help others. Here, hold her.
JOHNNY	It's all my fault. If I hadn't been so selfish I wouldn't have got her into this.

SCENERY	Stop snivelling. You're just a big baby.
JOHNNY	Now I'm a baby. A giant, a dwarf, a girl, Adam and now *(snivelling)* ...I'm a baby.
SCENERY	Oh, good grief, help me with her.

> JOHNNY *is largely ineffectual, as* SCENERY *picks* JOY *up in his arms.* LION *returns, on all fours.*

JOHNNY	Lion. Look what happened to Joy!
LION	*(unhappy)* Roar! *(holding up his paws in disgust)*
JOHNNY	You can't talk. Scenery, I not only can't find my identity, I've made everybody else lose theirs.

> *The* WHO *mask appears.*

WHO	Ha! Ha! Ha! Anxiety is very infectious. I'll have you all Who-doed before I'm done. Ha! Ha! Ha!

> *Blackout on the tableau.*

> *End of Act One.*

***

Act Two

The stage is bare except for the centred catafalque (ex-clock), on which rests the recumbent JOY— *unconscious.* JOHNNY, *now dressed in long pants and a sports shirt, paces back and forth in anxious frustration.* LION *is sitting on the floor to one side, still bereft of his clothes.* SCENERY *stands behind the catafalque, solemn, the same wiggy form as at the beginning of the play.*

JOHNNY   *(pausing)* Here's another one what happened to the duck that flew upside down?

SCENERY   I don't know. What happened to the duck that flew upside down?

JOHNNY   He quacked up.

JOHNNY and LION laugh, very forced laughs, then stare at JOY. She does not respond.

JOHNNY   It's no use. Even the laughter doesn't cure her this time.

SCENERY   A little knowledge is a dangerous thing — taken internally.

JOHNNY   Lion, do you know any funny jokes?

LION	*(rising wearily)* Me? Lord love you, lad, I'm fresh out of fun. Look at me. A plain African Lion. A region of economic distress. This cat's a sour puss.
JOHNNY	Scenery, you brought us back to the present. Couldn't you find the things that Lion lost when we went back in time?
SCENERY	Sorry. That's one scene I'm too old to make.
JOHNNY	It's all my fault. *(digging in his pocket)* Here, Lion, I have one gold coin left. I found it in my sock. You take it.
LION	Take your last nicket? I couldn't do that. It wouldn't be cricket. *(repelled)* Ugh, I said it.
JOHNNY	*(pressing the coin on him)* Please take it. It's no good to me.
LION	*(standing erect)* Well, bless you, guv, I'll give it to an under-developed notion: me.

LION *leaves.* JOHNNY *turns to* JOY.

JOHNNY	If I could only do something for *her.*
SCENERY	Maybe you'd better try a stronger remedy for young ladies who have been put under a spell.
JOHNNY	A stronger remedy? What's that?
SCENERY	Kiss her.
JOHNNY	Kiss her? Oh, I couldn't do that.
SCENERY	Why not?
JOHNNY	Why...I haven't got permission.
SCENERY	How can she give you permission when she's unconscious?

JOHNNY	I don't know, but it wouldn't seem polite.
SCENERY	It's not a matter of politeness. This is a medicinal kiss.
JOHNNY	Medicinal?
SCENERY	Yes. You know, like vitamins. Pretend you are a spoonful of cod liver oil. Go on.
JOHNNY	*(after an abortive start)* Why don't you kiss her?
SCENERY	Because I'm Scenery. I'm dew-kissed, sun-kissed and embraced by fog, but with a human being all I can contribute is a little atmosphere. *(snapping his fingers and the lighting mellows into the romantic; music is complementary)*
SCENERY	There. That's as kissy as I get.
JOHNNY	Me kiss her? Golly, I don't know...*(gingerly approaching* JOY, *bending over her and freezing)*
SCENERY	Go on! What are you waiting for?
JOHNNY	Her lips are two red rose petals. I can feel her breath on my face. It's as sweet as new clover.
SCENERY	Then kiss her! Kiss her, man!
JOHNNY	*(after a pause)* What flavour vitamin?
SCENERY	*Any* flavour! Wild cherry.
JOHNNY	*(closing his eyes to concentrate)* Wild cherry.
	JOHNNY *kisses* JOY *on the forehead and leaps back. As he and* SCENERY *watch,* JOY *stirs, groans, stretches, opens her eyes and finally sits up.*
JOHNNY	It's working!
SCENERY	Bravo!

JOY	What happened?
JOHNNY	I...I...
SCENERY	He kissed you.
JOHNNY	Medicinally.
JOY	*(standing)* Medicinally?
SCENERY	He shook well before applying.
JOHNNY	You were spellbound. We tried everything. Finally I kissed you.
JOY	*(smiling)* Thank you. My mother taught me that whenever I took something precious from somebody I should be sure to return it.

> JOY *goes up to* JOHNNY *and kisses him warmly. His eyes close and he topples onto the catafalque she has just left. Blissful but blotto.*

JOY	Oh! What have I done?
SCENERY	You've given him some of his own medicine.
JOY	Come back! Come back! *(chafing* JOHNNY's *wrist, making him sit up abruptly)*
JOHNNY	Sorry. What happened?
SCENERY	You collided with two rose petals.
JOHNNY	*(standing)* Oh? Joy! I'm so glad you're better.
JOY	Me, too. And only because you knew how to cure me.
SCENERY	Johnny on the spot.
JOHNNY	*(pleased)* Shucks, it was no —

	The stage goes black but for spotlights on the three faces. The WHO *mask appears.*
WHO	Johnny on the spot, is it? Now the spot is on Johnny — the spot-light! Heh, heh!
JOHNNY	*(sheltering* JOY *behind him)* I'm not afraid of you anymore, you old Who. Shoo!
WHO	My, aren't we the brave one! Full of fight are we, Mr. Johnny-come-lately? The gallant knight! Sir Name Missing! Well, I'd like you to meet a couple of *my* friends who have last names—the last names you'll ever hear. Destroy them!
	During this in the dark the catafalque has swung up on end. Now it opens outward and SNEER *and* SNORT *slither forth. The* WHO *vanishes as green light comes up. The two break into a duet.*
SNEER	I'm Sneer
SNORT	I'm Snort
BOTH	We aim to be a most unpleasant sort.
SNEER	He's Snort
SNORT	He's Sneer
BOTH	We've got you in our clutches, never fear.
	If you've a hope, please count on us to kill it, a cheery voice, our mission is to still it. Where life's a bowl of cherries we shall can it, or something merry verily we'll pan it. Our function is to make you feel inferior by taking you apart from your interior.

> BOTH *do a little dance of revilement,*
> *shaking their heads, motioning thumbs*
> *down, snooping and snickering and*
> *generally being snide.*

SNEER I'm Sneer

SNORT I'm Snort

BOTH To put you down is our big national sport.

SNEER He's Snort

SNORT He's Sneer

BOTH Abandon hope all ye who enter here.
When you have worked to make yourself a name,
we rub it out and make you take the blame.

SNEER Destroy!

SNORT Knock flat!

SNEER Kill Joy!

SNORT Brickbat!

BOTH That's us! Sneer and Snort the anti-hero.
When we get through with you, you'll be a zero!

> *The two uglies advance, each with a wet*
> *blanket held up to smother* JOHNNY *and*
> JOY,*who hides behind her champion.*
> JOHNNY *does some quick thinking.*

JOHNNY Wait!

> SNEER *and* SNORT *pause.*

JOHNNY (*to* SNEER*)* You're not so bad, but he's terrifying.

> SNORT *looks pleased.* SNEER *is discomfitted.*

SNEER What did you say?

JOHNNY He's the most frightening thing I've ever seen.

SNEER You mean you find him more horrible than me?

JOHNNY Oh, much.

SNORT *(admiring fingernails)* Some of us got it, some of us ain't.

SNEER *(to* SNORT*)* Just one moment. You don't mean to suggest that you agree with the victim's judgement?

SNORT Come, come, Sneer. Can I help it if he finds me less attractive than you? Let's get on with the smothering.

SNEER Hold it. I'm just as ghastly as you are, and you know it.

SNORT Now, see here, Sneer, you've got to learn to accept criticism.

SNEER Criticism!

SNORT Criticism.

SNEER From him? What does he know? A layman. *(to* JOHNNY*)* How many first-class monsters have you seen? I don't mean on television. I mean in person.

JOHNNY Oh, a lot. Lately I've seen hardly anything else.

SNORT There, you see, the kid's an authority. Let's face it, Sneer — on the surface you look fairly nasty, but deep down inside you're inoffensive. Basically, you're a pussycat.

SNEER	*(enraged)* A pussycat, am I? And who do you think you're fooling with that snorting act of yours? Everybody in the business knows that you are just compensating for a sinus condition.
SNORT	*(furious)* Why, you two-bit Sneer! You couldn't scare a fly if it was on the end of your sweet little nose.
SNEER	Miserable wretch! You're finished! Turn in your wet blanket.
SNORT	I'll show you where I'll turn it.
	SNEER *and* SNORT *hurl their blankets over one another's heads. There is much snarling and commotion.* JOHNNY *takes advantage of the covered heads, spinning first* SNEER, *then* SNORT, *then* SNEER *again, making them dizzy, so that at last both fall into the catafalque that* JOHNNY *has placed horizontal again. When they are both inside, he claps down the lid and sits on it. The lid bounces violently.*
JOHNNY	*(to* JOY*)* Quick! The blankets! Knot them together! Hurry! *(as* JOY *knots the blankets together to make a long rope)* Good. Can you get it under the box?
JOY	*(trying)* It's too heavy. I can't get it under.
JOHNNY	*(still bouncing)* Let me try. *(trying to loop the rope under the box while lying on it)*
	With one great heave, the lid throws JOHNNY *back and off and* SNEER *and* SNORT *stagger to theirf eet, side by side, facing* JOY.
SNEER	Ah-ha!
SNORT	Ho-ho!

JOHNNY	*(behind them)* Not so!
	JOHNNY *quickly throws a loop of the rope around the pair, pinning their arms. Then, with* JOY *grabbing the other end, they run in opposite directions to truss the* HOODS *up neatly.*
SNEER	You can't do this to us!
SNORT	We're too monstrous!
JOHNNY	*(pushing them down into the box)* There, all tucked into your blankets. Time for all boogie men to go bye-byes.
SNEER	I don't want to go bye-byes.
SNORT	*(last gasp)* I want a story!
JOHNNY	Night-night. *(clapping down the lid)* Scenery! Would you be kind enough to remove this bunk bed?
SCENERY	*(giving a hand)* Oof. Why couldn't you have picked a couple of light sleepers? *(getting the box offstage, returning during the following.*
JOY	Oh, Johnny, now that it's over, I'm shaking like a leaf.
JOHNNY	Now that you mention it, so I am.
SCENERY	But you used your head instead of your feet. That's an improvement.
JOHNNY	I've done with running away. I got rid of the Who's hooligans. Now I'm going to have a reckoning with the Who himself. Once and for all.

JOY   No, Johnny! Let's go away while we have the chance. We can go south, to a place where everybody knows who he is. Or we could go to the Indies, where nobody cares who you are. We can find a warm and happy land where that wicked old Who dries up in the sun and blows away on the tradewind. It's only here that the Who can live — in this dark, wet, cold, cruel country.

JOHNNY   I know, Joy. It is a dark, cold, wet, cruel country. But it's home, and I don't feel like running out on it.

SCENERY   Besides, the scenery is breath-taking.

JOHNNY   The scene I want to make is the one where the Who — the real Who — hangs out.

JOY   No!

SCENERY   You're sure you want to go *there?*

JOHNNY   Positive. I bet that if I can track down the Who I'll find my identity.

SCENERY   But that's the most dangerous part of the forest. The darkest. The oldest. The most full of the mysterious.

JOHNNY   I don't care. Let's go. *(to* JOY*) You* don't need to come. Stay where you'll be safe. *(to* SCENERY*)* Where can Joy be safe?

JOY   No! I'm coming with you.

> JOHNNY *and* JOY *clasp hands.*
> SCENERY *goes to the back curtain, and pauses.*

SCENERY   You're absolutely certain you want to be where the Who has his lair?

JOHNNY   I'm positive.

SCENERY	Very well. *(indicating a pull-cord)* Here is the cord. Pull it, and you'll have your scene. I'm off.
JOHNNY	Where are you going?
SCENERY	Out of range. When you're scenery you learn to shift for yourself. But I'll be pulling for you, kids. Everything but the cord.

> SCENERY *goes.* JOHNNY *approaches the cord and takes it in his hands.*

JOY	Johnny! Let's not. I don't care who you are. I still like you.
JOHNNY	Thanks, Joy, but I'm not sure that *I* like me. And there's only one way to find out.

> JOHNNY *reaches slowly for the cord. At this moment we hear, offstage*

JACQUES	Krowk.
JOY	What was that?
JACQUES	*(nearer)* Krowk, alors.
JOHNNY	Sounds like a frog.
JOY	Maybe it's the Who, in disguise again.
JOHNNY	*(releasing the cord)* Stand by me.
JACQUES	Krowk!

> JACQUES *hops on stage. He is a large frog, and he holds a sheaf of lily pads, one of which he throws before him to hop upon, proceeding in this manner right past* JOHNNY *and* JOY.

JACQUES	*(ignoring the couple)* Krowk, alors, Krowk, krowk, alors, Krowk.

JOHNNY	Excuse me. *(as* JACQUES *pauses, without turning)* Excuse me. Are you a frog?
	JACQUES *looks pained. He hops an about-turn and stares at the pair.*
JOHNNY	No offence, but we were wondering—
JACQUES	En français, s'il vous plait.
JOHNNY	*(flustered)* En français?
JOY	In French.
JOHNNY	Oh. Uh. Est-ce que vous etes une...une *(to* JOY) What's "frog" in French?
	JOY *shrugs.*
JACQUES	Assez!
JOHNNY	*(taking the cue)* Est-ce que vous etes une assez?
JACQUES	*(exasperated)* Krowk, alors.
	JACQUES *hops away from them, squats on a pad and produces his lunch — a sandwich of French bread and a bottle of wine. He eats with obvious gourmet pleasure, completely oblivious of the other two.*
JOY	He's going to eat his lunch.
JOHNNY	That reminds me, I'm hungry.
JOY	Me, too.
JOHNNY	It won't be easy, tackling the Who on an empty stomach.
JOY	I don't think I'd even have strength enough to pull the cord.

> *They move closer to* JACQUES,
> *watching him luxuriate in his picnic. At*
> *last, tortured beyond endurance...*

JOHNNY   Excuse me, but that is an awfully delicious-
looking sandwich.

> JACQUES *replies by taking a smug bite*
> *out of the sandwich.*

JOHNNY   May I ask what kind of sandwich it is?

JACQUES   *(in a French-Canadian accent, talking through a*
mouthful) It is a gnat sandwich.

JOHNNY   A nut sandwich! I love nuts.

JOY   Me too.

JACQUES   Not nut. Gnat. *(opening the sandwich to show the*
loathsome contents) Bzzz, bzzz, bzzz. Gnat.

JOHNNY   *(recoiling)* Oh, yes. Gnat.

JOY   *(revolted)* Delectable.

> JACQUES *wipes his lips and, after*
> *wafting the bottle under his nose to*
> *admire the bouquet, takes a swig,*
> *allowing the wine to run around his*
> *mouth a few times.* JOHNNY *and* JOY
> *are drawn in again.*

JOHNNY   I'll bet that is wine.

> JACQUES *confirms this by taking*
> *another drink.*

JOHNNY   Dry wine?

JACQUES   Non. Fly wine.

JOY   Fly wine?

JACQUES	Oui. *(admiring the colour)* Soixante-cinq. A good year for flies. Not great, but very satisfactory. *(yelding to a rare impulse of altruism)* May I offer you un petit coup?
JOY	No, thanks.
JOHNNY	Thanks just the same. Flies...go to my head.
	JACQUES *shrugs his shoulders dismissively — Philistines.* JOY *takes* JOHNNY *to one side.*
JOY	*(stage whisper)* He seems awfully sophisticated for a frog.
JOHNNY	He's awfully sophisticated for a person.
JOY	Do you suppose...Johnny, do you suppose he might be a prince, changed into a frog by a wicked witch?
JOHNNY	A prince?
JOY	Yes. Like the one in the fairy-tale. The frog who had to wait till a princess saw the beauty behind his frog face, and kissed him, and he turned back into the handsome prince.
JOHNNY	*(looking at JACQUES, who belches contentedly)* He doesn't sound like a bewitched prince.
JOY	Maybe he doesn't know. Why don't we find out?
JOHNNY	Find out?
JOY	Yes. If he is really a prince, he can help us fight the Who. He'll be strong and brave and handsome.
JOHNNY	*(hurt)* I thought I was strong and brave and handsome.

JOY	Oh, you *are*, JOHNNY. But a person can always use another prince.
	JOY *pulls him closer to* JACQUES.
JOHNNY	*(dubious)* I don't know.
JOY	Pardonnez-moi, Monsieur Frog.
JACQUES	Oui?
JOY	Etes-vous...Are you a prince that has been turned into a frog?
	JACQUES *stops chewing, while the enormity of this insult sinks in. The question has even put him off his lunch.*
JACQUES	*(trying to keep his cool)* Pardon, madame, but do I understand you to be enquiring whether I am a prince — a human being — that has been turned into a frog?
JOY	*(gung-ho)* Yes. Because, if you are, I'll kiss you, and maybe you'll change back into a prince.
JACQUES	Madame, for your information I am a fifth-generation frog. All my family have been frogs, and we are proud of being frogs. You people, always you are trying to change us. Everywhere I go, women are trying to kiss me. For myself? Non! To make me over into a prince, a person! Zut! How dare you insult a race that has been in this country longer than you?
JOY	*(crushed)* Oh, golly, I'm sorry —
JACQUES	*(building a head of steam)* You...you...humans! You don't even learn how to swim properly. All frogs are amphibian.
JOHNNY	You're what?
JACQUES	Amphibian!

JOHNNY	Never mind, I don't always tell the truth myself.
JACQUES	*(apoplectic)* Salaud! Espece de vache! Remove yourself from it!
JOY	From what?
JACQUES	My lunching pad!

> JOY *and* JOHNNY *hop backwards off the pad.* JACQUES *stares grumpily before him, and sings*

Je suis moi,
Voilà tout,
Je suis moi,
Je ne suis pas vous,
Vous n'etes pas moi,
Me voici,
Vous n'etes pas moi,
You ain't me,
Nous sommes nous,
Vous et moi,
Nous sommes differents,
Mais, pas de quoi,

Chorus.

Roquefort, roquefort
Roquefort et brie,
Gruyere, gruyere,
Tout ce que je suis.

JOY	I apologize, Mr. Frog. *(a flash)* Monsieur Grenouille. *(it's working)* Truly, I'm sorry. We wouldn't have mentioned it, except we hoped you might help us overcome the Who.
JACQUES	*(reacting to the proposition, packing up his lunch)* The Who?

JOHNNY	The Who.
JACQUES	You mean Le Qui.
JOHNNY	Qui?
JOY	Yes! Le qui. The Who-Qui.
JACQUES	This much we have in common Le Who-Qui. Vive Guy Lafleur!
JOY	You mean you'll help us?
JACQUES	Non! You will help *me*. I follow the Who-Qui more closely than you. He is my game.
JOY	Wonderful! We'll hunt him together.
JOHNNY	*(to* JACQUES*)* You're sure you want to do this? It is very dangerous.
JACQUES	Bien sur, I am sure. You think I wish to go through life only as Frère Jacques? Nom d'un nom! En avant! *(all packed now)*
ALL	*(singing)* Je suis moi, Voila tout, Je suis moi, Je ne suis pas vous, Vous n'etes pas moi, Me voici, Vous n'etes pas moi, You ain't me, Nous sommes nous, Vous et moi, Nous sommes differents, Mais, pas de quoi, Nous sommes differents, mais, All for one, We are different, but Tous pour un.
JOHNNY	Okay. Here goes.

JOHNNY	Okay. Here goes.
	JOHNNY *and* JACQUES *pull the cord together. The curtain parts to reveal a backdrop of question marks, which are supplemented by others that run out on leaders above the stage. Also revealed is an outsize cereal box, about eight feet high, against which leans a ladder. The three visitors are drawn to it. Accompanying music is a distorted version of "The Maple Leaf Forever", which is cut abruptly.*
JOY	What is it?
JOHNNY	Looks like a box of cereal. A huge box of cereal.
JOY	It says 'Shredded What'.
JACQUES	Krowk, alors.
	JOHNNY *mounts the ladder to read the side panel.*
JOHNNY	"Contains wheat, oats, barley, pork, Douglas Fir, fish, maple syrup, and water."
JACQUES	*(nauseated)* Euhh!
JOHNNY	*(reading the back panel)* "Hey kids! Free inside— an identity of your very own. Be the first in your block to be somebody. Made of sturdy plastic. Cannot chip or damage mental furniture."
JACQUES	"He, enfants! Gratuit."
JOHNNY	*(interrupting, to* JACQUES' *annoyance)* "To open, lift tab."
JACQUES	"Pour ouvrir, soulever la languette."
	JOHNNY *and* JACQUES *look at each other, weighing the risk.*

JACQUES	*(starting up the ladder)* My pleasure, monsieur.
JOHNNY	*(also) I'll* open it.
JOY	No! *(they halt)* Don't touch it. It's probably a booby trap.
JOHNNY	A booby trap?
JACQUES	Qu'est-ce que c'est —"booby trap"?
JOY	*(miming opening the box)* When you open the box — Boom!
JACQUES	Ah, boom! Pam, piff, poof. Snap, crackly, pop.
JOY	No, *not* snap, crackly, pop. Boom! Big boom. No more us. Finis.
JACQUES	Finis?
JOY	It's a trap set by the Who. I feel it.
JOHNNY	Maybe we can open it at long range. If we had a long pole
JOY	Here's a long pole.

> *A long pole is conveniently handy. The three wield it.*

JOHNNY	We'll knock it over and see what happens. One
JACQUES	Un. . .
JOHNNY	Two
JACQUES	Deux...
JOHNNY	Three!

> *Just as they swing the pole back for the push, on music chord, a large net falls over them. The webbing of the net is stiff enough, and of sufficiently large mesh, for us to observe the captives — a conical cage.*

JACQUES   *(flatly)* Trois.

> *After a brief pause, all three claw at the net, to no avail.*

JOHNNY   The Who! He's got us.

> *The struggle is halted by the amplified, disembodied voice of the* WHO.

WHO   Welcome! You have come to find the Who, and here is the net result, ha, ha. Now all your work is going for knots, eh? As I told you from the start, my friends, you are nothing but a netting. In a few moments I shall come, personally, to complete the operation, to dissipate you completely, like three drops of fat on a hot stove. *(drum beat, slow at first, which accelerates as the scene progresses)* When the drum beat stops, I shall be there, and you...nowhere. Au revoir.

JACQUES   *(numbly)* Au revoir.

JOHNNY   *(fighting to get out of the trap)* We've got to get out of here.

JOY   It's no use, Johnny. That rope is like steel.

JOHNNY   *(giving up)* You're right. We're done for.

JACQUES   Jamais! *(kicking at the netting with his frog's legs, without effect, breathing hard)* Formidable!

JOHNNY   Let's not give him the satisfaction of seeing us clawing at the net like trapped animals. We'll die like men...*(seeing the expressions of the two others)*...and girls...and frogs.

JACQUES   Courage, mes braves! Perhaps there is a hole at
           the top. *(getting down on his hands and knees)*
           Vite, stand on my back.

           JOHNNY climbs on JACQUES' back,
           and JOY clambers up both of them until
           she is perched on JOHNNY's shoulders.
           Just as she reaches this position, the
           drum stops, and the WHO sweeps
           onstage. He is dressed as a sinister
           magician, with cape and cane. At a flick
           of the cane, the net rises from the three
           prisoners, who freeze in their position.

WHO   Well! And what have we here? A totem pole, no
           less. And what an interesting story it tells !
           (addressing the audience) Observe, here we have
           the frog, first to come to the land — after the
           Indian and the Viking, of course — and standing
           on him, in a symbolic attitude of subjection, is
           our witless wonder, Johnny-kins, who in turn has
           the female of the species on his back — the
           Thunderbroad! What a pity this type of native
           artifact is doomed to extinction!

           JOHNNY jumps down, ready to do
           battle. The WHO stops him in mid-stride
           by pointing the cane, on the end of
           which glitters a mesmeric stone.

WHO   Ha! Not so fast, my young friend. This time your
           strong arms cannot help your weak head.

           WHO rotates the end of the wand, and
           JOHNNY's eyes follow the light,
           hypnotized.

WHO	Because, you are hypnotized by what you are — a zero...a cipher...nothing, to the first power...*(pointing at the cereal box)* There's the place for you, Mr. Fruit Loop. Into the box full of bland diet...
	JOHNNY *moves towards the ladder, the* WHO *leading him as if on an invisible leash.*
WHO	In with the sugar-coated nothing. In you go, quickly, quickly, because you never found your identity.
JOY	*(to the rescue)* He did too find his identity. He's my friend.
WHO	*(stricken)* No! Don't say that!
JOY	It's true! He's my friend, and he's brave, and he's thoughtful and kind. Isn't that an identity?
WHO	*(retreating up the ladder)* It's not true! He can't be! He's no —
JACQUES	C'est vrai! C'est un bon type, celui-la. Un peu stupide, mais tres aimable quand meme.
WHO	*(retreating)* Stop it! Both of you!
JOY	He's a hero!
JACQUES	Il est formidable!
	LION *comes on stage. He — or she — now wears a Union Jack muu-muu.*
LION	Hey, baby! Grab this! I'm not your father.
JOHNNY	You're not?
LION	No. I'm your *mother*. Mother England.

JOHNNY	Mummy! *(they embrace)* If you're my mother, who's my father?
LION	Your father is French.
WHO	No!
JACQUES	Mais si!
LION	He's also Scotch, Irish, Welsh, Ukrainian, Swedish, Norwegian, Italian, Polish, German, American, Chinese, Japanese, East Indian, West Indian, plain Indian and a lot of other interesting fatherlands.
JOHNNY	All those? Wow! I guess that makes me special.
WHO	No! Stop it! You're not! You're not!
	The WHO *now teeters at the top of the ladder.* SCENERY *has joined the group.*
SCENERY	And he's a man that enjoys a change of scenery.
ALL	*(except* WHO *and* JOHNNY*)* Vive Johnny! Vive Johnny!
	SCENERY *brings the audience into the chant. With a last despairing shriek, the* WHO *topples into the cereal box. His evaporation is marked by a puff of black smoke. In the sudden silence,* JOHNNY *runs up the ladder and looks into the box.*
JOHNNY	There's nothing! The Who blew!
ALL	Hurrah!
JOHNNY	*(sliding down)* Whee! I'm me!

ALL   That he be! *(all join hands and sing)*

You find yourself in what you do.
That's how to lick the Quickly Who.
Not who you are, but what you are
Will brighten up your special star.

LION   *(to* JACQUES*)* Kiss Auntie!

They embrace, JACQUES *somewhat
reluctantly. Auntie's kiss turns him into
a prince.*

JACQUES   Comment! I *was* a prince.

ALL   *(singing)*

Not who you are, but what you are
Will brighten up your special star.

The End.

The Copetown
City Kite Crisis

by Rex Deverell

Rex Deverell was raised in Orillia, Ontario. He holds a Bachelor of Arts and Bachelor of Divinity from McMaster University and McMaster Divinity College, as well as a Master of Sacred Theology (Theater and Theology) from the Union Theological College in New York City. He became playwright in residence at the Globe Theatre in Regina, where he continues to develop plays for both adult and young audiences including, among his 40 stage plays: *Boiler Room Suite, Black Powder: Estevan 1931*, and *Medicare*, as well as *Weird Kid, Switching Places, Melody Meets the Bag Lady*, and *You Want Me To Be Grown Up, Don't I?* He has also written for radio and television, served as dramaturge for the Saskatchewan Playwrights Centre, chair of the Playwrights Union of Canada, and playwright in residence at the Blyth Festival, Ontario. He now resides in Toronto.

The Copetown City Kite Crisis was first produced by the Globe Theatre, Regina, Saskatchewan, for the 1973-74 school tour with the following cast:

SOL	*Shaun MacNamara*
NANCY	*Kathryn Chandler*
THE MAYOR	*Pat Roberto*
MISS PLIMPTON/MRS. MALANOWSKI	*Lib Spry*
LEADER BAND/MR. HENLEY	*Les Stolzenberger*

Directed by Ken Kramer.
Costumes by Sue Kramer.

The Characters

SOL	*A boy, between 12 and 15.*
NANCY	*About the same age as Sol.*
THE MAYOR	
MISS PLIMPTON	*The town historian.*
MR. HENLEY	*Founder and president of the Copetown Kite Manufacturing Company.*
MRS. MALANOWSKI	*A painter of kites in the factory.*
MISS GURNSEY	*The Mayor's secretary - we hear only her voice.*

THE COPETOWN CITY KILTIE BAND

Production Notes

There are alternate endings for this script, according to the decision of the audience in Scene Three. Members of the audience can be selected to join the Copetown City Kiltie Band before the play begins. Actors not involved in scenes with the Band can join too. If necessary, the actor playing Mr. Henley or Mrs. Malanowski can double as Miss Plimpton.

The Copetwon City Kite Crisis

*The town square of Copetown City —
which is more of a town than a city in
spite of great ambitions. The Copetown
City Chamber of Commerce is holding
a promotional rally to which they have
invited prospective residents — the
audience. The Copetown City Kiltie
Band is present. It sounds suspiciously
like a comb and tissuepaper ensemble.
There are only two or three musical
phrases in the repertoire. Nevertheless,
it makes up in enthusiasm for what it
lacks in harmony. The maestro is given
to "striking up the band" at the drop of a
hat. Although this provides an
impromptu cheering section it also
disrupts the speeches. A large banner
proclaims: "Copetown City, A Place to
Work, Play and Stay!"*

*His worship the MAYOR is about to
welcome the audience. He is a large,
florid man and gives the impression of
being a dirigible balloon or some other
bag of wind. He and most of the other
Copetown citizens seem to be afflicted
with whooping cough, asthma and other
pulmonary diseases...the source of
which will be revealed later in the play.*

MAYOR	(*clearing his throat loudly and signalling to the band to cease their concert*) Welcome, ladies and gentlemen. Welcome to Copetown City. From the bottom of my heart, as Mayor of this fine metropolis and on behalf of the Chamber of Commerce and all the citizens of Copetown, I bid you welcome.

Applause — the band strikes up.

MAYOR	Now, we're here for only one thing — and that is to sell you on Copetown as a wonderful place to make your living, a wonderful place to live! (*pausing to appreciate the phrase and the band strikes up*) A wonderful place to make your living and a wonderful place to live! As we say in our city, "You come to Copetown to work or play — once you come you're here to stay."

Applause — a chorus from the band. The MAYOR *coughs, sips from a glass of water, makes a face at the taste of the water and goes on.*

MAYOR	Look about you, ladies and gentlemen, and observe our beautiful town. Over there you can see Copetown's tallest building, the Henley Building, towering majestically over the city, a full four stories in height; that fine edifice is named after C.G. Henley, founder and president of the Copetown Kite Company, but more about that later. Beyond the Henley Building, you can't see it from here, flows the mighty Cope Creek, surrounded by one and a half acres of lovely parkland — three quarters of an acre on either side of the creek.

More coughing and another sip of the foul-tasting water and more tootles from the band.

MAYOR	As you walk around the city, you'll notice two — no, I believe three — excuse me. *(aside to someone on the platform)* Spencer's house is finished, isn't it? I thought so. *(back to the audience)* Three brand new houses. We're having a population explosion here in Copetown City and we're inviting you to be a part of it! *(band strikes up)* Thank you. That, by the way, is the Copetown City Kiltie Band, a group of which we are justly proud. *(leading the applause but as "music" increases, glaring at band)* That's enough. *(as band stops, smiling at audience)* Now, may I introduce Miss Lilly Plimpton. Miss Plimpton is the President of the Copetown Historical Society. She may not look it but she is a vast repository of little-known facts about our fair city.
	Band plays appropriate music to accompany the arduous progress of MISS PLIMPTON *towards the platform — perhaps "When You And I Were Young, Maggie" or "The Old Grey Mare".*
PLIMPTON	*(who is as old as history)* Thank you, Mr. Mayor. You're pretty vast yourself, heh, heh. *(drawing herself up to address the audience)* I won't go into the... *(realizing the band is still playing)* Stop that noise! *(band does so)* Thank you. *(muttering to herself as she gets out her notes)* I won't go into the early history of our dear town. You may read all about that in the little pamphlet, *(holding up a sample copy)* "Pioneer Days Along the Cope Creek", published by the Copetown Historical Society. It'll set you back fifty cents a copy. *(putting the booklet back in her purse)* Ten years ago, our town was — well, to be brutal about it, our town was dying. Yes, it was. All the people were moving away to the bright lights of the big city. Even the Copetown Hotel, as it was quaintly called, had to close down for lack of business. It was a sorry kettle of fish, let me tell you.

PLIMPTON	Then in the year nineteen hundred and seventy, Mr. C. G. Henley came to town and set up his Copetown Kite Manufacturing Company. The transformation was miraculous. Our town became famous from coast to coast. There were new jobs, new businesses, new people and even a new picture show. Now Copetown is... *(cough)* Copetown is... *(cough — she has to take a sip of water)* Where in tarnation did you get this water? *(to audience)* And now, Copetown is "on the go"! *(snapping her fingers feebly)* And in appreciation thereof, I would like to sing a little ditty which I composed myself. I call it "Anthem to Copetown City". *(wheezing)*

SONG:

Copetown, Copetown, Copetown!
We praise your name, we sing your fame,
Our hearts are full of wonder.
Come snow, come hail, come rain, come thunder,
We know you'll never go under.

> MISS PLIMPTON *is as bad a singer as she is a lyricist.*

MAYOR	Thank you, Miss Plimpton.

Band strikes off on a different tune.

PLIMPTON	*(still singing)* Copetown, Copetown! Copetown!
MAYOR	Thank you !
PLIMPTON	But I'm not finished yet.
MAYOR	*(ushering her off)* Yes you are.

Exit MISS PLIMPTON.

MAYOR   As we say here, the past may belong to Miss Plimpton, but the future belongs to Copetown! Next on our agenda is the presentation of the Copetown Young Citizen of the Year Award. I know you are all waiting to know whom the judges have selected. May I have the envelope, please. *(as he opens the envelope we realize everyone is coughing a great deal)* This year's Young Citizen is... Sol Sims! Sol Sims, would you come to the platform, please.

                 SOL *arrives — a young, energetic, honest boy, but not overly goody-goody.*

MAYOR   Congratulations, Sol!

SOL   Thank you very much, sir.

MAYOR   And now the award itself — this year's model of the famous Copetown Super Kite! Bring on the kite! *(the kite is truly spectacular)* I name you Copetown Young Citizen of theYear, and present you with this kite. Congratulations.

SOL   *(eyes wide)* Thank you, sir!

MAYOR   *(admiring the kite)* What do you think of that, eh?

SOL   It's wonderful !

MAYOR   Wonderful? Of course it's wonderful! And the Copetown Kite is what makes...*(coughing and gagging)* Excuse me.That kite is what makes Copetown City *(to everyone)* such a wonderful place to live. So why don't you, you and you *(around to the audience)* pack up your old kit bag and move! Move to and *with* Copetown City!

                 The meeting breaks up in spasms of coughing. Sol is left onstage alone with his kite.

SOL   *(to the audience)* The only trouble with
       Copetown is that you can't drink the water and
       you can't breathe the air. Other than that, it is
       really a great place to live. It's the fastest
       growing town in this part of the country.
       Everybody says things have never been better.
       And it's all due to the Copetown Kite Company.
       (looking at the kite) Isn't she a beauty? Watch
       her catch the wind. Even on days that seem
       perfectly calm, when any other kite would stay
       on the ground — you can fly a Copetown
       Kite. On windy days, it's all a guy can do to
       hold on to them. Nobody knows exactly how
       they get to be like this. It's a secret process in
       the factory.

                   As he is talking, NANCY *enters. She is
                   a lively, likeable girl, about* SOL's
                   *age. She sneaks up behind him and
                   puts her hands over his eyes.*

SOL   Hey!

NANCY Guess who?

SOL   Let me go!

NANCY *(insistent)* Guess who?

SOL   All right, Nancy — let go!

NANCY *(disappointed, lets go)* How did you know?

SOL   How many serious silly people do I know??

                   *In spite of the banter, these two are on
                   good terms.*

NANCY Other than yourself?

SOL   *(fake laugh)* Ha, ha.

NANCY Hey, look at that, eh? *(the kite)* Congratulations.

SOL   Just lucky, I guess?

NANCY   Sure. Better you than old Harvey Peabody.

SOL   Harv's okay.

NANCY   He was trying to impress everybody so much. Last week, I saw him helping old Miss Plimpton across the road.

SOL   What's wrong with that?

NANCY   She didn't want to go! She was so mad she hit him with her umbrella...*(they laugh)* Will you let me fly your kite?

SOL   Maybe.

NANCY   When?

SOL   Someday, maybe....

NANCY   I thought the Young Citizen of the Year was supposed to be kind and generous and everything.

SOL   Nancy, I just got it. I haven't even tried it out myself yet.

NANCY   Well, try it out. *(coughing)*

SOL   Don't rush me.

NANCY   I'm your best friend, aren't I?

SOL   Don't be too sure.

NANCY   What was that?

SOL   I'm waiting for just the right kind of wind.

       NANCY *licks her finger and tests the wind.*

NANCY   What's wrong with this one? *(coughing again)*

SOL	Nancy, you're bugging me.
NANCY	Well?
SOL	*(losing patience)* It's too gusty! I want to try it in a gentle breeze — leastways for the first time.
NANCY	*(abrupt change)* I'm sorry. You're right.
SOL	*(puzzled)* How come you're so agreeable all of a sudden?
NANCY	There are more important things than whether or not you let me fly your kite or not.
SOL	Like what?
NANCY	*(coughing)* Nothing.
SOL	*(suspicious)* Nancy, you're not getting mushy, are you? *(backing away from her)*
NANCY	*(infinite disdain)* No, I am not getting "mushy".
SOL	Good.
NANCY	What a nerve!
SOL	I just wondered.
NANCY	You get to be Citizen of the Year and it goes to your head.*(coughing so violently that SOLbecomes alarmed)*
SOL	Are you all right, Nancy? Nancy?
NANCY	*(waving him away)* I'm okay.
SOL	You should see about that.
NANCY	I did see about it. My parents made me go to the doctor, yesterday!
SOL	And?

NANCY	And...*(she can't say it)*
SOL	Oh come on. It can't be that bad.
NANCY	*(flaring)* It is so!
SOL	Then tell me.
NANCY	We have to move away from Copetown, that's all.
SOL	*(astounded)* That's what the doctor told you?
NANCY	He said I'd never get better unless we move to a town where the air and the water are cleaner.
SOL	Are you going to go?
NANCY	My father said as soon as he can find a new job somewhere.
SOL	*(very sensitively)* You'll make new friends.
NANCY	That's what my parents said. *(not hopeful)*
SOL	*(getting an idea)* Do you want to fly the kite?
NANCY	You said the wind was too strong.
SOL	I know. *(looking up, anxiously)* Let's try it anyway.
NANCY	But you haven't even tried it yourself yet.
SOL	Ladies first. *(mischievously)* You second.
NANCY	*(cheered up)* Just for that I will fly your stupid old kite. What do I do?
SOL	*(disgusted)* You mean you've been pestering me like this and you don't even know what to do?
NANCY	It's your kite. You're in charge. Tell me what to do.

SOL	All right, hold the cord and I'll take it back where it can catch the wind. *(already having trouble holding onto the kite.*
	This scene could be tricky unless the performance is held outdoors and in a high wind. Both NANCY *and* SOL *could exit with the kite, then* NANCY *could re-enter, playing out the kite line in mime.*
SOL	*(calling from a distance)* Let out more line!
NANCY	More still?
SOL	Pardon? *(shouting over the wind.)*
NANCY	More still?
SOL	Just a little!
NANCY	Enough?
SOL	Are you ready? I'm having trouble holding it down.
NANCY	I'm ready!
SOL	Pull tight!
NANCY	Let go!
	Through mime, we see that the kite string has become taut. Suddenly there is a violent wrenching on the line. The wind is mounting in intensity.
NANCY	*(screaming)* Sol! You get down here, Sol! This instant!
	We assume from the direction of her gaze that the kite has taken off with SOL *attached.*

NANCY   Let go! Jump! No! Don't! Hold on — it's too
               high! *(to herself)* Look at him climb! *(almost
               letting go in amazement)* Gosh, the wind's
               getting stronger. *(grasping the cord tightly)* I've
               got to bring him down. *(pulling on the cord with
               all her strength, but a sudden gust drags her
               across the stage)* Sol! Can you hear?

                              No response — now NANCY *is in a
                              desperate battle with the wind — and
                              losing.*

NANCY   All right, wind, just take it easy. Calm down a
               little, okay? *(angry)* Calm down, I said! Let up!
               (desperate) Oh no. I can't...I'm not heavy enough!

                              *Audience participation suggestion:
                              perhaps the audience might be motivated
                              to help bring the kite down by
                              combined weight. Otherwise use the
                              following.*

NANCY   I've got to let out more string. *(doing so, while
               looking around frantically for help)* That old tree
               stump. If it's not too rotten, maybe...(working
               her way over to it)* Now — if I can only tie the
               cord around it...*(this is awkward, since she only
               has the use of one hand and the wind is
               constantly pulling the cord away)* Now stay
               there, you stupid cord. Stay there !

                              *Finally, after many failures, the cord
                              holds and* NANCY *is able to pull the
                              kite down, using the stump as a brace.*

NANCY   Sol, can you hear me? Hold on — just another
               few feet. Jump from there! Leave the kite and
               jump! *(pulling the line another few feet — it
               suddenly goes slack, and* NANCY *collapses)*

SOL   *(running towards her)* Wow, was that great!
               (NANCY *is speechless)* What's wrong with you?

NANCY   Are you all right?

SOL	Of course, I'm all right. Why did you have to bring me down so soon?
NANCY	*(exasperated)* Sol! You could have been killed!
SOL	Oh come on!
NANCY	You could have!
SOL	Yeah? *(looking upwards, alarmed)* I guess I could have! It was a long way up.
NANCY	You're telling me.
SOL	I didn't have time to think about it.
NANCY	I did.
SOL	I'm glad you did — thanks, Nancy.
NANCY	Boys — huh!
SOL	*(excited again)* I wish you could have been up there too. Ever neat!
NANCY	*(still grumpy)* I was scared half to death.
SOL	*(ignoring her)* But the thing is, I found out something important.
NANCY	I don't want to hear.
SOL	This is really important. I found out what's been making you sick!
NANCY	Oh, come on.
SOL	It's the Kite Factory!
NANCY	The Kite Factory?
SOL	I could see all kinds of smoke coming from a vent in the roof and this funny red stuff pouring into the creek!

NANCY	But that's where the town gets its water supply!
SOL	Exactly. So you see what this means? You won't have to move away after all!
NANCY	Huh?
SOL	All we have to do is tell them that they're causing the pollution and they'll stop and the air will get better and so will the water and then — you'll get better, see — and then...
NANCY	*(skeptical)* That's all we have to do.
SOL	Right.
NANCY	Easy?
SOL	Sure.
NANCY	We're just kids, Sol. They won't listen to us.
SOL	We'll start at the top. C'mon!
NANCY	Where?
SOL	City Hall!

They exit.

***

Scene Two

          The MAYOR *enters his office, carrying notes for a speech and maybe smoking a cigar.*

MAYOR   *(calling to his secretary, offstage)* I'm rehearsing my speech for the Save-the-Environment Club, Miss Gurnsey. Hold all calls.

GURNSEY   *(muffled, offstage)* Very good, your worship.

MAYOR   Now. *(examining the manuscript, jotting a note in the margin and clearing his throat)* "Ladies and gentlemen..." No. *(another note)* "Dear members of the Save-the-Environment Club: I stand before you this evening as a firm supporter of your efforts to preserve the environment. Bit I am more in favour of Progress.
It ill-behooves us..." I like that. *(majestically)* "Friends, it ill-behooves us to ignore the demands of Mother Nature. But it behooves us even less to ignore the demands of Progress. What is progress? Well my Friends, progress is having false teeth instead of being toothless, Progress is having a hearing aid instead of being deaf, Progress is having a hair transplant instead of being bald. That is progress, my friends. Who wants to give up the improvements of modern day life? Who wants to return to the Dark Ages?

GURNSEY	*(offstage)* I'm sorry, children — the Mayor doesn't want to be disturbed — no — you can't go in there!
MAYOR	*(breaking off, irritated)* Miss Gurnsey — what is it?
	SOL*and* NANCY *burst in.*
SOL	Mr. Mayor — you've got to do something!
MAYOR	I'm sorry. I don't have time. Please make an appointment with my secretary.
SOL	But this is an emergency!
MAYOR	An emergency? *(looking down at him)* Who are you, young man?
SOL	I'm Sol. Sol Sims.
MAYOR	*(blankly)* Do I know you?
SOL	I'm Young Citizen of the Year — remember?
MAYOR	Of course, I knew that.
SOL	And this is Nancy.
NANCY	Pleased to meet you, your Honour - Worship - Sir.
MAYOR	Indeed, well state your business.
SOL	I know what's causing all the pollution.
	This produces a strange effect on the MAYOR. *He is suddenly overly innocent.*
MAYOR	*(too carefully)* Pollution?
SOL	Yes.

MAYOR	What pollution?
SOL	Air and water.
MAYOR	Where?
NANCY	Here.
SOL	Right here...in Copetwon City. It's coming from...
MAYOR	Are you saying then that the air and water of Copetown City are polluted?
SOL	*(beginning to sense danger)* Y...yes, sir.
MAYOR	Nonsense.
NANCY	But it's almost impossible to breathe any more.
MAYOR	Nonsense.
SOL	And nobody swims in the old swimming hole any more.
MAYOR	Too dangerous.
SOL	Too dirty.
MAYOR	Nonsense. There's nothing wrong with our water. *(pouring himself a glass from a pitcher and holding it up to the light)*You see? Crystal clear. *(drinking the water at one gulp — hiding his reaction from* SOL. *(gasping)* Tastes fine! Copetown City is no more polluted than any other place. Better than some!
SOL	But that's not true.

MAYOR	Copetown Citizen of the Year Award and this is how you repay us? This is how you treat the city of your birth? *(starting to weep)* This is how you show gratitude to the community that has held you in her bosom from the days of your infancy, has nurtured you with tender care from the cradle...
SOL	But I
MAYOR	You heap upon her fiery coals of criticism and hot ashes of slander!
SOL	No!
MAYOR	*(sobbing)* Yes !
SOL	I just think we've got a problem and we should clean it up.
MAYOR	Leave my office.
SOL	But
MAYOR	Immediately.
SOL	*(defeated)* Yes, sir. *(turning to* NANCY*)* I guess you'll have to move away after all.
MAYOR	*(stopping them)* What?
SOL	Nancy's family is moving away.
MAYOR	Out of Copetown City?
NANCY	We have to — because of the air.
MAYOR	*(dumbfounded)* But there's no better place to live!
SOL	Doctor's orders.
MAYOR	Who's your doctor. I'll have his licence taken away.

SOL   Wouldn't it be better to take away the pollution? All you have to do is to tell them they're making pollution and they should figure out how to stop it.

MAYOR   They? They? Who are you talking about?

SOL   The Kite Factory.

The MAYOR *turns ashen.*

MAYOR   The Copetown Kite Manufacturing Company? Er — how do you know that it — er — what makes you think it is causing pollution, my boy?

NANCY   He saw it.

SOL   With my own eyes!

MAYOR   But that's impossible. Nobody —

SOL   I was testing out my new kite — the one that the city gave me — and it — uh — turned out to be such a good kite that I couldn't hold it down and the wind was very strong...

MAYOR   Yes?

SOL   Well, anyway — it lifted me into the air and I saw the junk coming from the Kite Factory.

MAYOR   You flew on a kite?

SOL   Yes, sir!

MAYOR   Ha, ha — that's a good story, my boy. You'll have to be a writer when you grow up! That's a fine story. *(patting him on the shoulder)*

NANCY   But it's true!

MAYOR	Now you've had your fun for the day — why don't you run along home, kiddies. I have a lot of work to do, you understand. The Mayor of Copetown is a busy, busy man.
SOL	But....
MAYOR	Run along now.
NANCY	Let's go, Sol.
SOL	But what about the factory?
MAYOR	*(angry)* I said, get out!
SOL	But why don't you tell them about the pollution?
MAYOR	They know already!!! *(realising what he has said and almost swallowing his cigar)* Ooops.
SOL	*(eyes widening)* How long have you known about it?
MAYOR	Er — not long. Two or three ah, years.
SOL	And you haven't done anything?
MAYOR	*(suddenly contrite)* Don't tell anyone, please. I've got a political career to think of! Don't let it out, Sims, my boy. There's nothing I can do about the pollution. The town depends on the Kite Factory.
SOL	Maybe I could talk to them.
MAYOR	You? They wouldn't even let you in the door.
NANCY	What if you gave him a note — like an introduction.
SOL	Yeah!
NANCY	They'd pay attention to you, wouldn't they?

MAYOR	Of course they would. I'm the Mayor.
NANCY	Right!
SOL	Well?
MAYOR	I'll write you a note. *(scribbling a note)* Here, take this to Mr. Henley at the factory. He'll talk to you.
SOL	*(in awe)* Mr. Henley?
MAYOR	*(snarl)* That's right. It's his factory.
SOL & NANCY	*(running off)* Thanks a lot, Mr. Mayor! *(exiting)*
MAYOR	*(left alone and anxious)* Not at all. *(half-heartedly picking up his speech and begining to read it as he leaves the stage)* Members of the Save-the-Environment Club, ladies and gentlemen. It illbehooves us to ignore the demands of Nature — but it behooves us even less to ignore... the demands of...Progess. *(exiting)*

***

Scene Three

*The Kite Factory. Audience
participation suggestion:* HENLEY*and*
MALANOWSKI *introduce a group of
new workers to their jobs. The workers
are audience members en masse, or
selected volunteers. They are mobilized
for the various phases of building the
kite: the operation of the Secret Process
Machine, testing, selling, shipping and
so on. Perhaps buyers from foreign
lands come to buy the kites in quantity.
Demonstrations can be given. In some
situations it may be possible to actually
build a kite or give out plans to the
workers. Directors will know how much
can be done without breaking down the
story line of the play itself .The
important point is that the audience
feels it has a stake in the factory and its
product.*

SOL *enters and asks one of the
employees to give the* MAYOR's *note
to* MR.HENLEY. MR. HENLEY*is
onstage. He is pleasant enough, but so
enthusiastic about kites that he seems a
little mad. A worker brings him* SOL's
note.

HENLEY	What's this? *(reading)* "Sol Sims, Copetown Young Citizen of the Year. Be nice to him but don't take him seriously.Your friend, the Mayor." *(delighted)* Of course. Quite happy to. Where is the young man? Show him in!
SOL	*(entering)* Mr. Henley?
HENLEY	Certainly, young man. How do you do?
SOL	I'm Sol Sims.
HENLEY	That's correct, and I'm C.G. Henley. Very pleased to know you. Very pleased.
SOL	Thank you, sir.
HENLEY	Not at all, my boy. Not at all. Now, where shall we begin? Mmm?
SOL	It's about your factory, sir.
HENLEY	Just what I thought. Exactly! A tour of the factory, yes?
SOL	No, sir, I —
HENLEY	Good.
SOL	But I —
HENLEY	I insist. Don't worry about my time.
SOL	I wasn't
HENLEY	My time is your time, my boy.
SOL	Thank you.
HENLEY	Not at all. Where shall we start?
SOL	With the air and water.

HENLEY	What about at the beginning? Begin with the beginning — I always say.
SOL	*(resigning himself)* Yes, sir.
HENLEY	When I was your age, I was exactly like you.
SOL	You were?
HENLEY	I was only interested in one thing, one thing, and only one thing.
SOL	You were?
HENLEY	I'll bet you are asking yourself what that one thing was.
SOL	What was it?
HENLEY	Kiting.
SOL	You liked to fly kites?
HENLEY	I was never without one. And then I said to myself, when I grow up, I'm going to make the biggest and the best kite that there ever was. What do you want to be when you grow up?
SOL	I —
HENLEY	*(interrupting)* And that's precisely what I did.
SOL	What?
HENLEY	I made the biggest and the best and the most colourful and the highest-flying kite in the whole world.
SOL	I know.
HENLEY	I'll bet you didn't know that, did you?
SOL	Yes.

HENLEY	*(leading him around the factory)* Now, here is the storage room for all the kite materials that come into the factory. Now don't be shy, young man. Ask any questions you like.
SOL	Sir, what kind of things do you use to make the kites?
HENLEY	Now this is the cutting room. Those people are busy cutting the material into the right size for kites. The struts have to be cut to the right length and — over here the fabric is being cut and sewn to the exact shape of a famous Copetown City Wonder Kite. Have you tried out our very latest model?
SOL	Yes, I have.
HENLEY	Why don't you? It's the best-flying kite we've ever made.
SOL	I know.
HENLEY	In this room the kites are being assembled. You see there, the struts attached to one another and the fabric stretched across them. *(no more responses from SOL)* I'm so glad you're enjoying yourself. Over here we have Mrs. Malanowski. Every one of our kites is hand-painted by Mrs. Malanowski. She's been with us longer than any other employee. Mrs. Malanowski?
MALANOWSKI	*(an elderly woman with a European accent)* Yes, Mr. Henley?
HENLEY	I'd like you to meet Copetown City's Young Citizen of theYear — er — *(fishing in his pocket for the note from the MAYOR)* Young Citizen of the Year —
SOL	*(to MALANOWSKI)* Sol. Sol Sims. I'm pleased to meet you, Mrs. Malanowski.
HENLEY	*(having found the name)* Sol Sims.

MALANOWSKI Pleased to meet you. You like kites?

SOL Very much. I like the way you paint them.

MALANOWSKI That's good. I like painting them.

HENLEY *(going off while the two are still chatting)* Now, in this area we have the kite strings. Every day we use five miles of string. Do you believe that? Five miles... *(exiting)*

SOL Is he always like that?

MALANOWSKI Well, you have to understand. The factory is his whole life.

SOL *(thoughtfully)* I guess it would be.

MALANOWSKI I'm very grateful to Mr. Henley. He gave me a job when I first came to this country. I didn't have a cent to my name. He's a good boss, Mr. Henley.

SOL Mrs. Malanowski. Could you tell me something?

MALANOWSKI I guess.

SOL What *is* it in this factory that makes the pollution?

HENLEY *(returning)* Ah! There you are!

MALANOWSKI *(frowning)* Pollution?

HENLEY *(continuing with the tour)* And there you can see our kite testing department...and over there is our sales division. People come from all over the world to buy kites. It's a sight to be proud of!

SOL *(aside to* MALANOWSKI*)* Yes. Somehow there's pollution coming from this factory.

HENLEY	And last, but certainly not least, here is our Secret Process Machine. *(stopping in front of a large machine)*
SOL	This is the secret process? What does it do?
HENLEY	Of course I can't tell you exactly. It's a secret.
SOL	Can you give me a hint?
HENLEY	*(looking at him)* Well, why not? You remind me of myself at your age. You can keep a confidence, can't you, my boy? I'll tell you. It's a special machine I invented myself. The kite goes through this end, you understand? And inside it is heated to a very high temperature. And then it is sprayed with a chemical that reacts with the kite fabric to create an entirely new molecular structure. Then the kite is cooled off with water and comes out this side almost as light as the air itself. Do you understand?
SOL	No.
HENLEY	I thought you would. You're a bright boy. Without this machine — our kites would be like any other kite ever made. But when it comes through here it becomes the best in the world: a Copetown Wonder Kite!
SOL	*(looking up)* What is that vent in the ceiling?
HENLEY	*(looking up)* That? That is a vent, my boy. Now, is there anything else I could show you?
SOL	When the kites are washed off — do you wash chemicals back into the river?
HENLEY	Would you like to see the employees' cafeteria?
SOL	Does that machine send off stuff into the air?
HENLEY	Or perhaps my executive office?

SOL *is frustrated* .

SOL	Listen to me!
HENLEY	What?
SOL	Will you stop talking and listen to me!
MALANOWSKI	How rude! (*grabbing* SOL's *ear*) Shame on you, boy!
SOL	Ow! My ear.!
HENLEY	I have been listening.
SOL	No you haven't! You've only been listening to yourself!
HENLEY	(*with admirable restraint*) Well, perhaps I do get carried away. At any rate, I'm listening to you now, you little rascal. What is it?
SOL	Your machine is causing pollution.
HENLEY	It is?
SOL	And you know it!
HENLEY	Who said so?
SOL	The Mayor said so, that's who. And I saw it with my very own eyes.
HENLEY	Well, maybe a little bit. Perhaps the tiniest bit of pollution. But the wind blows it away and the river takes it downstream. It's not enough to worry about. It's certainly not enough to deafen a man about!
MALANOWSKI	Without that machine, we'd go under.
HENLEY	That's right. We couldn't compete against cheap imported kites. Sol, you're a bright boy. You like to fly kites, don't you?

SOL	*(nodding)* Hm-mm.
HENLEY	Tell me. What's a little pollution? It's the price we have to pay for something as beautiful as that. *(indicating all the bright kites in the factory)* Now admit it. It's a small price.
SOL	*(wavering)* You're right. I like kiting. And you make the most beautiful kite in the whole world.
HENLEY	Well then...
SOL	This morning I even flew up over the city on one.
HENLEY	*(ecstatic)* You did what?
SOL	I flew on one.
HENLEY	I knew it! I knew it! *(dancing with* MRS. MALANOWSKI*)* Eureka! Eureka! We've reached the pinnacle. This year's kite is the one I've been working towards all my life!
MALANOWSKI	Congratulations, Mr. Henley! Congratulations!
HENLEY	I knew we'd get there someday. I knew it! I always told you...
SOL	That's when I saw the pollution!
HENLEY	*(gaily)* Forget the pollution!
SOL	*(deciding)* No !
HENLEY	*(more sober)* Please?
SOL	I have a friend — Nancy. And the doctor said that her family has to take her away from here because Copetown isn't healthy any more. So what good is the best kite in the world if you can't breathe the air or drink the water?

HENLEY	*(after a silence)* I feel sorry about your friend, son. Perhaps I could give them some money to help with their moving expenses.

SOL *turns away in disgust.*

HENLEY	But don't you see? Making kites is the only thing that makes me happy! It's the only thing I know how to do. I can't close down the factory.
SOL	Close it down?
MALANOWSKI	Think for a minute, boy. What about all the people who work here. We'd all be out of a job. *(if audience is being used as the workers, she indicates them)*
SOL	But if people can't live here, what's the use?
HENLEY	*(extremely agitated)* No. No! I won't have it, do you hear? I won't have you destroy the dreams of a lifetime. I will not have it!
MALANOWSKI	*(alarmed)* Aw, he's only a kid, boss. What can he do?
HENLEY	What can he do? He can let it out that we're polluting this town, that's what he can do. And then, you know how people are these days about "environment" and "ecology", "recycling, Blue Boxes, Green Products," and that stuff. They're liable to stop buying our kites — and then we'd be through. The plant would have to close.
SOL	*(idea)* That's right! I could start a boycott!
MAYOR	*(offstage)* Where is that little snort-ripper. I'll brain him, that's what! I'll brain him! *(bursting in)* There you are! I heard you were over here causing a ruckus — I ought to *(seeing* HENLEY*)* Hello, Mr. Henley, I'm sorry about this, I had no idea when I sent him here that he'd...

MAYOR	Don't pay any attention to this little idiot...none at all! And please accept my apologies, won't you, Mr. Henley?
HENLEY	Mr. Mayor, do you realize how important the Copetown Kite industry is to this town?
MAYOR	*(startled)* Oh — I do. Yes, I do, sir.
HENLEY	Do you understand that three-quarters of the citizens of Copetown get their salaries from me?
MAYOR	I know that, sir.
HENLEY	And that all the rest, the shopkeepers, and the service men, all the rest make their profits from people who do work for me?
MAYOR	Yes sir.
HENLEY	What would happen if we were to move our factory to another town?
MAYOR	Disaster.
HENLEY	Again?
MAYOR	Disaster.
HENLEY	*(shouting)* Then shut this boy up! *(turning and exiting)*
MAYOR	*(to SOL)* Now, see what you've done?
SOL	I was just trying to
MAYOR	Just trying to bring ruin and destruction on your own hometown — that's what you were just trying to do.
SOL	Not exactly.
MAYOR	Tell me exactly what you were trying to do?

SOL	I thought I —
MAYOR	Thought? You didn't think. That's the whole problem!
SOL	But this factory is spoiling our air and water!
MAYOR	It's also paying our bills and buying our food!
SOL	But it's wrong!
MAYOR	Now you listen to me, you young whippersnapper. Either you shut your mouth and keep quiet about this or I'll shut it for you.
SOL	I can't.
MAYOR	You'd better.
SOL	No.
MAYOR	I'm warning you
SOL	Make me.
MAYOR	All right then. First — I'm taking away your title. You are no longer Copetown's Young Citizen of the Year.
MALANOWSKI	*(who has been working nearby)* Now wait a minute! That's not fair.
MAYOR	Who are you?
MALANOWSKI	I'm the kite painter.
MAYOR	Well then, go paint a kite. I'm dealing with this town traitor here.
SOL	*(stung)* I'm not a traitor!
MAYOR	Where's the kite the city gave you?
SOL	*(pointing off)* Over there.

MAYOR	Over where?
MAYOR	*(going off to get it)* I'll show you what we do with ungrateful boys who kick a gift horse in the mouth. I won't stand for it. No ! *(we hear the sound of cracking and ripping)*
SOL	Not my kite!
	The MAYOR *brings the remains of the kite back and throws them at* SOL.
MAYOR	Now will you keep quiet?
SOL	*(defiantly)* No.
MAYOR	I'm going to spread rumours, then. I'm going to tell people that you are a liar and a cheat and when I'm finished, see if anyone will believe a thing you say.
SOL	Nobody will trust me?
MAYOR	Not a soul. Sorry, but you leave me no choice
SOL	Then I can't do anything about the pollution.
MAYOR	Afraid not.
SOL	*(walking away)* I might as well go and help Nancy and her family pack their suitcases.
MAYOR	Afraid so..
MALANOWSKI	I don't like the way you're treating the kid, Mr. Mayor. Why are you being so mean?
MAYOR	I don't want to be mean, but I'm trying to sAve your job *(to other workers and the audience)* and yours, and yours. I'm trying to save Copetown City. I'm doing it for you.
MALANOWSKI	For us?

SOL	(*an idea starting*) You're thinking of them?
MAYOR	Yes, yes! I want veryone in Copetown to have decent jobs, and make bags of money, and have a wonderful future.
SOL	Why not ask them then? Ask them what they want.
MAYOR	What?
MALANOWSKI	A workers' meeting!
SOL	Right!
MAYOR	What?
MALANOWSKI	All right, everybody — a union meeting.
MAYOR	Uh-oh.
MALANOWSKI	(*addressing the workers*) Fellow workers, you all know me. I'm not a troublemaker. I'm the first to say the company's been good to us, right?
WORKERS	*Right!*
MALANOWSKI	They've given us raises every year, bonuses some years. Mr. Henley is a good man, right?
WORKERS	*Right!*
MALANOWSKI	But every year the air in our town is getting a little harder to breathe, and the water — well, kinda hard to drink. We didn't want to admit it, right, but we sorta *knew* that the Secret Process Machine was behind the whole thing. Now this young lad here says people are getting sick because of it. We don't want any trouble, right? Our lives depend on this factory. But we gotta face up to this sooner or later and it might as well be now. We could call a strike over the pollution — but don't get too excited over that. If we went on strike the factory might close and

MALANOWSKI	that'd be it. No more kites. No more jobs. No more money. Finished. So we'll take a vote —
MAYOR	Excuse me. May I say a few words?
MALANOWSKI	Certainly — it's a democracy.
MAYOR	*(very humbly)* It's just that I've seen Copetown grow from a one-horse little milk-stop to the wonderful place that it is now. And I don't want it to end here. I want Copetown to be a city we can be proud of! *(his eyes begin to shine)* Think of it! Majestic broad streets shaded by spreading elm trees, tall, beautiful buildings, museums, galleries, libraries, fine restaurants, theatres. We could have our own sports stadium and our own football team. Think of it — the Copetown Blue Jays! *(or the most evocative team name for the particular audience)* That's what I want for Copetown! Now, I've talked to Mr.Henley about his Secret Process Machine and he says he can't for the life of him figure out how to make it work without the pollution. So, I guess the future of Copetown City is in your hands. I hope — well, you understand what I hope — but it's all up to you. *(sitting down)*
MALANOWSKI	Sol? Why don't you say what you think?
SOL	I don't know whether going on strike will work or not, but I think...well, I'd like to have Copetown be like what the Mayor thinks it should be...still, I think people have to be able to stay healthy. *(shrugging)* I don't know.
MALANOWSKI	Now why don't you discuss it among yourselves — and when you're ready to make a serious decision, we'll have a vote. Should we go on strike, yes or no?

Discussion.

MALANOWSKI   Well, if nobody else wants to say anything we'd better put the question. All those for going on strike and stopping work until Mr. Henley stops the pollution?

                  Response.

MALANOWSKI   Those against?

                  Response. The MAYOR *exits.*

MALANOWSKI   We go on strike...

                  If the answer is "no strike" proceed to the alternate ending on page 43.

MALANOWSKI   All right, turn off all the machines and let's see how quiet this factory can be.

                  A variety of strike actions can be organized, such as picketing, sitting on the floor with arms folded, singing labour songs, forming bargaining committees, etc, etc. The MAYOR *has exited and now he returns with* HENLEY.

HENLEY   What's the meaning of this? Why aren't you at work?

                  AUDIENCE MEMBERS *should tell* MR. HENLEY *that they are on strike.*

HENLEY   A strike? But this is impossible. Nobody has ever gone on strike in my factory! Why? Do something, Mrs. Malanowski!

MALANOWSKI   I'm sorry, Mr. Henley — but until you do something about the pollution, I'm out of here. (*exiting with her paint brush*)

HENLEY	But I can't, Mrs. Malanowski. (*to the others*) Enough of this nonsense. Get back to work. The Japanese delegation is coming to tour the plant at four o'clock !
SOL	(*to the audience*) Are you going back to work?
AUDIENCE	No.
HENLEY	Yes.
AUDIENCE	No.
HENLEY	What do you want out of me?
SOL	Just take care of the problem.
HENLEY	(*weeping*) I can't. I can't. Oh, what am I going to do? The whole factory's shut down. I'm ruined. I'm ruined.
SOL	Don't cry, sir.
HENLEY	I know you were trying to do the right thing — but that's not the only thing to think of.
MAYOR	True, true! My point exactly.
HENLEY	(*to the* MAYOR) And you! You! I told you to shut this boy up — not my factory.
MAYOR	I — I didn't realize what I was doing
HENLEY	You never do !
MAYOR	Yes, sir. I mean no, sir! I mean
SOL	Well, Mr. Henley?
HENLEY	We've had it. We're through. I can't make a secret process that won't pollute. I've tried — and I can't and without the secret process - no more Wonder Kite...(*suddenly sniffs the air*) What's that?

MAYOR	What?
HENLEY	That strange odour.
MAYOR	*(sniffing)* I don't smell anything.

Everyone sniffs.

SOL	Yeah. There is something, It's not a bad smell.
HENLEY	It's getting stronger.
MAYOR	*(panicking)* Hold your nose, everybody. We're being gassed. Aaaargh, I'm choking to death!
HENLEY	It's rather pleasant, actually. I remember a long time ago, something that smelled just like this. What was it?
NANCY	*(running in)* Sol! Sol!
SOL	Nancy! How did you get here?
NANCY	I had to come, Sol. You've done it!
SOL	Done what?
HENLEY	Who is this young lady?
SOL	My friend, Nancy. Remember? I told you about her. Nancy, this is Mr. Henley.
NANCY	*(throwing her arms around HENLEY)* Mr. Henley, thank you !
HENLEY	*(disengaging himself)* This is all very nice — but what are you talking about?
NANCY	Can't you tell?
SOL	Tell what, Nancy?
NANCY	It's the air! It's fresh again!

MAYOR	*(disappointed)* You mean we're not being gassed?
HENLEY	*(taking a breath)* So that's what it is. Good clean fresh air. I haven't breathed air like this in years.
NANCY	And look out the window.
SOL	The river — all that red stuff is washing downstream.
NANCY	It's starting to turn clean again.
MAYOR	*(looking in amazement)* I'd forgotten how beautiful it used to look. It makes a man want to go for a swim!
NANCY	And now I can stay in Copetown. I've even stopped coughing, see? *(taking a deep breath and no cough)*
HENLEY	Just a second. Don't enjoy yourselves too much. We have to get this factory back into operation.
NANCY	*(her hopes suddenly dashed)* You mean this isn't permanent?
HENLEY	That's exactly what I mean. *(taking another breath)* Wait a minute.
	Everyone waits, anxiously, another testing out of the air. HENLEY begins to smile beatifically — but tries to control himself.
HENLEY	No, it isn't worth it. *(another breath)* Or is it? *(another breath)* Maybe it is. *(changing his mind)* No, it couldn't be. But would it work? Oh, I couldn't do that. *(pacing back and forth)* Then why not? *(coming to a decision)* Yes! Why not?
EVRYONE	What?
HENLEY	Who says we have to make the very *best* kites in the world?

EVERYONE	Who says?
HENLEY	Our kites could just be among the very best kites in the world.
EVERYONE	Right!
HENLEY	A non-polluting kind of kite!
EVERYONE	Right!
HENLEY	Nancy and her family could stay in town
NANCY & SOL	Hurray!
HENLEY	We wouldn't be able to bring as much business into the town
MAYOR	I object.
EVERYONE	*(to the* MAYOR*)* Sssshhh.
HENLEY	But we'd all be happier and healthier.
EVERYONE	Hurray! *(the* MAYOR*starts to leave in disgust)*
HENLEY	And I suppose we owe it all to this Young Citizen of the Year. Don't you agree, Mr. Mayor?
MAYOR	*(curt)* What?
HENLEY	Don't you agree? Take a deep breath.*(as the* MAYOR *does)* Don't you agree?
MAYOR	I suppose I do, at that..
SOL	But you took my title away...
MAYOR	No, no. Shhh. I changed my er...mind. *(seeing the ruins of the kite)*. I suppose we'd better get you another kite, eh?

SOL	Thank you, Mr. Mayor.
MAYOR	*(beaming)* Not at all.
HENLEY	In honour of the occasion, I'd like to give everyone a holiday — but now — I'm afraid we're all going to have to work very hard to keep ahead of the competition. It's the price we have to pay for non-pollution.
MALANOWSKI	It's worth it, Mr. Henley. It's worth it! All right, everybody, let's get to work!

> *Cheers. Everyone exits, leaving* SOL *onstage flying a kite.*

SOL	Well, that's the story of the great Copetown City Kite Crisis.*(pointing up)* How do you like my new kite? Of course, it isn't like the old one. It won't lift me into the air or anything — and I have to work hard to keep it flying. But so what? In a way, it's better than the old one — because of everything that's happened. You know what I mean? Oh, about Copetown, since the factory stopped using the Secret Process Machine, Copetown didn't actually become the boom town that the Mayor was hoping for. But it's a good place to live. The air is fresh, the water is clean. And it's a fine, fine place to fly a kite. Goodbye — come and see us again, won't you?

> *The End — Alternate Ending on next page.*

Alternate Ending

MALANOWSKI	The decision is "No strike"! Sorry Sol. I guess I'd better get back to my painting. (*exiting*)
MAYOR	Very good. I thank you from the bottom of my heart. Don't feel bad, Sol. I know you meant well. To tell the truth, I admire you boy.
HENLEY	(*rushing in*) What's this? The Secret Process Machine is stopped. Why is nobody working?
SOL	The workers just had a meeting, Mr. Henley. But it's alright. Everyone decided they could put up with the pollution.
HENLEY	I'm glad. (*to everybody*) You won't regret it, I promise you. Now, get the machines started again. We have to fill today's quota. And I have the Japanese delegation coming at four o'clock(*sniffing the air*) What's that?
MAYOR	What?
HENLEY	That strange odour?
MAYOR	(*sniffing*) I don't smell anything.

Everyone sniffs.

SOL	Yeah — there is something, It's not a bad smell.
HENLEY	It's getting stronger.

MAYOR	*(panicking)* Hold your nose, everybody! We're being gassed.
MAYOR	Aaargh, I'm choking to death.
HENLEY	It's rather pleasant, actually. I remember a long time ago, something that smelled just like this. What was it?
NANCY	*(rushing in)* Sol! Sol!
SOL	Nancy! What are you doing here?
NANCY	I had to come, Sol. You've done it!
SOL	Done what?
HENLEY	Who is this young lady?
SOL	My friend, Nancy. Remember? I told you about her. Nancy, this is Mr. Henley.
NANCY	*(throuing her arms around* HENLEY*)* Mr. Henley, thank you!
HENLEY	*(disengaging himself)* This is all very nice — but what are you talking about?
NANCY	Can't you tell?
SOL	Tell what, Nancy?
NANCY	It's the air! It's fresh again!
MAYOR	*(di.sappointed)* You mean we're not being gassed?
HENLEY	*(taking a breath)* So that's what it is. Good clean fresh air. I haven't breathed air like this in years.
NANCY	And look out the window.
SOL	The river — all that red stuff is washing down stream.

MAYOR *(looking in amazement)* I'd forgotten how beautiful it used to look. It makes a man want to go for a swim!

NANCY And now I can stay in Copetown. I've even stopped coughing, see? *(taking a deep breath and no cough)*

HENLEY Just a second. Don't enjoy yourselves too much. We have to get this factory back into operation.

NANCY *(her hopes suddenly dashed)* You mean this isn't permanent?

HENLEY That's exactly what I mean. Start up the Secret Process Machine.

NANCY But Mr. Henley

SOL It's no use, Nancy. Let's go

NANCY *(seeing the factory starting to operate again)* I guess not.

HENLEY Children, I'm sorry I couldn't help you out. I truly am. But Sol, you understand, don't you?

SOL I'm not sure I do, sir.

HENLEY *(looking at him intently)* No, I suppose you can't. Well, keep on trying, son. Don't lose your ideals.

MAYOR You can't have your cake and eat it too.

HENLEY What the Mayor means, son, is...sometimes choosing is real hard. No matter which way you go, you'll lose something. This time everybody chose the factory insted of the air and water. It was the best choice under the circumstances.

SOL I'm not so sure it was the best.*(pause)* Goodbye, Mr. Henley. *(to NANCY)* Come on *(both exiting)*

MAYOR	Very good, Mr. Henley. That's certainly the way to deal with that nonsense. Let me say that I agree with you completely.
HENLEY	*(obviously deeply sorry for what he has had to do)* Mr. Mayor, haven't you said enough already?
MAYOR	What? Well, I...*(speechless)*
HENLEY	Good day. *(exiting)*
MAYOR	Well, I...I...Hrumph. *(exiting)*
SOL	*(returning to address the audience)* So that is the story of the Copetown City Kite Crisis. What will happen to Copetown City now? Well, it will get bigger and bigger until it has all the good things and bad things that really big cities have. Professional sports and traffic jams, great restaurants and huge garbage problems, art galleries and smog, nice parks and buildings so tall that they shut out the sky. Nancy and her family move away, of course — but me? I'll still be here, fighting battles — losing some, winning some — but trying eh? For me it will always be like...like keeping a good kite high in the wind. See you around.

The End.

My Best Friend is Twelve Feet High

by Carol Bolt

Carol Bolt was born in Winnipeg, and graduated from the University of British Columbia after growing up in that province. In the early seventies, she moved to Toronto and developed scripts through the collective creation process at Theatre Passe Muraille and Toronto Workshop Productions. Adult works such as *Gabe, Red Emma,* and *Buffalo Jump* are interpretaions of historical events and flamboyant figures. Her most-produced play, the comedy thriller, *One Night Stand* was made into a film starring Brent Carver. Other plays include *Shelter* and *Escape Entertainment.* Plays for children include: *Tangleflags, Cyclone Jack,* and *Ice Time* — winner of the 1988 Chalmers Best Play for Children Award. In 1988, she received a scholarship to attend Norman Jewison's School for Advanced Film Studies in Toronto, where she now resides.

My Best Friend is Twelve Feet High was commissioned by the Ontario Youtheatre Company and produced by Young People's Theatre in July 1972 with the following cast:

FLIP	*Andy Platel*
FRANK	*Charlie McIntosh*
ALICE	*Georgie Johnson*
CAPTAIN KING	*Guy Laprade*
PIP	*Karen Waterman*

Directed by Ray Whelan.
Costumes by Michael Rutland.
Music composed by Jane Vasey.

The Set

The set should be flexible; it could resemble an adventure playground. The cast should be able to arrange its modules to create the locations called for in the script: clubhouse, ship. bridge, etc.

The Characters

The characters are children trying to act as adult as possible, but they need not be played by child actors.

My Best Friend is Twelve Feet High

The COMPANY *sings.*

I saw a pigeon baking bread
I saw a baker coloured red
I saw a towel one mile square
I saw a playground in the air
I saw a rocket walk a mile
I saw a pony with a smile
I saw my best friend twelve feet high
I saw a ladder in a pie
I saw an apple fly away
I saw a sparrow making hay
I saw a farmer like a dog
I saw a puppy catch a frog
I saw a boy with bright green hair
I saw a rag doll hunt a bear
I saw three men who saw these too
And they'll tell you that it's all true.

The GANG *enters the clubhouse. There
is a round of ritualistic handshakes. A
game is begun.* CAPTAIN KING *the
President, is not included .*

FLIP   The 543rd meeting of the Royal Loyal Gymnasts
Lodge will come to order.

FRANK   The Royal Loyal Gymnasts, Engineers and
Storytellers Lodge.

FLIP	It's shorter my way.
	ALICE *has not been included in the game, but she is pretending she doesn't much care.*
ALICE	Big deal. Big deal.
FRANK	*(To* FLIP*) You* aren't supposed to announce the meeting. President King is supposed to announce the meeting.
KING	That's right.
ALICE	We should have a pet-lover's club.
KING	We should have order.
ALICE	I'm working on my pet-lover's badge.
KING	Thank you, Alice.
FRANK	We should have a dog.
KING	I don't like dogs.
ALICE	*(singing)* Big deal. Big deal. Big de-he-he-he-al.
FLIP	We should have elections.
KING	We had elections last week.
ALICE	Big deal.
KING	I won.
FLIP	I didn't know that.
KING	It was a secret ballot.
ALICE	Big deal. Big deal.

CAPTAIN KING *blows his whistle to stop the game.*

KING   President King presiding. The secretary will call the roll.

FRANK   Frank, the chief engineer. That's me. I'm here. Flip, the chief gymnast'?

FLIP   Chief gymnast, sergeant-at-arms and major-general. Grey Cup All-Star, also represented in the Hockey Hall of Fame.

FRANK   Pip the Storyteller.

KING   Assistant Storyteller.

PIP   Here.

FRANK   President King?

KING   Is that all? President King and Chief Storyteller King presiding.

FRANK   And Alice.

KING   Alice is not a member of our lodge.

ALICE   Why don't I get to do anything?

FRANK   You can sing, Alice.

KING   She doesn't belong.

ALICE   There's not much point in trying to sing when you're trying to sing to President King.

KING   I don't like music.

ALICE   You don't like anything.

KING   I like everything and everything likes me.

FLIP	He likes being president. Actually, the chief gymnast should be the president.
ALICE	President King should walk around on his hands. He sees everything upside down.
FRANK	We should have a dog. Its name could be Mope.
FLIP	We should have a club which is totally devoted to gymnastics. To swordfighting, tree-climbing, horseback riding, deep-breathing and health foods.
ALICE	We should have a new president.
KING	Alice can be the dog, Mope.
ALICE	No!
KING	All in favour? Carried. Alice is Mope.
ALICE	I am not.
KING	Call the roll, Frank.
FRANK	Mope-the-dog.
ALICE	I'm Alice.
KING	Alice is not a member of our lodge.
PIP	Mope-the-dog was not her real name.
ALICE	No?
PIP	Her real name was Noble.
ALICE	Yes?
PIP	She had spent her life rescuing mountain climbers and explorers in the Canadian Arctic.
ALICE	Yes.

PIP	She found hundreds of lost explorers and every time she foundone, she also found the new mountain he was climbing or thenew lake he had discovered and they were all named after her.
	ALICE is enchanted with the possibilities of being Mope-the-dog. Her transformation is complete.
ALICE	There was Lake Noblemope. There was the lost island of Mopenoble. There was Mount Killamannoblemope. Mopenoble River. Noblemope Desert, Mopenoble Dessert. Noblemope Ice Cream! Yes, ice cream, my favourite flavours, and I could eat it...
PIP	She also worked in Europe as a police dog for Interpol, tracking down dangerous criminals. People gave her medals. She was interviewed on television.
FRANK	*(as interviewer)* How is the case progressing?
KING	*(as police chief)* Well, I...
FLIP	How is the case progressing, Mope?
ALICE	Woof. W-oo-oo-f. Grr. Woof.
PIP	She was in a movie which told about some of her greatest adventures.
FLIP	*(as director)* All right, Mope. In this scene, the lost boy is trapped inside the burning building. You look up. Listen. You hear his call.
PIP	*(as lost boy)* Help!
ALICE	Woof?
FLIP	*(as director)* Print it.
PIP	She had so many adventures, she could sing about them.

KING   Instead of singing "big deal" all the time.

PIP   My greatest adventure. A song by Mope-the-dog.

ALICE   Yes?

PIP   I was working in the South of France...

ALICE   *(following)* I was working in the South of France

PIP   ...from my base just east of Nice.

         ALICE's *song is illustrated in a series*
         of tableaux.

ALICE   *(singing)*
         I was working in the South of France
         From my base just east of Nice
         The jewel thieves had kidnapped
         The inspector of police

         They tied him to the railway tracks
         Of the Orient Express
         Inspector Marc was frightened
         But I heard his SOS

         Inspector Marc was frightened
         And I could not bear his shrieks
         I rushed in and untied him
         And he kissed me on both cheeks

         The jewel thieves' invention
         Was a bright green smoke machine
         I looked around, Inspector Marc
         Was nowhere to be seen

         The thieves jumped in a hydrofoil
         I jumped in my canoe
         It wasn't very fast but it
         Was Mediterranean blue

The thieves reached land, they beached
their boat
They transferred to a jet
I would have tried to follow but
I'm not an air cadet

They took off down the runway
They went higher and still higher
As I watched them, the left engine—
All the engines were on fire

The inspector was thrown from the crash
He landed at my feet
And the jewel thieves' Ferrari
Was careering down the street

So we jumped in our Alpha Romeo
And my ears flew straight back in the breeze
And I followed their scent
Yes, I knew where they went
Yes, I know the woods from the trees

> *The story is over, but the participants
> are still very pleased and excited.
> Applause, cheers.*

FRANK	We could have a choral society and marching band.
KING	No.
PIP	Then Alice could be the conductor.
KING	Her name is Mope-the-dog.
FLIP	Then Mope-the-dog can be the conductor.
KING	It isn't that I don't like music. It's because I sing so well myself.
FRANK	I wish we had a dog like that.
KING	Call the roll.

FRANK   Mope-the-dog?

ALICE   Woof.

> FLIP, FRANK *and* PIP *begin to*
> *call:"Here, Mope. Nice fellow. Come*
> *on, girl", etc .* ALICE *is thrilled. She*
> *has never had so much attention.* KING
> *is more annoyed than ever.*

KING   We'll have the minutes of the last meeting.

FRANK   There are no minutes.

KING   There must be.

FRANK   I forgot to take them. Pip can tell a story now.

KING   That comes later.

FRANK   Now.

ALICE   Why not?

FLIP   All in favour?

> *All vote "Aye" including* ALICE, *who*
> *votes loudest.*

KING   Dogs don't vote, Mope.

ALICE   Arf. Arf. Arf. Arf. Arf. Woof. Arrouuuuuuu!

KING   First I will read the club rules. First rule. No one
               is allowed in the club who is under five years
               old. (*to* Alice) That means you.

PIP   Mope's a dog.

KING   Mope doesn't make the rules.

PIP   I'm not staying if Mope can't stay.

KING	That's fine. It isn't that I don't like stories. It's only that I tell them well myself.
PIP	I mean it.
KING	Second rule.
PIP	Come on, Mope.
KING	No one is allowed in the club who doesn't know the secret password. (*to* FRANK) What is it?
FRANK	I don't know.
PIP	There isn't any secret password.
KING	Who's in charge here?
FRANK	Well, I'm not staying if Pip's not staying.
KING	That's fine. That's perfectly all right. There's no use having a club if nobody in it knows the secret password. The club will go on without you. With Flip and me. Goodbye.
	The following song is a competition between FLIP *and* KING.
FLIP	Why should you be President? Why should you be King? Why should such a nobody be anything?*(repeat)* I've never been self-seeking And I've studied public speaking And I don't believe in sneaking I can stop a tent from leaking
KING	I'm a good administrator I'm a rapid calculator I'm a very skilled speed skater I could be an aviator

FLIP But why should you be President?
Why should you be King?
Why should such a nobody be
anything? *(repeat)*

FLIP I discovered Argentina
I can play the concertina
I can laugh like a hyena
I can dance and I can sing

KING My teeth are so much pearlier
My hair is so much curlier
I get up so much earlier
No use arguing
I could be an astronaut
Fly to the moon
I could get to there and back in one
afternoon
I have been to Jupiter, I have seen Mars
Almost all my life has been spent in the stars
I was greeted with affection
At our latest club election
I'm the closest to perfection
And I'm anti-vivesection

FLIP I'm by far the most athletic
And I'm also sympathetic
I'm frenetic, energetic
I'm magnetic and poetic
Once I won a rodeo championship
All the way to Calgary—short pleasure trip
Busted all their bronchos and I roped all their
steers
Best all-round cowboy that they'd seen in
years

KING I'm a very fine musician
And I'm free from superstition
At the risk of repetition
I'm the best for this position

FLIP

No one else has even seen a
Finer prima ballerina
No one else has ever been a
Star at Maple Leaf Arena
So why should you be President?
Why should you be King?
Why should such a nobody be anything?

FLIP

(spoken) I'm going to form a new club. I'll ask Pip and Frank and Mope to join. I'm going to be President.

KING

So am I.

Meanwhile, in another area, PIP *and* MOPE *and* FRANK *are playing an imaginary game.*

PIP

(throwing an imaginary ball) Here, Frank, catch.

FRANK

I can't.

PIP

Why not? We're only pretending.

FRANK

I'm busy.

PIP

What are you doing?

FRANK

I'm building a new clubhouse in this tree.

PIP

What if we were hunting?

FRANK

Hunting what?

PIP

Buffalo. What if we were Indians and you had to climb this tree and it was the only tree on the wide prairie? You climbed the tree to look for buffalo.

FRANK

I see one.

FRANK sees KING, *building his own clubhouse with pieces from the main structure.*

PIP	I knew you would.
FRANK	We could build a buffalo trap. Like this. With one box there and one box here. And a rope strung between them. And when the buffalo walked past, we could catch him in the rope and tie him up!
KING	*(trapped)* I am not a buffalo.
FRANK	Yes sir, President King, sir.
KING	I never have been a buffalo. And I never will be a buffalo. I thought we were all building my new clubhouse. Get to work. I want the walls to go right out to here. And in this corner there will be a lookout tower and there will be an elevator going upto it. And here, there will be a fireplace and right here, Mope can dig a hole and we can have a swimming pool. Here, Mope. Here, Mope.
PIP	*(to the others)* What if we were on board a ship and you had to climb up the mast to look for land? And a storm came upand the mast was swaying back and forth, back and forth.
KING	This isn't a ship, it's a clubhouse.
PIP	Let me go up. *(climbing further than FRANK)* This is wonderful. You can see for miles.
KING	Build the clubhouse.
PIP	I'm twelve feet high.
FRANK	So am I.
KING	I can build my own ship.
PIP	I can see the top of the trees. I can see the sky and the sun and the edge of the park and the city and the lake.
KING	And my ship is the flagship. It will lead the fleet.

PIP   There's a whale on the lake.

KING   Captain King. That has a good ring to it.

PIP   There's a boat called *Maid of the Mist* and it's
                       chasing the whale.

KING   I sailed all around the world. Alone. There were
                       storms...

FRANK   We could build a boat called *Maid of the Mist*.

PIP   We could build any boat.

KING   I build the best boats and that's why I'm the
                       Captain.

ALL   *(singing)*
                       Climb the mast and hoist a sail
                       Time to catch yourself a whale
                       A big grey whale and sandy beaches
                       Is a song to sing instead of speeches

                       I've always been a rover
                       Travelled the wide world over
                       When I was eight, I went to sea
                       I never left my grandad's knee
                       (*Chorus*)

                       The rare old whale mid storm and gale
                       In his ocean home will be
                       A giant in might, where might is right
                       And monarch of the boundless sea.
                       (*Chorus*)

KING   There she blows. Three points off the lee bow.
                       Raise up your wheel. Steady! Mast ahead, ahoy!

PIP   Do you see the whale? *(meaning KING)*

FRANK   Yes.

PIP   I knew you would.

KING	Keep her full before the wind!
FRANK	If we had a rope we could attach it to a harpoon and shoot it from the harpoon gun.
KING	Stand by to lower the boats. Lower away!
FRANK	Maybe we could herd the whale into some kind of net. Maybe we could sneak quietly up behind him and...grab him!
KING	*(trapped)* I am not a whale. I never have been a whale and I never will be a whale.
PIP	Now say we were in a circus and we'd climbed right to the top of the tent and we had to dive off into the net.

> ALL *jump, doing forward somersaults when they land.* KING *is more and more determined to take over.*

FRANK	How do you know what's real and what isn't?
PIP	I tell stories, that's all.
FRANK	I know that.
PIP	Because building a clubhouse you are never going to finish is not very interesting.
FRANK	No.
KING	No?
PIP	*(ignoring* KING*)* So I make up a story about it.
FRANK	What kind?
PIP	Any kind. How do you know what to build next?
FRANK	I build useful things.

PIP	I tell any kind of story. Whatever comes into my head.
KING	Oh, sure.
FRANK	For example?
KING	For example?
PIP	For example, last week Mope and I were playing in Mr. Roberts' front yard.
FRANK	You aren't supposed to play in Mr. Roberts' yard.
KING	That's right.
PIP	We were pretending. It was the dead of night. There was no light. Anywhere. Except the moon, sometimes, coming out from behind a cloud, just for a moment. There's a tree in Mr. Roberts' yard and there was something moving behind the tree. Maybe it was just a shadow. We didn't know for sure. We stopped and listened. There was a strange sound.

> *There is a strange sound from* KING. *He is making his bid for control.*

FRANK	That was Mr. Roberts.
PIP	Mr. Roberts doesn't sound like that. The sound came from behind the tree and Mope and I decided that no matter how frightened we were, we would have to look behind that tree and see what it was

> PIP *and* MOPE *advance toward* KING.
> FLIP *decides to start his own game.*

FLIP	Keep off the grass. Keep off the grass.
FRANK	That's Mr. Roberts.

> MOPE *is very scared, and* PIP *is so far into her story that she is startled.*

PIP	What?
FLIP	No dogs on the grass. No people on the grass. No trespassing.
PIP	It was awful, Frank. There was a huge flash of light and suddenly, Mr. Roberts turned into a dragon.
KING	And the tree turned into a dragon!
FLIP	That's not the way the story goes. You turned into a dragon egg.
KING	An egg!
FLIP	Yes.
KING	I didn't.
FLIP	You did.
KING	I hatched!
FLIP	You hatch next January.
FRANK	*(to* PIP*) You* were scared, eh?
PIP	Yes. And Mope was scared. A little.
FRANK	What kind of dragon was he?
PIP	The worst kind. He ate dogs and people.
FLIP	*(as a dragon)* Whereas trespassing on the grass or the path in front of my cave is absolutely forbidden and completely prohibited, it is hereby announced that dogs and people who walk or run or jump or hop or crawl or stand or sit...*(Roberts notices* PIP*)* Who are you?
PIP	Who are you?
FLIP	Roberts, the dragon.

PIP

Roberts, the huge, green, fire-breathing, people and dog-eating dragon?

FLIP

Yes.

PIP

Who do you think I am?

FLIP

Dinner.

PIP

I'm your nephew, Pip.

FLIP

You aren't a dragon.

PIP

Well, if I'm not a dragon, then you aren't a dragon. You look just like me.

FLIP

No, I don't.

PIP

Here's a mirror.

> As PIP *pretends to be* FLIPs *reflection,* MOPE *growls.* FLIP *jabs and* PIP *misses the move.*

FLIP

I don't have a nephew.

PIP

Yes, you do.

FLIP

I don't have any relatives. I have one dragon egg that won't hatch till January.

KING

Happy New Year! I'm Captain King, the world's largest dragon and you are my nephew, Pip.

PIP

What?

KING

Roberts doesn't know anything about dragons. He's only pretending. He doesn't know soup from soap. He doesn't know a bicycle from a fire engine. He doesn't know anything.

> FLIP, *playing Roberts, spins* PIP *around.*

FLIP	Of course. Pip! My nephew!
PIP	After all these years.
FLIP	And no one ever mentioned you.
PIP	Surprise. *(stopping on the wrong side of the mirror)*
FLIP	*(meaning* MOPE/ALICE*)* Who's that?
PIP	That's my dog, Mope.
FLIP	I like dogs.
PIP	That's good.
FLIP	I like to eat dogs.
PIP	No, wait! Stop! Uncle Roberts!

KING *blows his whistle.*

KING	Neutral corners!
FRANK	Neutral corners !
KING	I'm the referee.
FRANK	I'm the referee.
FLIP	I don't need a referee. I've never fought fair and I'm not starting now.
KING	I'm the television announcer. This is the CBC Sports Final bringing live coverage of the fight between Roberts and Pip and we join the action just as round one begins. Pip, on your right, is bowing to his opponent.

> *Obviously, The dragon fight can include any number of special turns.*

> *The original production included a karate*
> *contest, a reel, a couple of amazing high*
> *leaps, a fashion show, a tango and a*
> *tug-of-war in the first round. and a*
> *simultaneous French commentary. If the*
> *latter isn't practical, either* FRANK *or*
> KING *can act as cameraman, technician,*
> *scorekeeper or cheerleader.*

FRANK   And they are bowing to the audience. They are bowing to the announcers . . .

KING   Bonjour, mesdames et messieurs, ici Radio Canada, ils vous salutent, ils nous salutent...

FRANK   Pip was born in Toronto. He's a rookie. This is his first appearance in the ring but he seems to be getting a lot of support from the crowd. Roberts the Dragon is an old hand at this sort of contest, although last year he was suspended for six months for roughing. There has been no roughing this afternoon. Pip is staying well clear of Roberts in this first round, which, as usual, is hand-to-hand combat. They're circling each other.

KING   Ils se circlent.

FRANK   They're circling each other.

KING   Ils se circlent.

FRANK   They're circling each other.

> *As the first reel begins,* KING *is*
> *enchanted by the action and right in*
> *there with them, slapping his thighs and*
> *singing.*

KING   Ils sautent...Ils sautent, ils sautent. Ils sautent.

FRANK   This is most unusual, ladies and gentlemen...

KING   Ah, oui, ah oui, ma p'tit, p'tit, p'tit. Ah, oui, ah oui, ma p'tit, p'tit, p'tit.

ROBERTS:	Hai!
FRANK	Roberts is a karate black belt, so this should be a most exciting part of the contest...Oh, he missed. Pip has stepped clear of his attack. Wait, her hat has fallen off. Pip picks up her hat.
KING	Pip porte un beau chapeau jaune, un blouson jaune...
FRANK	A yellow blouse and blue overalls.
KING	Roberts, a l'autre main, porte une belle uniforme de baseball, blanche et rouge.
FRANK	...and Pip has kicked Roberts. Roberts looks angry. He turns. He attacks. They're dancing again, ladies and gentlemen.
KING	...une bataille passionelle...ils s'embracent
FRANK	They've tripped on the rope. They've picked up the rope. They're pulling on the rope.
KING	...Pip tire, Roberts tire...
FRANK	And the bell rings to end the first round. Now, for half-time entertainment, we'll talk to Mope, the reason for this fight. What do you think of the fight so far, Mope?
KING	Que pense-tu du premier rond, Mope?
ALICE	*(to PIP, with some affection)* Woof. Woof. Woof. Woof. *(to Roberts with some anger)* Woof. Woof. Woof. Woof. Woof.
KING	C'est ca, mesdames et messieurs, de la bouche du chien.

FRANK   There you have it, ladies and gentlemen, straight from the dog's mouth. In the second round, it is customary for Pip to be handed the magic sword *(someone does)* and we expect that Roberts will concede at that point. Yes, Pip has the sword now. She is drawing the sword. Roberts retreats. Yes, Roberts has conceded.

> MOPE, FRANK *and Roberts*
> *congratulate* PIP *on the fight.*

KING   *(singing)*
I could kill dragons if
I had the time
Heroes in a comic book are three for a dime
Hour after hour in a President's day
Is obligation, duty...it is work and not play.

(spoken) Clean. Clean. This clubhouse should be clean.

FRANK   That's Captain King.

KING   We've cleaned the sheets and the streets and everybody's feeta nd the wheels of the automobiles and now all this green grass should be clean.

FRANK   Come on, Pip. It's Captain King.

PIP   So?

FRANK   So we better start cleaning.

> FRANK *and* FLIP *and* MOPE *all clean*
> *furiously.*

KING   This is wonderful. We've been working all summer. Because we all knew that if we did work all summer we would build a new clubhouse. And here it is. Just as I pictured it. Now all we have to do is carry in the winter provisions. The popcorn and the popsicles and the popovers and the soda pop. The ketchup, the mustard and the

KING	mayonnaise. And clean everything. Absolutely, positively, definitely, completely and utterly clean. Clean as a whistle. *(blowing it)* Then we'll be ready for winter. Get to work, everybody.
FRANK	This is my friend Pip, Captain King, and his dog Mope.
KING	How do you do? What do you do?
PIP	Do?
KING	You aren't cleaning.
PIP	No sir, Captain President, sir.
KING	My name is Captain King.
FRANK	Pip and Mope would like to stay with us this winter, Captain King.
KING	What does he do?
FRANK	Do?
KING	Do. Do. Do.
FLIP	*(picking it musically)* Do. Do. Do. Do. Do. Do. Do. Do. Do. Do.
KING	Everyone does something. Flip is working. Flip likes working. Flip is singing while he works.
FRANK	Well...
KING	Is he a house painter?
FRANK	No.
KING	Is he a bean picker?
FRANK	No.
KING	Is he a window washer?

KING
That's the silliest story I ever heard. Come on, everybody. *(blowing his whistle until everyone is lined up in front of him)*

FRANK
I'm sorry, Pip.

PIP
That's all right.

FRANK
I have to go with him.

PIP
I understand.

FRANK
I'll see you next summer?

PIP
Sure you will. And Mope and I will do just as we always do

KING
The doors are mine to open and the doors are mine to close, so I close them in the winter when it snows. *(leading his club members offstage)*

PIP
Just as we always do, won't we, Mope? *(continuing the story, but slower, much less animated, not so sure of herself)*

She skated and slid
on the ice and the snow
Her feet were so big
like the wind she could go
But the East Wind would howl
and the North Wind would blow

And she thought she had frozen an ear and a toe
She waited for summer she paced to and fro
She was looking for someone who might say hello...

(spoken) Don't be sad, Mope. We could pretend we're discovering the South Pole. And we're lost in a blizzard and I go through the ice and you have to go for help, Mope. Help!

ALICE	Woof!
PIP	I guess it's more fun with more people pretending. Mope, do you believe what Captain King says? That everybody has to do something, and telling stories doesn't count?
ALICE	Woof?
PIP	It's lonely, Mope, isn't it? Maybe we should pretend we're inside with Frank and Flip and Captain King.

> *And if* PIP *pretends something, it happens. But as we might have suspected, all is not well with* KING *and* FRANK *and* FLIP. *They are bored.* KING *is trying his best to be entertaining, without really admitting that anything is wrong. There is a certain amount of desperation to his good humour.*

KING	Cheer up, everybody! Let's all do a few exercises. One. Two. Three. Four. No? Well. Well, since we have nothing to do, I'm going to tell you a story. It was a dark and stormy night. It was very cold. It was so cold that it wasn't raining rain, and it wasn't sleeting sleet and it wasn't snowing snow. It was icing icicles. I had icicles hanging from my arms and I couldn't move my arms. I had a big icicle hanging from my nose and I couldn't move my head. And every time I opened my mouth to catch my breath, I got a mouthful of icicles. I looked up. I saw a huge family of penguins, so I knew I was in Antarctica.

> FRANK *and* FLIP *grab at penguins.*

FRANK	Penguins?
FLIP	Penguins?
KING	Antarctica

FRANK   Penguins?

KING   *(realising he finally has their attention)* Yes. Penguins. Of course. That's what I said.

FRANK   What are penguins like?

FLIP   They walk like this. *(waddling)*

KING   That's right. Penguins. They were short, stubby penguins. They were cold. They were hungry. But over here...there was a beautiful beach. And picnic tables with heaping plates of penguin food.

> FRANK *and* FLIP *are now totally into the penguin game and they rush for the food on the imaginary tables.*

KING   But you can't come.

FRANK   Why not?

KING   Because there is a river here. There are rocks. There are rapids. So what can you do?

FLIP   Build a bridge.

KING   That's right! So the penguins built the bridge across the river so that they could cross to the picnic tables and the penguin food.

FRANK   And then what happened?

KING   Then the first penguin crossed the bridge!

> *The first penguin does.*

FLIP   And then what happened?

KING   Well, the second penguin crossed the bridge!

> *The second penguin crosses* the *bridge.*

FRANK   And then what happened?

KING   And the third penguin crossed the bridge! I'm the third penguin.

> *The third penguin crossing the bridge is a big production number which is greeted with enthusiasm and applause by* FRANK *and* FLIP, *still as penguins.*

FLIP   And then what happened?

FRANK   And then what happened?

KING   *(carried away with the success of his story)* The fourth penguin crossed the bridge.

BOTH   *(a little confused but willing)* Fourth? The fourth?

KING   On the other side. And he was a very cowardly penguin and he was afraid to cross.

> *Someone is delegated fourth penguin and runs back to do the cross.*

FRANK   Then what happened?

KING   And the fifth penguin, who was also a very cowardly penguin, crossed the bridge.

> *No one* except KING *is interested in being fifth penguin. No one is very interested in his production number cross.*

KING   When he was halfway across the bridge, his foot got caught on the ice, and the sixth penguin...

FRANK   Then what happened?

FLIP   What happened after you got across?

KING   The sixth penguin...

FLIP   And the sixth penguin got across.

KING   Well, the seventh penguin crossed the bridge.

FLIP   After that.

KING   The eighth and the ninth

FRANK   After all the penguins were across.

KING   Well, the partridges started across...the first partridge.

FLIP   No.

KING   And the snowbirds?

FRANK   What happened after the bridge fell down?

FLIP   No bridge.

              The penguins destroy the bridge,
              thinking it will help.

KING   But the bridge didn't fall down.

FRANK   I wish you knew better stories.

KING   There was a herd of walrus and the first walrus —

FRANK   I wish Pip were here.

KING   I'll tell another story.

FLIP   Never mind, Captain King.

FRANK   It's all right. We'll just sit here.

KING   Any kind of story. Your favourite kind of story. What kind of story do you want? Flip, you can pick it.

FLIP   Don't ask me. I'm not going to help you.

KING	All right. Frank?
FRANK	Ask somebody else.
KING	All right. I don't need you. *(to the audience)* What can I tell a story about?

> KING *and the kids in the audience decide on the subject of a story.* KING*s role in this dialogue should be helpful and enthusiastic.* FRANK *and* FLIP *can turn down as uninteresting any ideas that seem unpromising, or can choose from a number of suggestions. The format of the improvisation that follows is another shaggy-dog type story which never quite gets off the ground. The improvisation is better if* FRANK *and* FLIP *are given the opportunity for movement. If the suggestion is a dog, cat, fish, etc., this is easy. If the story is supposed to be about a tree or grass or some other immovable object, then that object can be lost and* FRANK *and* FLIP, *playing kings or football players or storekeepers or whatever, can go and look for it. The possibilities are limited only by your facilities. The following story is fairly adaptable for any number of suggestions.*

KING   Once upon a time there was a king *(...of Mars, or whatever the suggestion is)* and he had a box he couldn't open. *(to FLIP)* You be the king. Inside the box was the magic *(grass or foot-ball, etc.)* and the king sat on his box and looked out his window. He saw three pyramids and he knew that in one pyramid there was a golden key that would open the box. The king had a servant. *(to FRANK)* You be the servant. And he called him and said, "Go and open the pyramids and find the key and bring it back to me and we can open the box."

FLIP	Go and open the pyramids and find the key and bring it back to me and we can open the box.
KING	And the servant said, "All right."
FRANK	All right.
KING	And he went to the first pyramid and he opened it up and he found...That's right. He found a hat to shade him from the sun and a bell to ward off evil spirits. And he went to the second pyramid and he found...That's right. Nothing. And he didn't touch it. Don't touch it. And he went to the third pyramid and he found a strange creature *(from Mars, etc.)* who made a strange *(Martian)* sound. *(This is* KING's *part in the the story and he enjoys it)*
FLIP	Then what happened?
KING	Then the servant came back to the king and the king said, "Did you find the key?"
FLIP	Did you find the key?
KING	And the servant said, "No."
FRANK	No.
	KING *is getting more and more involved in the story but* FRANK *and* FLIP *are more and more annoyed.*
KING	So the king said: Well I know the key is there so you go back and look again.
FLIP	I'm tired of sitting here, Captain King.
FRANK	And I'm tired of looking in boxes.
FLIP	Pip knows better stories than that.

> *In the fury of improvisation, it is better
> to avoid saying: I don't want to do this
> any more, or, I don't want to be the dog,
> because the kids in the audience will
> occasionally volunteer.*

KING   I'm going to sing a song for you.

(singing)
My name is Captain King
I really like to sing
I sing throughout the night and the day
When I walk down the street
The people that I meet
Say: What is your name?
And I say:

My name is Captain King
I really like to sing
I sing throughout the night and day
When I walk down the street
The people that I meet
Say: What is your name?
And I say:

My name is Captain King
I really like to sing...

> *Sometime after it becomes obvious that
> this song is never going to go anywhere
> and might just never end, FLIP and
> FRANK, who have not been enjoying
> themselves, begin to chant.*

**FLIP &
FRANK**   We want Pip! We want Pip!

> *The kids in the audience may begin to
> chant as well. KING has to be prepared
> to control this.*

KING   All right. Go and find him. Find Mope too. Or
          Alice! Find all three of them. I shouldn't have
          sung that song. I can't sing. I shouldn't have told
          those stories, either. I've never been able to tell
          stories. Sometimes I think I'm only the president
          because I talk the loudest. It's lonely being a
          president without a club. I wish Pip were here.
          Or Mope. Here, Mope. Here, Mope.

                    ALICE *is a little suspicious. She*
                    growls.

KING   Hi, Mope. I wish you were my dog. A dog can
          be a good friend and a friend in need is a friend
          indeed. We could talk to each other.

ALICE   Woof.

KING   Where's Pip?

ALICE   *(agitated)* Woof. Woof.

KING   You can tell Pip she can join my club again,
          even if she doesn't do anything useful.

ALICE   *(agitated)* Woof. Woof.

KING   No, I didn't mean that. You can tell her that she
          can join. Even if she does tell silly stories.

                    ALICE *is worried. She is trying to lead*
                    KING *somewhere.*

KING   No, I didn't mean that. Tell her I want to be
          friends. And when she comes back, we'll have a
          party. In the club house. What's the matter,
          Mope?

                    ALICE *is barking. Running in circle.*
                    PIP's *"drowning", like all the other*
                    stories, is mimed.

PIP   Help!

KING	Pip is in trouble.
FRANK	Pip is drowning in a pool of quicksand.
PIP	Help!
FLIP	There is no way we can reach her from the edge of the quicksand. I fly over her. I try to reach down for her but I'm going too fast.
FRANK	And I try to build a bridge out to her, but the bridge sinks into the quicksand and I fall.
ALICE	And I save you. I save Frank and pull him to shore.
FLIP	And we make a human chain, from the edge of the quicksand out to the middle of the pool.
PIP	Help.
FLIP	Flip and Alice and Frank.
FRANK	But we can't reach her.
KING	And I help. I hold on to a tree.
FLIP	Flip and Alice.
ALICE	And Frank and Captain King.
FRANK	And we reach her. We pull her to shore.

> *The rescue is accomplished. The* COMPANY *sings:*

Surprise, surprise, surprise, surprise
Clap your hands, slap your thighs
Welcome home, welcome home
Ever more welcome, however you roam.

Captain King will bring you
At incredible expense
This fantastic celebration
This supreme experience.

It's a real extravaganza
An incredible display
It's liberal, it's lavish
Your red letter day.
(*Chorus*)

Captain King will bring you
His wild horses, his brass band
It's a party for our best friend
It is glorious and grand.

This magnificent attraction
Brought to you by Captain King
Is a song of praise to raise hoorays
And make the rafters ring.
(*Chorus*)

KING   I did it. I made up a story.

PIP   We all made up the story together, Captain King.

KING   That's a good way to do it. When one person
       can't think of what to say. I could make up a
       song about the story.

       (singing)
       The day that Pip fell in the quicksand
       She couldn't reach land
       She couldn't stand...

       (spoken) No. That's the silliest song I ever heard.

ALICE   Woof!

KING   You could help me, Alice.

ALICE   Woof!

KING   You don't have to be the dog all the time, Alice.

ALICE   I don't?

KING   You could help me make up a song.

ALICE   I could?

KING   If you want to.

> ALICE *and* COMPANY *sing the*
> *closing song.*

My best friend is twelve feet high
Hey, my best friend
I like milk and apple pie
Hey, my best friend
Why does Flip think he can fly?
Hey, my best friend
Don't know how and don't know why.

Hey, my best friend,
Hey my best friend,
Hey my best friend.

Slap my knee and slap my thigh
I know how to multiply
Got a nickel, what'll I buy
How many stars are in the sky?

Way up in the clouds so high
Saw a dragon in the sky
Caught a bird as it flew by
I've been here since last July.

Sometimes I'm afraid and shy,
Got an apple in my eye
Turned it into apple pie
I might bake it next July.

I can wear a shirt and tie
I wish I were dignified
No, I wouldn't tell a lie
I laughed so hard I split my side.

Saw a pretty butterfly
No green dragons need apply
Had to give this song a try
Now it's time to say goodbye.

The End.

FRANK	No.
KING	Is he a storekeeper or a postman?
PIP	No sir, Captain Prince, sir.
KING	My name is Captain King.
FRANK	Well, he —
KING	Is he a lawnmower or a mixmaster? Is he a toaster?
FRANK	He kills dragons and tells stories.
KING	There are no dragons.
FRANK	He tells stories about them.
KING	Anyone can tell stories.
FRANK	She tells good stories.
KING	No. She can't stay.
FRANK	*(disappointed)* But Captain —
KING	Nose to the wheel and shoulder to the grindstone.
PIP	That's all right, Captain General, sir.
KING	My name is Captain King.
PIP	Mope and I will do just what we always do.
KING	And that's impossible.
PIP	What?
KING	What you need in the winter is a clean, warm house full of food. A big warm fire in the fireplace. A big warm rug in front of the fire. A toasted cheese sandwich and a mug of cocoa before you go to bed, just to wet your whistle so

KING   to speak. *(blowing his whistle)* Lots of blankets. Porridge for breakfast. Or pancakes would be nice. That's what you need in the winter time. Stories won't keep you through the winter time and if you think they will, you are whistling in the dark. *(blowing his whistle)* and you will soon be whistling another tune. *(blowing his whistle)*

FRANK   Pip will tell you a story.

KING   No time. Not interested.

PIP   A story about winter.

KING   I know them all.

FRANK   He'll make it up. Right now. You've never heard it before.

KING   Ha!

FRANK   Just one story.

KING   One story. That's all. I've got time for one story and I'm watching my watch.

PIP   *(singing)*
My friend's feet are so big
that they flap in the breeze
She can bend her toes backward
they come to her knees
So she's glad on the days
that the leaves leave the trees
And the day that the cold
in the air makes her sneeze
When school started she went back
as quick as you please
She was glad when the hockey rink
started to freeze
She can slide down the hills
with the greatest of ease
Since her feet are so big
that she doesn't need skis